THE FLOWER GIRL MURDER

Mags —

Hope you like it!

Keith Hirshland

ISBN: 0692046682
ISBN 13: 9780692046685
Library of Congress Control Number: 2017919498
Keith Hirshland, Peapack, NJ

When you finally hit rock bottom
Will you do what's wrong or right
You're gonna find out what you're made of
In the middle of the night

—Pat Green

"Always."

"I won't keep you," he promised, "but I wanted you to know BA called again."

"Oh boy." Two words this time. She knew BA was William "Billy" Atkinson, Lancaster's agent.

"It's good news," he started to say.

"For you," she interrupted.

"For us."

"Let's talk about it tonight, okay?"

"Of course." Some of the excitement had exited his system and his voice.

"I want to hear all about it," she said, but he had already hung up. "I really do."

He set the phone on the top step and used both hands in an attempt to rub the irritation from his thoughts. Nothing about Lancaster Heart was average. He had once had a full head of brown and black hair that was now silver around more than just the edges. That transformation had started before he said good-bye to his thirties. The healthy hair was a genetic gift from his father, who took his own magnificent mane to his grave at eighty-seven. His mother's side of the family was much more follicularly challenged. He had seen pictures of his maternal grandfather and knew his uncle personally; both were, as they say, "bald as a bean." The skin around Heart's eyes, mostly underneath, was about a size too big. More so, it seemed, with each passing birthday. This was the bestowal from his mother, the thing she left him to constantly remind him of her when he looked into the makeup mirror. The rest was all Harry Heart.

Mary Virginia Heart passed away seven months after her beloved husband. As far as Lancaster could tell, they had never spent more than two nights apart, and his mother wasn't about to endure one night more than the two hundred that followed his dad's death. Those who knew his parents well couldn't help but tell

When you finally hit rock bottom
Will you do what's wrong or right
You're gonna find out what you're made of
In the middle of the night

—Pat Green

CHAPTER ONE

Lancaster Heart continued to stare at his mobile phone. The fella on the other end had long since signed off. He diverted his attention, momentarily, to the computer screen in front of him. The script for the lead story of that evening's newscast was only a paragraph. A glance at the Rolex on his left wrist told him he still had plenty of time; the big red ticking numbers on the digital clock on the wall confirmed it. His gaze returned to the phone still in his hand, blank screen staring back. He exhaled.

"I'll be damned," he said with a shake of his head.

A couple of hours later, scripts all written, Heart sat on the concrete steps that led from the side of the building to the parking lot. Those stairs were next to a big metal garage door that opened and closed when the television station's various live trucks or news vans needed to come and go. None was doing that now. In the relative peace and quiet, Lancaster Heart pulled his phone from his pocket, found his favorites, and from that list tapped *his* favorite.

"Hey," she answered curtly.

"Hi, doll," he said back. "You busy?" he asked, knowing the answer.

"Always."

"I won't keep you," he promised, "but I wanted you to know BA called again."

"Oh boy." Two words this time. She knew BA was William "Billy" Atkinson, Lancaster's agent.

"It's good news," he started to say.

"For you," she interrupted.

"For us."

"Let's talk about it tonight, okay?"

"Of course." Some of the excitement had exited his system and his voice.

"I want to hear all about it," she said, but he had already hung up. "I really do."

He set the phone on the top step and used both hands in an attempt to rub the irritation from his thoughts. Nothing about Lancaster Heart was average. He had once had a full head of brown and black hair that was now silver around more than just the edges. That transformation had started before he said good-bye to his thirties. The healthy hair was a genetic gift from his father, who took his own magnificent mane to his grave at eighty-seven. His mother's side of the family was much more follicularly challenged. He had seen pictures of his maternal grandfather and knew his uncle personally; both were, as they say, "bald as a bean." The skin around Heart's eyes, mostly underneath, was about a size too big. More so, it seemed, with each passing birthday. This was the bestowal from his mother, the thing she left him to constantly remind him of her when he looked into the makeup mirror. The rest was all Harry Heart.

Mary Virginia Heart passed away seven months after her beloved husband. As far as Lancaster could tell, they had never spent more than two nights apart, and his mother wasn't about to endure one night more than the two hundred that followed his dad's death. Those who knew his parents well couldn't help but tell

Heart he "looked like both of them"; then they'd add, with a smile or a hand on his shoulder, "especially your dad." Nothing made him feel better. He liked to say he was six feet tall, but that was not exactly true. Heart was closer to six foot one, and everyone would swear he was even taller than that. In a meeting, or a room, or a restaurant, with similar-sized men, folks would always leave with the impression that Heart stood above the rest. Often they'd say so if asked. He had never regarded himself as particularly handsome, but every day he lived with the realization that he was good looking enough to be on TV every night.

The metal garage door squawked to life and began to rise. A more-than-slightly-beat-up Chevy Suburban, with the station's call letters painted on the side, started to back out. The driver hit the brakes when she came parallel to Heart.

"Hey, Denise," he greeted the person behind the wheel. She had circa 1993 Andie MacDowell hair and was the best and most creative camera operator on the staff.

"Hey, Caster," she returned. Thanks to his job as a broadcaster, the moniker was a nickname no brainer.

"Where you headed?"

"Huge wreck on Four Forty," she answered. "Big rig, bunch of cars, and we thought we heard school bus on the scanner." She took a quick drag on the cigarette she was, against company policy, smoking. "Wanna come?" The words raced to pass a cloud of smoke.

"I'll wait for the movie."

"Suit yourself, superstar." She waved, backing out and away from him.

CHAPTER TWO

Brodie Murdoch was brilliant. She was also very pretty. Not one feature, from the color of her hair to the arch of her feet, stood out above the rest, but when the whole package came together, she turned heads. She was athletic enough, more than playful, and despite being the smartest person in almost every room, she never wore her intelligence on her sleeve; she didn't have to.

Brodie and her mother, Claire Hooper Murdoch, were two peas in a pod. Though they were mother and daughter, they were easily, and often, mistaken for sisters, and that suited both just fine. By contrast, there wasn't much of Parker Murdoch in Brodie's mirror; those genes manifested themselves in other ways.

After attending a small, prestigious prep school in Denver, Colorado, she had headed east for college to change the world. Brodie was going to be a doctor. She excitedly lit off down that path at a prestigious institution of higher learning in the Carolinas until an epiphany changed her mind and her life. One day, she realized two things: she took everyone's pain personally, and she couldn't stomach the sight of blood. But having already invested a great deal of time, effort, and money, she graduated with a degree in biology that she would never use. With a diploma in her hand and a head full of confidence, Brodie Murdoch headed down a different path. She teamed up with several classmates and business-school-graduate friends in combining a burgeoning technology world with a rabid sports fan base. The group came up with the construct that would allow her school and others to disseminate scores, information, and more to aficionados, devotees, and followers all over the world. It didn't take long for other schools in the area to take notice and partake in the enterprise. From there, it spread to the entire conference, and ultimately around the country. Consensus called it a breakthrough, and capital poured in.

They all made a nice chunk of change, but Brodie, by virtue of being a driving force as well as the most appealing of the group, also earned a reputation that developed into a consulting business. She had heard the expression "those that can't do, teach, and those that can't teach, consult," but she dismissed that as horse-and-buggy ideology in a space-shuttle world. Her worldview saw consulting as an integral part of shaping a business's operating philosophy and helping to maximize profitability. In the *real* world, it was a safe bet neither was completely correct, and the truth probably existed somewhere in the middle. When the new business also boomed, she took the advice of another classmate and invested a large portion of her original commission in gold before the precious commodity's value went through the roof. Then, thanks to the same friend, she reinvested her profits just before the market self-corrected. She hadn't spoken to that friend in years—had no way of knowing he was serving five to ten in a medium-security correctional facility.

Along the way, she found an outlet to slow her always racing, constantly busy brain. She put pen or pencil to paper. Some called it sketching; a few even labeled it art; she thought of it as doodling when she thought about it at all. She was working on a particularly intricate one when Lancaster Heart walked into her life and sat across from her at a conference table in a rented office space. He was there to do a story for the station's weekly newsmagazine broadcast on the group she headed. She was there because some-one in PR told her she had to be. It was a match made in heaven.

CHAPTER THREE

The group at the television station responsible for putting together and delivering the evening newscast was packing up, at least a couple of them deciding at which local haunt they would have dinner and a drink. Bobby "Buck" Gates, a former pro basketball player turned sportscaster, was an immediate out. He had already ordered General Tso's chicken from Dang's Good Chinese and was settling in and waiting for a full slate of games to start on TV. Buck had been a star player at a small college a couple of hundred miles southeast of Raleigh, and he had performed well enough one postseason to help lead his school to the national championship game. Much to his—and his team's fan base's—chagrin, he had his career-worst game in the game that mattered most. He missed an astounding 80 percent of his field goal attempts as well as two crucial free throws near the end. So what little chance he had to advance to the NBA diminished thanks to doubts about his "ability to handle the big moments," resulting in a precipitous drop in his professional draft value.

Undrafted, he went to play in Europe and performed well enough there to earn a trip back to the States and a ten-day contract with the Greensboro Swarm, an NBA Developmental League team. Gates finally got the chance to play in a blowout victory, contributing nine points on three of four three-pointers and blocking a shot to boot. Then, with less than a minute left in the game, he jumped for a rebound and came down awkwardly on the size twenty-two shoe of a seven-foot-six opponent and ruptured his Achilles tendon. Now he delivered sports at a local Raleigh TV station, during an increasingly shrinking segment at six and eleven o'clock. Buck still loved his hoops, so that's why tonight, and most nights, he was a "no go" on dinner.

The rest of the crew, two cameramen and the studio stage manager, surprised exactly nobody by choosing a dive called Archibald Moore's for wings, beer, and maybe a shot or two of Jägermeister. That night's no-nonsense, no-fun producer extended her streak of never going out with her coworkers to another record, while their happy-go-lucky director kept his slate of always going alive and well. It never mattered if any or all of them had to be back for the late newscast.

Lancaster was hit or miss, and tonight he chose the latter and grabbed his car keys off the desk.

"I'm out tonight," he announced, heading for the door.

"I'll have a Jägerbomb in your honor," someone said to his back.

"Have two," Heart offered with a wave.

"If you insist," was the reply, and everybody had a chuckle over that.

CHAPTER FOUR

When he arrived home, the house was dark except for the glow from the sixty-inch TV in the living room. He turned the corner and saw images from a show about people arguing over wedding dresses. Brodie was sitting on the couch, legs under her, wrapped in a TV-station-branded throw. Without taking her eyes off the screen, she dipped a silver spoon into a pint of ice cream.

Uh-oh, Heart thought.

"Hey, darling," he said. She sucked a bit of ice cream off the spoon and set it inside the nearly empty container. Lancaster had bought the confection the day before. Brodie took her eyes off the television and turned toward her boyfriend.

"Sorry," she said.

He had made it to the couch and plopped down next to her. He reached for her left hand. It was cold from holding the ice cream container.

"For what?"

"For being a bitch. For being that person, *that* girlfriend." She rested her head on his shoulder.

"You're not."

"I was."

"I'm starving." He kissed the top of her head. She looked up at him, smiled, and then looked at what was left of the ice cream.

"I already ate."

CHAPTER FIVE

"You rang, Boss?" Cody Switzer walked through the office door, talking. He stopped in front of the desk, having asked his question to an empty chair.

"Do these glasses make me look smarter?" The "boss," Tanner Goochly Jr., asked a question of his own. The words came from behind and to the right of Switzer. The kid nearly jumped out of his skin.

"Crap, Boss!" He spun to face his bespectacled employer. "Don't spook me like that."

"Well?" Goochly asked impatiently.

"Well, what?"

"Do these glasses make me look smarter?"

Smarter than what? Switzer wondered. *Smarter than me? Smarter than you looked this morning when I saw you? Smarter than that asshole old man of yours? No, they make you look like an idiot.*

"Sure do," he said.

Goochly pushed the glasses farther up his face with an index finger, strolled back to his desk, and plopped down in the

11

high-backed chair. He whirled around like a child and then stopped his momentum by putting both hands on the desk.

"You rang?" Switzer repeated.

"Lurch, right? *The Addams Family?*"

"Boss?"

"Never mind." Goochly reached down near the bottom right drawer of the desk and lifted out a nylon bag, the kind the dry cleaner might use for dirty clothes. It was tied at the top. He plopped it down in front of the errand boy. "Take this," he said, pointing at the bag, "out to the homestead, and give it to my uncle." He looked past the boy's left shoulder. "And take that," he added, pointing the same finger at an electronic blackjack machine, a little smaller than a standard slot machine, "to the Squeaky Wheel out on Two Sixty-Four."

"Will Miss Teri be there?" The boy blushed a bit and looked down at his shoe tops.

"At the Squeaky Wheel? No idea," Goochly said, teasing the uncomfortable kid.

"No, sir," Cody mostly whispered, eyes still downcast. "At the homestead."

"I know what you meant, dipshit," he scolded. "And the answer's the same: no idea. Now take this stuff and get the hell out of here."

Without making eye contact, Switzer grabbed the bag and exited the office as quickly as he could.

"Not yet," Goochly said into thin air. Moments later, Cody came in again, hefted the gambling machine off the table, and struggled back out the door. Goochly never considered an offer to help. Knowing both reasons for the boy to be in the office were gone, he spoke to nobody again: "All clear." The nobody to whom he was not speaking emerged from the door to the bathroom in Goochly's office. Teri Hickox smiled at the man behind the desk.

"He's cute," she said as she approached Goochly and sat on his lap.

"He's twelve," Goochly grunted.

"Don't be jealous now," she said before leaning in and kissing her cousin hard on the mouth. "He's not as cute as you." She slid off his lap and headed for the door, lifting up her skirt to reveal a panties-less bottom on the way out. She stopped at the door and looked back over her shoulder. "And lose the glasses. They look silly." She blew him a second kiss and resumed her exit.

"Call your dad and tell him a delivery is on the way," he shouted to the lingering image of her perfect backside.

CHAPTER SIX

They were lying in bed, his body on top of the covers, hers underneath, watching TV. For the first half-a-dozen years of their live-in relationship, Brodie had resisted—in fact, laid down the law about—having a television set in the bedroom. Heart couldn't remember why she changed her mind, but he was happy she did. He could now watch his favorite baseball team play its West Coast home games from the comfort of the bed he shared with the love of his life. There remained rules, however; for example, the sound had to be all the way down, which it was at the moment.

"Aw, crud." He voiced his displeasure at the 6-4-3 double play he had just witnessed. Brodie opened her right eye.

"You all right?" she asked softly.

"Fine, doll. Just another inning-ending double play. I didn't mean to wake you."

"Wasn't sleeping." She continued to look at him through one brilliant blue eye. "Did you get your ears shortened?"

His chuckle manifested itself as a burst of air though his nostrils. Brodie Murdoch just might have been the smartest person

Heart had ever met, but she had a penchant for conflating colloquialisms and screwing up sayings. Friends, associates, and colleagues appeared to ignore this, while Lancaster Heart found it adorable. It reminded him of Norm Crosby, a comedian his mom and dad enjoyed. He could still hear them laughing during one of Crosby's late-night television appearances. Mixing up well-known phrases was one of the things Lancaster loved most about Brodie. One of a million things. He looked at her, still looking at him.

"I believe the parlance for getting a haircut is 'getting your ears lowered,' not shortened."

"You know what I meant." Her reply was so sweet and so loving, it instantly made him feel guilty for correcting her. "You *always* know what I mean." She kissed his chest, then rolled over onto her right side. He did always know what she meant. He turned his attention back to the ball game and watched his team's lefty ace strike out a batter on three pitches.

"You wanna know what BA had to say?" he asked Brodie's back. She snored lightly in response.

CHAPTER SEVEN

It felt to Cody as if he had made this drive a hundred times. Always with one kind of bag or another, sometimes more than one. He knew it was full of money but had no idea how much. He never looked, never cared, never hung around long enough to find out what Goochly's uncle Hank did with it.

He didn't much like Hank Hickox. He liked both of the Goochlys less, but he liked what they paid him, and he liked that they paid him in cash. There were two members of the family he *did* like: the dog, Duke, and Miss Teri, Hank's only daughter. He knew she knew he was stuck on her. He also knew his boss, Tanner Goochly Jr., knew he was sweet on her too. He figured Miss Teri's father, Hank, had no idea, because he guessed the old guy wouldn't take too kindly to that and Mr. Hank had always been kind to Cody.

The pickup kicked up dust in its wake as he made the turn off the paved road and onto the dirt and gravel that led to the Hickox house, the homestead. It was about a half a mile from the beginning of the road to the end. A wooden fence bordered the route on both sides the entire way. Some of the posts were topped with birdhouses, but during the hundred or so trips Cody had made up and down this strip, he had never seen a bird fly in, out, or around any of them. He didn't know why, but he did know some of the birdhouses contained cameras so somebody could keep an eye on who or what was coming and going. Driving in this time, the memory came back like a love letter with a return to sender stamp. It involved Teri Hickox and an incident that happened months ago, but to Cody, it always felt like yesterday. Every time he drove in now, he couldn't help but remember.

That time Teri had obviously been aware of his approach, because she had been standing in the doorway when Cody pulled up. He put the truck in park, checked his lap to make sure there were no obvious signs of his affection for Teri, and grabbed the bag of money before exiting the driver's side door. Teri greeted him with a smile and a peck on the cheek and said Mr. Hank was out in the field. Then she insisted Cody come inside. He said he shouldn't; she said he should. She won. Teri made him sit on the sofa and brought him a glass of sweet tea. Claimed she had made it herself, but it tasted store bought to him. His mom made the world's best sweet tea, but he lied and told her how good it was. She thanked him and plopped down on the sofa by his side. He tried his best to look calm, but she smelled so good. Lilacs and honey and a hint of summer sweat filled his nostrils, and he thought he might faint. Then she leaned over and placed her hand on his crotch and whispered in his ear all the things she'd like to do to him but said there were cameras *everywhere*, including in some of the birdhouses on the fence line outside. He heard about every third word because the blood rushing through his veins drowned out the other two. Her lips brushed against his ear. Her tongue flicked out to tickle it now and again. Her hand stayed in his lap. He felt himself grow hard as marble.

Cody Switzer had had sex twice, with the same girl, and he was all too aware that neither time had started out feeling anything like this. He was sure he was going to explode, so he shifted his weight, set his glass on the coffee table, and stood slowly on unsteady legs. He managed to stammer out a thank-you and hustled, stiff legged, out the door to his truck. He imagined she just stayed on the couch, smiling.

Driving among the birdhouses this time, Cody thought about that time. He couldn't stop thinking about Miss Teri Hickox. He spent just about every waking moment—and, if he was lucky, some nonwaking moments—thinking about her too. He pulled up to the house and killed the truck's engine. To his disappointment, Mr. Hank, not Miss Teri, greeted him, sitting in a rocking chair on the porch, shotgun across his lap, the 120-pound black-and-tan Rottweiler at his feet. Cody left the keys in the ignition and climbed out of the cab. The dog raised its heavy head, gave him little more than a cursory glance, and yawned.

"Hey, Mr. Hank," Cody said with a wave.

"Howdy, Cody. How was traffic?"

"Not too bad." Mr. Hank always asked him about the traffic, every single time, and Cody couldn't figure out why. It had no effect on either of them. Hank had no idea the route he traveled to get there or where he was headed once he left. As far as Cody could tell, Mr. Hank rarely, if ever, left the homestead himself, and if he did, he didn't go very far. Regardless, he *always* wanted to know how the traffic was.

"Got something for me?" It was another question the old man always asked even though he knew the answer was always yes. Why else would Cody Switzer come all the way out here? Cody knew there was another reason, but Hank didn't.

"Yes, sir." Cody walked around the back of the truck and came alongside the passenger door. From the rocking chair, Hank watched. From the porch, so did the Rottweiler. Cody opened the door and pulled out the canvas bag. Then he closed the door, shifted the bag from his left hand to his right, and headed toward the house.

"Right there is just fine." Hank had stopped rocking and was pointing the business end of the shotgun in Cody's direction. The dog was suddenly standing at attention. Cody knew this was also standard operating procedure, so he did what he always did; he dropped the bag on the ground. Normally the next step would be for him to retrace his steps, get back in the pickup, and hightail it out of there, but on this day, he stood his ground for an extra few seconds.

"Something on your mind, son?" Hank almost growled. The Rottweiler's tail wagged.

"No, sir." Cody tried his best to stay calm; then he smiled. "Is Miss Teri home?" He attempted to sound nonchalant but was fairly certain he had probably given up his secret. If Hank Hickox was any the wiser, it didn't appear that way to Cody.

"No, son, she's not. Law school today."

"Of course, thank you, sir. Sorry to bother you, sir. Adios, Duke." Cody walked backward to the truck.

"No bother."

Cody climbed inside, turned the key, and rolled down the window. After executing a U turn, he headed out the way he had come with a wave. In the rearview mirror, he saw the dog trot out to the canvas bag, wrap its drool-filled jaws around the top, and carry it back to his master. Cody reached the main road and turned left to make his second delivery of the afternoon. He noticed traffic was light.

CHAPTER EIGHT

Parker Murdoch watched the sun slowly set in the western sky. His bare feet, crossed at the ankles, were propped up on a wooden table. A seven-inch scar, tissue several shades lighter than the rest of his deeply tanned skin, ran up the outside of his left leg. In his left hand was an ice-cold bottle of imported beer; the right hand had just set aside a shot glass that, until seconds ago, was filled with his favorite brand of añejo tequila. A chime rang from somewhere inside the house, indicating that one of the several doors, hooked up to an intricate alarm system, had been opened.

"I'm out here, Claire," he called, assuming it was his wife. If it wasn't, he'd know soon enough. Murdoch had been a world-class athlete and still stayed in great shape. He was the classic multisport star growing up in a tiny Colorado town. Captain and quarterback of the football team, leading scorer on the basketball team, and the homerun-hitting centerfielder during baseball season. He was good at everything, and he was also smart. Smart enough to know, despite all the accolades and idolatry, that a big fish in a small pond usually struggles in the deeper waters of a more populated lake. So he took up cycling.

That more-even playing field led to Parker Murdoch scaling majestic heights. He trained in the Rockies and competed all over the globe. He won, among others, the Nevada City Classic Race and even shared the podium during a stage or two of a couple of Tour de France appearances. But the last time he competed in the most famous of all cycling spectacles, Murdoch found himself in the middle of the peloton with dozens of other pumping, sweating, grunting riders more than twenty minutes off the breakaway's pace during the 159-kilometer fifteenth stage. One moment he was reaching behind his back for a protein pack; the next he was face first on the French Alps asphalt road, bleeding, left leg twisted unnaturally and tangled between his bicycle frame and a mangled rear wheel. He covered up as best he could and rode out the wave of riders trying to avoid the heap of flesh, spokes, metal, and rubber in the road. Then he rode away from professional cycling and toward the hospital in an ambulance.

He spent the next several years rehabbing both mentally and physically. He started with a stint in the Hawaiian surf and sun, then made his way to Mexico, where he immersed himself in both the creation and consumption of tequila. The moneyed friends who helped sponsor his cycling career felt a debt of gratitude as well as a modicum of benevolence, and they pitched in to help Parker start a new tequila brand that would become internationally popular. Before the agave ascendancy, he spent about eighteen months introducing the spirit, and his spirit, to the masses. He was doing exactly that when Claire Hooper entered his life. They came together at a chili cook off in the historic mining town of Virginia City, Nevada.

She had hitchhiked from her home in rural Pennsylvania, determined to make her way west with the goal of becoming a world-class chef in San Francisco. She had impeccable taste and culinary gifts—everybody said so, so she believed it to be true and set out to prove it. One of her specialties was chili, and she helped support her cross-country sojourn by participating in, and almost always winning, cook offs at county competitions and state fairs. The Chili on the Comstock contest was the biggest, best, and most lucrative in the Silver State and the perfect opportunity to refill her purse. She noticed the slightly rugged, certainly handsome tequila rep with the nearly imperceptible limp immediately. As it turned out, he liked chili, and she liked tequila. They had been together ever since, including right now in their Aspen home.

"Hey, Park." Claire used the shortened version of his name as she leaned above him and kissed the top of his head. It was what she had called him from that very first night they were together.

"Hello, hot stuff." He answered with the term of endearment he had bestowed upon her the first time he tasted her delicacy.

"Want another beer?"

"Nah, I'm good. But grab one for yourself and come watch this gorgeous sunset with me."

"Sounds good." She turned to head back to the kitchen. "Have you heard from Brodie today?" she called back over her shoulder.

He pulled his phone out of his pocket and checked. "Not today. Why?"

She pulled a bottle from the fridge and headed back his way.

"No reason." She took a long sip. "Just got one of those feelings that something was up."

Parker mulled that for a moment as Claire pulled her chair a little closer to his. Claire's intuition had proved over the years to be unimpeachable.

"Maybe we should call." He took her hand. "Those feelings of yours are rarely wrong." She smiled a simple smile and clinked the top of his bottle with her own.

CHAPTER NINE

"What did you decide?" Heart heard the question despite an inordinate amount of wind and a less-than-ideal connection.

"Where are you?" He answered his agent's question with one of his own.

"Fourteenth green. Hang on, it's my turn."

"Of course it is," Lancaster said dismissively to suddenly no one.

"That putt can*not* break that way!" Heart's agent complained in the distance. Then after a few more seconds, BA was back on the line. "Sorry about that, Lancaster. Thought I made that one. Now, where were we?"

"You asked if I had come to a decision, and the answer is no."

"Really? I thought this was something you wanted." What *this* happened to be was an opportunity to return to his roots. He was being offered a job at his father's old television station serving the town in which he had spent most of his young life. The station where he got his start in the business. But this wasn't another reporter position or anchorman role. They wanted—were practically begging—him to come back and run the entire news department. Be the managing editor and director of news. It was indeed something Lancaster Heart wanted. He wanted it very much.

"It is," he said matter of factly. "But I haven't spoken to Brodie about it yet."

"Well, what are you waiting for?" Heart didn't have a good answer for that.

"Gotta go," BA interjected. "Reachable par five. Give me a buzz when you have something to give me a buzz about. I'll let them know we're working on it, but I can't keep them at arm's length forever." The agent ended the conversation and the connection.

Heart leaned back in his chair and looked up at the crater-like surface of the acoustic white-tile ceiling. There were half a dozen number-two pencils, erasers pointed his way, embedded in one of the squares directly above his head. He picked up another Ticonderoga, flung it upward, and watched it stick in a tight grouping with the others. His dad's former station had fallen on ratings hard times in recent years. It all started when the new owners, a media conglomerate that bought the enterprise from his parents, hired what they thought was a hotshot general manager. The GM, in turn, gave the station's longtime news director and Heart's mentor, Pierce Edwards, his walking papers. Then he replaced 90 percent of the veteran newsroom staff. A new news director, a fraternity brother of the GM, was hired, and he immediately began steering the broadcasts in a more tabloid direction. It turned out to be a complete misreading of the mostly rural, more-than-slightly-conservative viewership, and the ratings in northern Nevada almost immediately started to go south. Then they fell off a cliff.

It took a while, but the owners finally realized the root of the problem and decided to take action. They hoped a big part of the solution would be Lancaster Heart. The GM approached him through his agent and began the courting process. After the initial back and forth, both BA and Heart came to the conclusion that money was not going to be a sticking point. Heart wanted the job, but he had conditions that were nonnegotiable. First and foremost was almost complete autonomy to run the department and the authority to bring back Pierce Edwards, the man who had taught him everything he knew about the news business, as a consultant, sounding board, and mentor to a new breed of newsmen and newswomen. The station immediately agreed to that demand, so Heart made a phone call to find out if Edwards would be interested. "Not just yes, but *hell* yes!" was the response.

That pushed Heart closer to the point of no return, but what about Brodie? He had little to no interest in a long-distance relationship and even less enthusiasm about going anywhere without her, but he wasn't certain she would want to go. He pulled out one of the blue graph-paper legal pads that had been a constant throughout his entire career, and for what felt like the millionth time, he listed what he considered to be all of the pros and cons about the move.

At the end of the exercise, the "pro" side had more than a dozen reasons listed, while the "cons" column revealed only one: "Brodie likes North Carolina." He lifted the black phone from its cradle and punched the buttons for Brodie's direct line at work, knowing he'd get her voice mail.

"Hi, dorgeous," he said, combining the words "doll" and "gorgeous" on purpose. He had done it the first time by accident many moons ago, and the term of endearment stuck. "It's me." As if she wouldn't recognize his voice. "I really need to talk to you tonight. Love you." *Well, that sounded fucking ominous*, he thought as he replaced the phone.

A clause in his current contract allowed him to take a number of days or newscasts off at his discretion. Today would be one of those days, so his wannabe replacement, Ric (no *k*) Hammer (real name Richie Hammelstein), would suit up and start the telecast by letting viewers know Lancaster Heart was "on assignment." The assignment was to set the groundwork for getting the heck out of there for good. On the way to the grocery store to pick up ingredients for the dinner he would prepare for himself and Brodie, he reminisced about the day he had signed the contract under which he was now bound.

A local magazine had just named him the region's most popular television personality for the fourth straight year, and BA was quick to use that as leverage. Heart was happy with the money he made and told his agent to tell the station he didn't need all that much more, but he did insist on an out clause. He remembered BA looking at him skeptically for a second before quizzing him on what his particular out might be.

Heart was quick to respond, saying if he received an offer to become the managing editor or news director at another station or network, *other than* one in his current market, he could leave without penalty or repercussions. His agent nodded and said he couldn't imagine that being a problem. And as it turned out, it wasn't.

CHAPTER TEN

Hank Hickox stared at the twenty-, fifty-, and hundred-dollar bills floating in the laundry sink he had installed in the barn. As soon as Cody's truck was out of sight, he brought the bag of currency into the house and dumped it all out onto the table in his kitchen. It was more money than usual. He separated out a small pile and put the rest back in the bag, retied it, and set it aside. He took less this time than last, making a mental note to take more next time.

"That looks about right, don't it, Duke?" The dog ignored his master. His mind was purely on getting at the marrow inside some big bone. Hickox had been skimming money from his brother- and nephew-in-law for years. The first couple of times, it made him nervous, but it turned out to be so easy, for a number of reasons. First of all, the Goochlys were an extremely loyal clan, and while they didn't warm to Hank in the beginning stages of his courtship with their daughter, sister, aunt, they decided they liked him if she liked him. When Betty Lou Goochly became Betty Lou Hickox, they loved him.

Another reason taking the candy from these particular babies ended up being easy was that neither Tanner Goochly Sr. nor Jr. was very smart. For example, Hickox learned that both father and son assumed the other counted the money, when neither actually could be bothered. They just stuffed it in bags and gave it to that snot-nosed kid, Cody, who gave it to Hank. It was then his job to leave it in a Dumpster or trash can behind whichever business the Goochlys decided was that week's drop, to be picked up by one of many unknown, unnamed delivery delinquents. And because of reason number one, even if they realized that some of the money was being siphoned out of the system, Hank Hickox would have been the last person they suspected.

A third reason was the lack of a paper trail. Hank never put any of the stolen Jacksons, Grants, or Benjamins in a bank. His preference was coffee cans, a variety of Folgers, Taster's Choice and Maxwell House, buried a few feet deep around the vast acreage that composed the Hickox estate. He had already taken this week's take—he figured about $7,500—and run it through a small cement mixer filled with a couple of shovels full of Carolina dirt, and now he was rinsing it in the sink. It made the bills appear older, more well worn, used. He chuckled the first time he thought of himself as a "money launderer." Then he realized he was just a plain old thief, stealing from other thieves. After the money dried, he'd roll it up, wrap a rubber band around it, then go out to the south forty and find a can. Over the years, he figured he had put several hundred thousand bucks of the Goochlys' illegal gambling earnings in Hickox family ground. It was a fairly steady stream of income that was interrupted for about thirty-five months when Tanner Goochly Sr. was in the hoosegow.

The betrayal all started the day after he lost his Betty Lou to a shocking, sudden illness. The doc said a blood vessel burst near the base of her brain, killing her instantly. Called it a cerebral aneurysm and said she wouldn't have felt any pain. *How the hell could he know that?* Hank thought. He had no way of knowing if she suffered any pain, or how long it took her to die. Nobody did. Hank found her on the kitchen floor, soup pot boiling on the stove, after he had come in from working one of the fields. All he had wanted was a drink of cold water and a kiss. He'd never get one of those two things again.

Hank's heart broke, and then it broke again when he had to tell his ten-year-old little girl when she came home from school and wondered where Mommy was. Hank never had a way with words, and holding back tears, he simply said, "She died, honey. Mommy just died." He told the Goochlys too, both Tanners and Betty Lou's father, Gus, who took it the hardest. In fact, four days later, Gus Goochly blew his brains out in his car, a picture of a teenage Betty Lou in his lap, so they had ended up burying two Goochlys in one day.

Hank, with the money in a front pocket of his overalls and a shovel over his shoulder, headed away from the back of the house. The Rottweiler was by his side. Somehow the dog knew exactly where there was a half-full coffee can and made a beeline for it.

"Good boy." Hickox patted the dog on the head when he caught up to it. He pulled a hunk of beef jerky from another pocket and took a bite. Gave what was left to the dog. Then he unearthed the can, dropped in the cash, and covered it up with dirt again. When they got back to the house, Teri was on the porch.

"Hi, Daddy."

"Hello, angel."

"Hey, Duke!" She clapped her hands. "Come here, boy." The dog, stubby tail wagging, obliged.

"How was school today?"

"Just fine. We had a guest lecturer talk to us about the economics of evaluation, as well as debt and leverage."

"How did you get so smart?" he asked with pride after her words went in one ear and out the other.

"Good genes," she said and kissed him on the forehead.

CHAPTER ELEVEN

H eart was whisking egg whites. Heart hated whisking egg whites, but he knew, thanks to Claire Murdoch, that properly whisked egg whites were the key to ideal waffle batter. Waffles were Brodie's favorite thing to eat, which was information also gleaned from Claire Murdoch. To get his mind off the tedious task of whisking, Heart recalled special moments spent with Brodie. He remembered the time they went engagement-ring shopping on a lark. Over ice cream cones, they both separately but at the same time professed the opinion that marriage was not in the cards.

"Why do it?" she had asked after a lick of her cone.

"Why indeed?" he replied.

Both meant it at the time—at least he was certain he did. He was also becoming more and more attuned to the feeling that, marriage or not, he didn't want any part of a life without Brodie Murdoch in it. There was a high-end jewelry store catty corner from the ice cream shop, and they decided to go inside.

"Neither one of us wants to get married, but if we did, what kind of ring would you want?" He held the door open, then followed her to the diamond display. The salesperson said they made a beautiful couple.

"Aren't you on TV?" she asked Heart.

"We do, and I am."

"We're just looking," Brodie interjected.

She tried on several beautiful, brilliant rings and *really* liked one of them, and then they left. Four days later, Heart had returned and purchased the ring, just in case they decided to revisit the whole marriage thing.

He whisked and reminisced, and then his phone rang. He recognized the number, pushed the green button to accept, and then hit the icon image of a speaker.

"Hello, Park." It was Brodie's dad calling. "Sorry to put you on speaker, but I'm whisking egg whites." He called Parker Murdoch by his nickname because when they first met the man had asked him to.

"Waffles?" A hint of envy from the other end of the phone. "What's the occasion?"

"Thursday," Heart answered. "What can I do for you, sir?"

"I didn't mean to trouble you, but I tried Brodie's cell, and it went straight to voice mail."

"No trouble at all. She should be home any minute. Is everything okay? Is Claire okay?"

"Everything is copacetic," Park reassured Heart. "Brodie's mother just wanted to check in. And so did I."

"I'll have her call as soon as she walks in the door."

"Much appreciated. By the way, when are you going to make an honest woman out of my little girl? I'm not real big on the two of you living in sin."

"Says the guy who lived with Claire Hooper for three years."

"Two and a half," was the rapid response. "And my advice would be to do as I say, not as I did." They both laughed.

"Actually, if I'm being completely honest, I am afraid you won't give me your blessing and Brodie won't give me the answer I'm hoping for."

"Good reasons, both." Park paused a little longer than Heart liked, making him wonder how serious the man was. "Have Brodie call her mother." With that, Parker Murdoch hung up.

A half an hour later, the egg whites were whisked, the batter perfectly mixed, and the flowers he had picked up along with the ingredients for dinner were trimmed and in a vase. Brodie walked in the door with her right hand behind her back. She looked past him, into the kitchen.

"Waffles?" she asked excitedly. "For me?"

"Waffles." He smiled. "And no, they're not for you. They're for Mr. Rosenberg," he chided, referring to their next-door neighbor.

"What's the occasion?" She asked the same question her father had, which, for a fleeting instant, reminded him to tell her to call her mother.

"It's Thursday." He gave the same answer.

"No, it's not; it's Wednesday." She cocked her head, then saw the flowers. "*And* flowers?"

"It is?" For some reason he looked at his watch. "No, it's Thursday. What do you have behind your back?" She smiled, then showed him. He recognized the bottle of scotch immediately. It was a 1973 Ladyburn, extremely rare and expensive. The scotch was a product of the now-defunct Girvan distillery in the Ayrshire area of Scotland. That part of the country was the ancestral home of the Murdoch clan, and he and Brodie had visited it a number of years ago. They had fallen in love with the land, the people, and the place. Heart had an affinity for the scotch, the 1973 Ladyburn in particular, but it had proved impossible to find since the distillery had closed and was subsequently demolished. Impossible for him, apparently not for Brodie.

"Seventy-three Ladyburn? For me?"

"No, silly, for Mr. Rosenberg."

He took her in his arms.

CHAPTER TWELVE

Fast-food wrappers shared the top of the coffee table with two semiautomatic Beretta handguns. The 92 model belonged to Tanner Goochly Jr.; he had procured the 8000 Cougar for her. Goochly's grandfather had taught his father how to handle firearms; Tanner Sr. had taught Tanner Jr. Now Junior was teaching Teri Hickox. The table was pushed out of the way to make room for her to get between his legs. Her head bobbed back and forth while his stayed perfectly still. Both their eyes were closed—his due to delight, hers disgust.

For him it was an opportunity to get his rocks off. For her it was a necessary evil, a means to an end. Men were so stupid, she had come to realize, and so easy. She had figured out a good butt and an even better blow job could get almost every one of them to do just about anything. Like giving up secure passwords to multimillion-dollar accounts at a prestigious law firm. Or getting access to and being taught how to use a gun.

"You're getting good," Junior said in delight. Teri wiped her mouth with a Taco Bell napkin.

"At this?" She licked her lips. That made Tanner Goochly Jr. laugh.

"No. At shooting that little Cougar." His eyes lit on the gun and then found their way back to hers. "You've always been good at this."

She almost threw up in her mouth as he buttoned his Levi's. She couldn't wait to blow his mind literally, not just figuratively, but that would have to wait. For now, she needed her dimwit cousin to be the conduit for her to get deeper inside his father's—her uncle's—operation. She'd get in by continuing to get him off; then she'd get rid of them both. Her mother's death was still fresh in some part of her mind, and so was the blame she placed on the Goochlys, all of them. In her mind, they had made her mom's too-short life a living hell. She knew about the baggage, the belittling, the beatings, and worse. Her mother, in a rare moment of openness, had confided in Teri. Told her things she wouldn't, couldn't ever tell Hank. Gus Goochly was an evil, twisted man. A taker, a manipulator, a demon. Teri was glad the bastard had left this earth full of guilt when he put a gun in his mouth and pulled the trigger. She would never forgive him. She would never forgive any of them. She would make them pay.

CHAPTER THIRTEEN

Brodie had wanted to do the dishes. Heart thought they could wait. Brodie won. To expedite the procedure, he helped, and the entire exercise made each want the other even more. With the last dish done, they decided the now-clean kitchen island was as good a place as any.

"You want some more champagne?" They had moved to the living room couch, and he was stroking a bare leg draped over his. He took a sip of scotch, savored it.

"Sure, but I'll get it."

Heart watched her go back toward the kitchen and the bottle of Veuve Clicquot. He marveled, as always, at how beautiful she was. She poured more bubbly into her glass, took a sip, and headed back his way.

"Let's do it!" She referred back to the postcoital conversation just moments ago. He had laid it all out—the new job offer, the deal, his desires, but no demands on her.

"Really?"

"Of course." She set the flute down, sat herself down, and kissed him on the mouth. "I mean, you gotta take the bull by the tail." He couldn't decide if she was trying to say "the bull by the horns" or "a tiger by the tail" but realized it didn't matter because in this instance they both meant pretty much the same thing. "We've been saying we want to move back west."

That was "pro" number four, thought Lancaster.

"And I can do my job from anywhere as long as there's an airport."

Number nine. Heart reached for and held her hand.

"Oh shit!" he blurted out.

"What?"

"I forgot to tell you to call your mom."

"Go get my phone." She laughed and kicked him off the couch.

CHAPTER FOURTEEN

Teri Hickox walked out of the gun store with an extra spring in her step. She had just picked up her brand-new Sig Sauer P238 semiautomatic 9mm handgun. She came to the immediate conclusion that the high she now found herself on was better and less destructive than any blast of Tanner's cocaine. And Tanner's cocaine was always primo. Her thoughts returned to the gun: *unless, of course, I accidentally shoot myself.* Then she giggled at the thought.

That nitwit Tanner Goochly Jr. thought he was teaching her how to shoot with the Beretta he kept for her. The truth was she had been meeting up with a gun-enthusiast colleague from the law firm once or sometimes twice a week at a local gun club. She was the one who introduced Teri to the Sig, and Teri had loved the way it felt in her hand the moment she put it there. It weighed about a pound, a little more with a full magazine, and fought back with minimal recoil. Plus, it fit perfectly in her purse or the back pocket of her favorite jeans. She even loved the cute leather thigh holster her law-firm friend had given her as a present. Teri had enthusiastically thanked her for the gift for a little more than an hour in a motel room on the outskirts of town one hot, lazy afternoon.

She filled out all the forms, submitted to a comprehensive background check, and counted out ten crisp, clean hundred-dollar bills for the weapon and some ammunition. She registered the gun, applied for and received a concealed-carry permit, and was suddenly ready, willing, and able to defend herself if she had to or to kill somebody in cold blood if she wanted to. The latter was exactly what she intended to do.

Teri had been hanging around Tanner Goochly Jr. for as long as she could remember. That's what cousins do in the South. The two had only just recently started having sex. Some closed-minded folks might say that's another thing cousins do in the South. Junior had once admitted that the fact they were related was one of the things that excited him about their physical relationship. That and the fact that she had great tits and a perfect ass. Teri didn't have any qualms about it at all. She liked having sex with Tanner. He could be surprisingly caring and gentle, and he had a decent-sized dick. She knew he wouldn't hurt her or mistreat her. She also knew he wasn't really her cousin.

It was sometime around the third grade that Teri Hickox had started feeling like she was different from her mom and dad. She noticed that her friends and classmates looked and acted a lot like their parents when they were picked up from school. She saw them move and sound alike when she went for playdates. But when she looked in the mirror, she didn't see any part of her mom or her dad looking back. She had blond hair; they didn't. She had freckles; they didn't. She had bright-blue eyes; theirs were brown. She wondered why but didn't ask because she was loved. Then her mom, days before death, told her the truth. It helped her stop worrying, *Is what killed my mom waiting to kill me one day?* But it made her start wanting to find her real mom.

She allowed resentment a shelter, a place to hang and grow. It provided the tools to paint her birth mother as a monster, someone who would give a baby away, leave it behind, abandon it, because this woman was a person who cared more about herself than the innocent, helpless baby she was responsible for bringing into the world. At least that's the way Teri saw it. Her fake mother had loved her and left her because she died. Her real mother didn't want anything to do with her because a baby would ruin her own life. At least that's the way Teri had it figured. Then she found out the bitch still only lived about forty miles away, with her rich second husband and his twin spoiled, bratty boys. The mom she had known growing up never got the chance to see her graduate from high school or college or share in the excitement of being accepted to law school. They would never get to shop for a prom dress or a wedding dress together. She never got the chance to say good-bye. She vowed that wouldn't happen with her birth mother. She'd look the woman right in the eyes when she shot her. She'd smile as the light of life left those eyes. At least that's the way Teri had it planned.

She had driven the forty miles more than a dozen times. Found the target, stalked her, knew exactly when and where she'd be. Then decided how she would get her alone, and that's exactly what she did.

Teri Hickox surprised Daisy Burns on the sidewalk as the woman exited the beauty salon. The daughter knew the mother immediately; after all, she had been studying her movements for months. The mother recognized the daughter immediately too. She hadn't seen her since walking out the shelter door, without as much as a glance back, but the resemblance was unmistakable.

"Oh my God!" Daisy's hand went to her mouth in perfect southern fashion.

"Hello, Mother," a steely eyed Teri replied.

"Oh my God," the woman said again, absolute fear replacing surprise. "How?"

Your god doesn't exist, lady, Teri thought, *and even if he did, he can't help you now.* "Can I buy you a cup of coffee?" Teri said. "Or something stronger?"

Daisy Burns didn't live long enough to tell her husband, or anybody else, about the reunion.

CHAPTER FIFTEEN

Heart was beating golf balls on the practice range of the club to which both he and Brodie belonged. About fifty yards away, the head pro David Gerald was finishing up with a lesson. Lancaster knew there were country clubs where he and Brodie were headed—heck, his parents had belonged to one—but he'd miss this place. It was a golf-only club that featured a great course, a friendly enough "mind your own business" membership, and a respect for Brodie and all the female members. All things Heart both expected and appreciated. He had worked his way through the short irons in his bag and next reached for his six iron.

He had played golf competitively as a junior and in high school—at least as competitively as a kid from northern Nevada could. The season at the base of the Sierra Nevada Mountains was short compared to a lot of places, and the kids who played in those places were just better. He got a taste of that reality at the few national junior tournaments in which he competed, and a steadier diet of it when he played college golf in the Pacific Northwest. His occasional sixty-eight was no match for a constant barrage of sixty-fours and sixty-fives fired by most of his opponents and a few of his own teammates.

In reality his younger brother was the family's best player, consistently whooping Heart head to head and earning a spot on the golf team at a prestigious southwestern school. But in the end even he couldn't make a go of it. There were just too many really, really good players out there. One of his brother's chief competitors was a talented kid from southern Nevada named David Gerald. Small world.

"Hello, Mr. Heart." The pro, who greeted every member formally, had made his way down the line at the practice tee.

"Mayor," Heart replied. Gerald wasn't actually the mayor of anything, but he had earned the nickname by being the most social and sociable player on the mini tour circuit when he played as a pro. He was everybody's buddy, a lot of people's confidant, and a heck of a player, winning a time or two on various tours, including the one that was one step away from the PGA TOUR. Injuries and attitude kept him from attaining the ultimate highest heights as a professional golfer, but he did what he always had; he landed on his feet. This time, it happened to be at this club and David Gerald was as well liked here as he had been out there.

"What are you working on?" Gerald asked as he rolled another slightly beaten-up Titleist at Heart's feet.

"Nothing in particular, just beating balls."

"Now, now." The pro shook his index finger back and forth. "Remember you need to practice with a purpose." Heart took a big swing and intentionally dug his six iron into the ground a couple of inches behind the ball. A tuft of grass flew about five feet; the golf ball stayed put.

"What am I doing wrong, Pro?" he asked with mock sincerity.

"Not a thing. Looks good." They both laughed.

An hour or so later, Heart was in the grill room having a Cobb salad when the pro appeared again.

"When are you guys leaving?"

"How did you know?"

"Brodie told me."

"Girl just can't keep a secret," Heart said before shoving another forkful of salad into his mouth. He chewed and swallowed. "But that's okay. She's got a million other redeeming qualities."

Once upon a time Heart had wondered if Brodie and Gerald were an item. Heart noticed they appeared to be awfully chummy when he first joined the club. That was before he and Gerald put the common pieces of each other's past together and he realized the pro was chummy with everybody. It's not that there wasn't a connection. There was; it just wasn't an attraction. Then Brodie Murdoch fell in love with him, and David Gerald didn't matter. Bottom line was Brodie and Heart had something in common with just about everybody who crossed paths with Gerald; they genuinely liked the guy.

"We're hoping to leave in a month, six weeks max," he said, answering the original question. "We gotta get the house ready to put on the market, among other things." Brodie had purchased her home a couple of months before she and Heart started dating. He moved in, at her request, less than a year later. Legally it was her place, but they split all of the expenses, including the mortgage, fifty-fifty. Heart, Brodie, and her parents wouldn't have it any other way.

"Why not rent it?" Heart and Brodie hadn't considered that. "My sister has a coworker at the law firm who might be looking for a place. Your house could be perfect."

"I'll speak with Brodie about it," Heart said as he suddenly considered becoming a landlord. Then he took one last bite of his salad.

"Sure. Just let me know if I can help." The pro gently slapped the table with the fingers of his right hand and got up to leave. As he wandered over to greet another table of members, Heart remembered there was something else he needed to do that day. He pulled his phone out of his pocket and dialed United Airlines. Next, he called the man he hoped would be his future father-in-law.

CHAPTER SIXTEEN

Lancaster Heart was a terrible liar. As a rule, he didn't practice the offense, mainly because he believed in telling the truth but partly because he knew he was just so bad at lying. And Brodie knew it too. Because of all of that, he hated it when he felt he had to hide the truth from her. He was packing an overnight bag when he heard the door to the house open and close. He took a deep breath and steeled himself for the discomfort that was about to come.

"Going somewhere?" She had quickly and silently come up the stairs.

"Jesus, doll! You scared the crap out of me."

"Going somewhere without me?" She added two words to the question.

Heart tried to conceal another deep breath—he couldn't—and then attempted to put on his most sincere face as he turned and found the woman he loved.

"Reno." He reached her in one long stride and gave her a kiss. "Why? When?"

"Tomorrow." He truthfully answered the second question first. "To meet with Pierce." He added the lie and finished it off with another truth. "Just for a day."

He watched Brodie take a bite out of the lie sandwich, decide she recognized the flavor, and figure she'd swallow it anyway. Heart knew she knew that he was an incompetent liar. But she had also told him he was the most loving, honest, faithful man she'd ever met.

Please don't ask to come along, thought Heart. He hoped she'd let it be, let him go. He'd bought a ticket to Reno, making sure it included a stop in Denver, because he was aware that she'd see the credit card receipt. But he had no intention of continuing to the "Biggest Little City in the World," even though he realized she would also see the one-way ticket from Denver to Raleigh somewhere on the same receipt. He was counting on the fact that the reason for the deception would far outweigh the actual betrayal. A classic case of the ends justifying the means.

"What's for dinner?" she asked. Then she kissed him on the forehead, spun on her right heel, and headed back downstairs. As he stood there, he knew she had to have noticed the sweat circles that had soaked through his shirt at his armpits. As she walked away, he couldn't see the smile on her face.

Brodie would have loved to go to Reno with Caster. Lake Tahoe was one of her favorite places, and she knew she'd have no problem spending a day there while he met with his mentor. But he wasn't going anywhere near Reno on this particular trip. She was mildly curious about where he really was headed, but it wasn't that big a deal. She trusted him. She was also looking forward to a little alone time. They both knew how much she enjoyed her "me" time.

"Salmon," he called as he closed and zipped the overnighter. "I'll fire up the grill."

CHAPTER SEVENTEEN

Teri tried to pay attention on her drive home. She kept the speedometer at exactly four miles an hour over the speed limit but forgot to use her indicator whenever she changed lanes. Confronting her birth mother had gone, in some respects, exactly as she had for so long planned, but in other ways the "conversation" they'd had and the moves Teri had made came as a complete surprise. She turned off her phone to avoid any potential distractions, but she did turn on the radio. For some reason, she tuned it to an oldies station and tried to hum along to songs she really didn't know. Out of the blue she giggled, then chuckled, then laughed out loud. Despite following—practically stalking—her birth mother for months and memorizing every physical feature, she reveled in the knowledge that she would never have to see her again.

CHAPTER EIGHTEEN

As a decades-long veteran of the police force, Marc Allen had seen his share of dead people. But this one struck him as a little strange. The body, from what he could tell, belonged to a once relatively attractive female. That determination was more difficult because the victim had been shot three times at point-blank range. Once in the face, once in the heart, and once right between the legs. Someone would eventually tell him in what order those shots had been delivered and which one may have been most responsible for the victim's death. He guessed it was the shot to the heart, but he'd let the experts confirm that. For some sick reason, he started humming the famous Bon Jovi song, popular when he was in high school, while he continued to examine the crime scene. Another expert, or maybe the same expert, would also give him a best estimation on time of death. It had clearly been a while, but how much of a while had yet to be determined. He noticed it had been long enough for some four-legged and feathered scavengers to get a meal but not long enough for any major decomposition to take place. He'd get the information on all of it soon enough, but in the meantime, he contemplated the crime scene. He knew from experience it wasn't very often that bodies of full-grown adults were found near the Dumpsters behind the Planned Parenthood office in this North Carolina town. Especially full-grown adult bodies that were well past the age of the clinic's usual customers.

Allen jotted down another note in his black leather sheathed notebook. "Employee? Doctor? Volunteer?" he scribbled, indicating a line of questioning he would later pursue. One of the first things they had taught him at the academy was not to jump to conclusions. "The best cops make determinations based on facts," they preached. Seemed obvious, he thought at the time, but he never forgot those words as he worked his way up the institutional ladder from beat cop to detective. They had served him well in his service to the people of the community as well as to his fellow cops. But staring down at the bloodied corpse, one unpecked eye staring back, he couldn't help but jump to the conclusion that somebody *really* hated this woman. "You give love a bad name." The words of Jon Bon Jovi, Richie Sambora, and Desmond Child returned, and he whistled softly.

"Hey, Detective." Allen recognized the voice and turned slowly to face the camera operator from one of the local TV stations.

"Denise, you can't be back here."

"I know, Marc." She betrayed a familiarity by using his first name. "But at least I left the camera in the truck."

"That's big of you, Guy." He used the French pronunciation of the male name.

"I'm a giver." She shrugged and smiled. "Whadda you got?"

He knew she knew exactly what he had. "Possible homicide," he deadpanned.

"Possible?" she deadpanned back.

He remembered Denise Clawsew could deadpan with the best of them. The two had dated briefly—in reality it was a one-night hookup years ago. They went out a few times after that, but both came to the decision, almost simultaneously, that work was going to complicate things and maybe they were better suited being friends instead of lovers. And they had been friends, good ones, until recently. They had been spending quite a bit more time together lately, and Allen decided he was okay with that. Her last name conjured up visions for him of the bumbling French police inspector Clouseau, played expertly by Peter Sellers in the old *Pink Panther* movies. One of the characters the goofball cop assumed in the films was named Guy Gadois, pronounced "Gee Gadwah." Since her last name reminded him of the fictional cop's last name, she immediately became "Guy" to him. She didn't care as long as he was the only one who called her that and he did it when nobody else was around. So far he was and he had.

"How did you know I was here?"

"Scanner," she said. "But I didn't know it was you until I pulled up and saw your car. Do we have a story here?"

"I would say that's a given," he replied, "but give me a day or two, okay, Guy?" He knew she would. "I just want to get a little better handle on this."

"Not a problem, Marc." The quick response let the detective know she was confident that her rivals, the other two stations in the market, weren't anywhere near being aware of the story yet. Allen would make sure it stayed that way. "Forty-eight hours." She started to walk away, but after three steps, she turned back.

"I'm just going to shoot some B-roll—front of the building, signage, that kind of thing—so I don't have to come back."

"Fine, but not too close."

Clawsew looked past him for the first time, to the dead woman's body lying on the ground. "Man, somebody had a hard on for her." She shook her head, then pulled out a pack of cigarettes, shook one loose, and popped it in her mouth. "I need a smoke."

"Don't light it up here," Allen warned, and then he went back to work. So did Denise Clawsew. When she got back to the station's

Suburban, she called Lancaster Heart. His phone went straight to voice mail.

"Caster, it's Denise. We got a homicide about a half an hour outside of town. Woman, murdered in what looks like execution style, near the Dumpster behind a PP. Marc Allen is the detective, and he asked for a little time, but he said when he's ready the story is ours. Call me back." She clicked off and finally lit the cigarette still hanging in her mouth.

CHAPTER NINETEEN

Heart loved flying into Denver. The Rocky Mountains made it one of the prettiest places in the country. He normally chose aisle seats when he flew (unless he flew with Brodie—then he gave her the aisle and he took the middle seat), but when he traveled to Denver, he sat by the window if he could. Just after landing, he pulled his phone out and checked his messages. He had two. The first was from Brodie, who hoped he had a good flight and told him she missed and loved him. It was one of those romantic ritual things they shared when either traveled without the other. He had started it when they first began dating and had been relieved when she didn't find it too corny to continue. Or if she did, she continued it anyway, which made him like—then love—her even more. The second and only other message was from Denise Clawsew. Something about a murder that might turn out to be an exclusive. People were more than occasionally found dead in and around Raleigh, but this one appeared to be of particular interest to the station's top camera operator. He'd call both back when he got in his rental car. After all, he had a three-and-a-half-hour, two-hundred-plus-mile drive ahead of him. He made sure to up-grade his rental car to include satellite radio and spent the better part of the first hour of his trip bouncing back and forth from one cable news outlet to another. It saddened him to listen to the same stories told from completely opposite ends of the political and ideological spectrum.

He was a newsman, and he wanted to hear the news, not a con-stantly interjected stream of less-than-objective opinions. He never forgot the words of his mentor Pierce Edwards, who told everyone who would listen, "There are two things that make up a newscast. One is stories, dispassionately delivered and balanced by views espoused by all sides. The other is commentary, punctuated by both a disclaimer and an identifier. One belongs at the beginning of the broadcast, the other at the end." Pierce practiced what he preached even if it meant an occasional summons to the general manager's office, Lancaster's father's office. Heart was proud to have followed in those footsteps. His frustration growing, he gave up on the radio altogether.

He had made this trek many times before, almost always with Brodie, but never alone. Most times, including the most recent, Heart and Brodie simply headed west for about 150 miles on Interstate 70 toward Glenwood Springs. Along the way, they'd pass through the Eisenhower Tunnel on the way to the towns of Frisco and Vail and Eagle before hooking up with the Colorado River. He recalled Brodie, with her left arm dangling out the open driv-er-side window and her right hand on the wheel, reminding him that the tunnel, an engineering marvel, represented the highest point (11,158 feet) along the national interstate highway system. Then she'd add, "Did you know the section of the road through Glenwood Canyon is one of the final pieces of the entire system to open to traffic? And," she'd excitedly add, "one of the most expen-sive stretches of rural highway ever built in the United States." The only time he hadn't known these facts was right before the first time she'd told him. He figured it was Claire or Park or both who had given her the facts on more than one occasion too.

But he decided he wasn't going that way this time, on this day. He was going to take the even more scenic route over Independence Pass. It might take a little longer, depending on traffic, but that was okay; he needed as much time as possible to figure out exactly what he wanted to say when he reached his destination. Brodie hadn't answered her phone when he called, so he had left a brief message. Denise's line had gone directly to voice mail without a ring, so he had hung up and decided to try later. It was later, so he tried again. This time she picked up on the first ring.

"Superstar!"

Heart chuckled because she always sounded happy to hear from him.

"Where are you? I looked on the schedule and saw that Ric 'the Dick' was filling in again." The nickname for his fill-in was appropriate, and Heart knew Denise wasn't the only one who called him that. She was, however, the only one who called him that to his face.

"Outta town for a couple of days. I got your message. Tell me about this murder."

"It was gross, Caster. You should have seen the scene."

"I'm all ears."

"I couldn't get a great look because Allen was doing everything he could to make sure I didn't. But what I did see was a woman, maybe midforties, shot point blank at least a couple of times, including once in the head. Looked pretty methodical, even professional."

"Sure sounds like it. And you said the body was behind a Planned Parenthood building?"

"Yup. Right next to the Dumpster."

"Next to it but not *in* it?"

"That's right. Is that important?"

"No idea. You said Allen caught the case?"

"I did. He did."

"That's good. He's a solid guy."

"And he owes me one now." He could see the smile on her face from thousands of miles away. Denise loved it when somebody owed her one.

"Even better."

"Gotta go, Caster. Duty calls. Enjoy the mountain air." And she was gone, leaving him to wonder if she knew where he was or if she was just guessing.

CHAPTER TWENTY

Teri Hickox rode a high throughout the entire weekend. She couldn't sleep more than an hour or two at a time, but she didn't feel the least bit tired. An hour earlier she had cleaned her gun for the third time. The weapon was in her purse along with rolls of cash she had removed from one of the Folgers cans on her old man's property. Teri wanted another gun and figured Hank wouldn't miss a few bills from each of a handful of buried cans strewn about the farm. She resisted the urge to get in her car and go back to the same gun store at which she had purchased the Sig Sauer, and she succeeded for the better part of a day and a half. Teri didn't know what kind of gun to buy but thought maybe Tanner could help with that. She hit the icon on her phone for her favorites and then tapped Tanner Goochly's name.

"Hey." Man of few words, she thought.

"Hi, Tan Man." She used a nickname she knew bugged him. "Whatcha doin'?"

"Workin'. Don't call me that."

"On Sunday?" She knew he was much more likely to be at the lake with some buddies or at the gun range by himself.

"One of the damn poker machines at Lou's is broke. Dad told me I had to fix it before Monday."

Lou's was one of the watering holes that the Goochlys used to house their illegal gambling operations, and it was one of the more lucrative spots. The cop responsible for keeping law and order in the little town where Lou's was located was the namesake's brother-in-law. Free drinks and a little something extra for the effort every month did wonders for helping the relative with the badge look the other way. But Teri was aware that the wolf was more than occasionally at the door. Tanner had told her more than once that the Raleigh cops were constantly poking around and breathing down their necks. *That's what happens when you've already been arrested once for doing something,* she had thought but hadn't said.

"Interested in taking a break?" She tried to be coy.

"Not really," was his unaffected reply.

Teri actually wasn't all that interested in Tanner at the moment either, but she had zero intention of taking no for an answer. She wanted the hillbilly to help her with something, and she knew she could get him to do it if she gave him something else to do first.

"I got a six-pack of cold PBR and nothin' under my jeans but what the good lord gave me." She used a more direct approach this time.

"How long will it take you to get here?"

CHAPTER TWENTY-ONE

Heart made good time, even as he made sure to observe the speed limit heading into both Twin Lakes and Leadville. He chuckled at the police vehicle parked on the outskirts of the first tiny town, dummy behind the wheel. The decoy had been there long before Heart saw it with the Murdochs so many years ago. The highway that took him to and over Independence Pass proved the perfect place to clear his head and practice the speech he had been working on for days. The pass officially started at 9,200 feet above sea level, then rose up to the heavens. The aspen trees gave way to the pines, which gave way to the tundra. He recalled another earlier trip with Brodie. She was driving; he was gazing out the window at the trees. He grew up out west, but in the high desert of Reno, home to towering pine trees and tumbling sagebrush. He'd seen plenty of photographs of aspens, but in person they were much more beautiful and impressive.

"Those trees are cool," he recalled saying sophomorically.

"Aspens are magical." Heart thought she sounded like a poet. "And they're a natural phenomenon. Did you know that big copse that you're admiring"—she pointed at the same trees—"they all come from the same single root." It was the first time he could remember hearing the word "copse" used in a sentence. A little later he looked up her statement about the solitary-root system and discovered Brodie was correct about that as well. He wasn't surprised.

Back in the present, he was nearing the summit. At the top, he pulled off to the side of the road, got out of the rental, and took several long deep breaths of the sweetest air on the planet. He watched as folks took or asked strangers to take pictures of themselves hard against the Parks Service monument. Independence Pass, elevation 12,095 feet, Continental Divide. He recalled Claire snapping a photo of him and Brodie at the very same spot. He could see peaks in the distance and knew they were Grizzly Peak, Mount Champion, and Casco Peak, but for the life of him he couldn't remember which was which. *Claire and Park would be so disappointed,* he thought. Then he chuckled and climbed back behind the wheel. It was all downhill into Aspen from there.

A little more than half an hour later, he pulled into the iconic mountain village. He turned off of Main and onto Bleeker Street and followed it to the Murdochs' house at the corner of Bleeker and Third. Heart didn't want to announce his presence, so he rolled through the intersection, parked the rental on the street in front of Pioneer Park, and doubled back on foot. Claire's white Range Rover was parked in front of the house. Heart knew there were two more automobiles behind the closed garage doors—Parker Murdoch's babies, a 1997 Porsche 911, 993 series Turbo and a 1964 Mercedes Benz 230 SL. Lancaster had seen both, been in neither. He wandered around to the side of the beautiful—*was it recently painted?*—Victorian home. Claire Murdoch was on her knees, back to Heart, wide-brim hat on her head, working on a flower bed. Lancaster's shadow covered several of the blooming mountain harebells in the garden.

"If you're a Jehovah's Witness, I'm way beyond salvation. If you're a thief, go inside, door's open, and see the guy with the guns." Claire Hooper Murdoch didn't turn around.

"Hello, Claire." She turned around.

"Lancaster?"

Hugs were quickly exchanged, and Claire got right to the point.

"What are you doing here?"

"I need to talk to Park." He looked toward the house, then back at Claire. "And you."

She grabbed his shoulder and gave it a loving squeeze.

"He's inside."

Heart took a deep breath, smiled at his future mother-in-law, and headed for the front door.

CHAPTER TWENTY-TWO

"That was special." Teri was on her back. Tanner sat on the edge of the bed.

"Don't be a bitch."

"Can't help it," she said as she rolled off the mattress and made a beeline for the bathroom. On the way, she stopped, turned toward Tanner, and gave him her best kissing-cousin smile. "I want to buy a gun of my own." She conveniently left out the fact that she already had one. Tanner looked up but was silent for a few seconds.

"What the hell for?" he said a little too defensively. "What's wrong with the Cougar?"

"Nothing is *wrong* with the Cougar." She turned toward the bathroom, sounding exasperated. "But it's not *mine*; it's yours." Tanner stared after her.

"Why do you need a gun of your own?" He asked the same question in a slightly different way. "You can use the Beretta any time you want. Hell, keep it for all I care."

"Never mind." She had emerged from the bathroom and was standing, still naked, in front of him now. "I'll figure it out myself."

Then she grabbed his ears and pulled his face into the recently shaved smooth spot between her legs. With his tongue, Tanner Goochly Jr. attempted to do what he hadn't been able to do moments earlier.

CHAPTER TWENTY-THREE

Parker Murdoch was on the phone, feet up on his desk. Heart stood in the doorway at the entrance to his office. Murdoch's eyes found him, and without a smile he waved Lancaster into the room.

"Gotta go," he said to whoever was on the other end of the line. "Apparently I'm in demand." He hung up the phone and brought his feet to the floor. "Hello, Lancaster."

"Mr. Murdoch."

"Good lord, son, why so formal?" he asked, even though he thought he knew.

"I was in the neighborhood." Heart attempted a smile. Park didn't bite.

Heart cleared his throat and dove right in.

"Park—uh, Mr. Murdoch." Park leaned in. "I love your daughter. I realize that you and Mrs. Murdoch had—I'm sure still have—hopes, dreams, and aspirations for Brodie. I want you to know that I have hopes, dreams, and aspirations for her as well." Heart looked right at Parker Murdoch but, as usual, couldn't get a read on the man. He took a second to envy that, and then he pressed on. "What I'm not sure about is whether yours and mine are the same, and while the hopes, dreams, and aspirations you have may not include a slightly older, nowhere near as intelligent kid from Reno, I'm here to tell you that mine do. Mr. Murdoch, I love your daughter with all my heart, and when I get home, I plan to ask her to be my wife. I would be honored to have yours and Claire's—uh, Mrs. Murdoch's—blessings in that endeavor." Heart stopped, having said none of what he had rehearsed. From behind the desk, Parker Murdoch stayed silent.

"Welcome to the family, son." It was Claire, standing in the doorway, beaming.

"Now, hold on a second!" Parker Murdoch objected. "I have not given my answer."

"Your answer matters not one lick," Claire lovingly scolded her husband and approached Heart for a hug. "We"—she looked at Park one more time—"are thrilled."

"You're assuming my little girl is going to say yes." Park, having lost one fight, chose another.

"Actually, I'm assuming nothing of the sort," Heart offered. "But I'm hopeful."

"My guess is you have nothing to worry about," Claire said. Park reached into a desk drawer and lifted out a bottle of his signature tequila. Claire moved around and retrieved three glasses from a shelf behind her husband's desk. Heart thought for a moment, then spoke.

"I know how Claire feels, sir, but can I head back home with your blessing too?"

"I'm still considering your request," Brodie's dad said with a straight face. "And I am pleased that at least one of you thinks my yea or nay is important." He looked at Heart, then at his wife, and then back at Heart. Giving up any pretense of faux outrage, he smiled. "I'd be proud to call you son," he said and poured three healthy shots of the clear liquid. "And I am very impressed you came all this way to ask a question to which you already knew the answer." Claire grabbed two of the glasses and handed one to Heart.

"To Brodie and Lancaster," she said.

"Welcome aboard," Park added, and they all drank.

"There is one more thing I need to tell you," Heart said as he placed his glass on Parker's desk. "Brodie and I are moving to Reno."

CHAPTER TWENTY-FOUR

Still far from satisfied, Teri Hickox left Goochly's place and headed downtown to her favorite bar. She refocused on her new mission: her next gun. She could ask her old man but decided she probably didn't want to open up that can of worms. She could do some research online, but that would only give her limited information. Suddenly she knew where to turn. A place to kill two birds with one stone. She'd get the skinny on a new weapon *and* satisfy the itch Tanner Goochly had twice failed to scratch.

She stopped at a red light, turned down the radio, grabbed her phone, and called Harper Madison, her "friend" from the law firm.

"Hey, it's me. You up for a drink?" The response from the other end of the line was positive. "I'll be there in fifteen." Teri clicked off and smiled for what felt like the first time all day.

CHAPTER TWENTY-FIVE

Heart spent another couple of hours with Claire and Park Murdoch. He marveled at how comfortable he felt around them and how much he enjoyed their company. He honestly believed they felt the same about him. Better still was the feeling he had that they enjoyed each other's company even more. Park gave him shit to be sure, but Heart knew he gave everybody shit—everybody he was fond of, that is. They had a few laughs, one more shot of tequila, and Heart told them both about the upcoming move and the new job. He realized in the seconds after he had popped the question that Brodie's parents were thrilled for him. Thrilled for them. They had told him they appreciated the fire in his eyes and the passion in his voice when he talked about being able to influence young journalists. He told them a chance to continue his father's legacy was hugely important to him, and they were genuinely happy that he would have a chance to do just that. They told Heart they knew Brodie would help and admitted, selfishly, they were overjoyed that their only child would now be thousands of miles closer.

"Brodie and I will probably head out there soon and find a place for us to live." Heart looked from Park to Claire. "And she might want her mom there to help."

"I'd like that." Claire gave her husband's hand a squeeze. "I'll help her look for a place with enough room and rooms that we can visit without them being able to hear you snoring."

"What are you going to do with the house in Raleigh?" Park changed the subject.

"Good question. Brodie and I have been going back and forth. The market stinks right now, but neither one of us is crazy about being landlords."

"Especially not from three thousand miles away," Claire added.

"There's that." Heart nodded.

"There's that," Park parroted. "If you can't get close to what you think it's worth, it might make sense to take the rental income."

"I agree," Heart told his future father-in-law. "We'll definitely take a hit if we sell, but we'll get at least the mortgage payment if we rent."

"There's bound to be a pool of responsible tenants there. Between the state capitol, all the government offices, and the three major universities in the area."

"You'd think," Heart said hopefully.

"Doesn't Brodie have a friend who's a realtor in Raleigh?"

"That's right, she does," Heart remembered. "Dana Sutton."

"Probably worth a call."

"You better think about hitting the road." It was Claire. Both Heart and Park looked at their watches.

"Guess I better." Heart stood. Park stayed seated.

"You gonna pop the question as soon as you get home?" Dad wanted to know the details.

"Friday night," Heart answered. "I made a reservation at Revolution." Claire smiled at the memory of the restaurant. The look on her husband's face when the chef brought out the "especially for them" raw-quail-egg appetizer was forever burned in her mind.

"One of my favorite meals, ever!" Park said sarcastically.

Thirty minutes later, Heart was back on the road, this time taking Colorado Highway 82 East to Interstate 70. He was happy. He was relieved. He had been pretty sure he knew what Park's and Claire's answers were going to be, but he hadn't been certain. Now that he had gotten the Murdoch seal of approval, that weight was lifted from his shoulders. He was running the Friday night proposal through his mind when his phone rang. It was Denise Clawsew.

"Heart here." He answered on the third ring.

"Hey, Caster. How's it going?"

"Couldn't be better."

"Good to hear," she shot back. "Are you in town?"

"Not yet, but I will be bright and early tomorrow morning."

"Cool." She paused for a brief moment. "Can you meet Allen and I at Big Eddie's for breakfast?"

"Allen and me." Heart couldn't help but correct her grammar.

"What?"

"Allen and me, not Allen and I," Heart explained.

"Oh, for goodness sake, don't be such a dick," Clawsew scolded. "Can you meet Allen and *me* at Big Eddie's for breakfast?"

"Of course." Heart was smiling. "What time?"

"Nine."

"I'll be there."

She hung up without saying good-bye. Heart wondered for a second what that was all about but then remembered the homicide that Denise was all lathered up about. She loved her scoops. He also wondered why a face to face with the detective was required but figured he'd find out soon enough. He picked up his phone again and this time called home.

"Hi," Brodie answered.

"Hi, doll." Heart loved the sound of her voice. "Whatcha doin'?"

"Having a glass of wine and watching *Fixer Upper.*"

"Sounds fun," he said, though it really didn't. "Any shiplap?" He had sat through his share of *Fixer Upper* episodes.

"What do you think?" She giggled. "How's the trip?"

"Over," he said happily. "I'm headed to the airport. Cut my visit short because I miss you too damn much. Rebooked on a red-eye."

"Aw, you're sweet. And you're full of it." He could hear the smile in her voice. "A red-eye out of Reno?" Her tone proved she knew just how full of it he was. Heart was momentarily caught off guard. He could feel his heart rate tick up a notch or two; then he lied.

"No such thing, but I found one out of Sacramento, so I'll be home in the morning."

"Excellent," she said. He knew if she opened up her laptop and searched for a Sacramento to Raleigh red-eye, she wouldn't find one. He was counting on her not caring. He hoped she was just happy that he was coming home, and he was well aware of the fact that she'd get the truth out of him eventually.

"Gotta go," she added. "They're about to show the big reveal."

"Far be it from me to interrupt that!" Heart laughed. "Sweet dreams. I love you."

"Love you too, Lancaster. Travel safe."

Heart realized he was exhausted and was looking forward to dozing off on the plane even though it was only a three-and-a-half-hour flight. After getting through the maze that is DIA security, Lancaster settled into his slightly ratty, moderately comfortable aisle seat. His boarding and preflight strategy was simple and consistent: get on early, get settled, but don't buckle up. Row mates would be getting on after him. Grab the latest read, usually a book, sometimes a newspaper, never a magazine. Stuff his backpack under the seat in front of him and stick his nose in the reading material. Lastly, and most importantly, avoid eye contact.

Mission accomplished most times and, so far, this time. Out of the corner of his right eye, he noticed a pair of black Converse Chuck Taylor All Stars had stopped in the aisle, toes pointed into his row. *Window or middle seat*, Heart wondered as he rose. The shoes covered what looked to be average-sized feet, so having the newcomer plop down in the middle probably wouldn't be the worst thing in the world. Without looking at the passenger's face, Heart made room for him to enter the row. He shoved his overpriced backpack, which would easily fit on the floor, into the overhead, taking up room unnecessarily, and slid all the way to the window. Heart eased back down into his own seat, hoping that would be it for row ten. The flight appeared to be nowhere near full, so he felt confident that he wouldn't have to share an armrest. He stuck his nose back into his book.

"Baseball book?" It was Mr. Black Converse.

Oh crap, thought Heart. "Sorry?" he said, looking at his traveling companion for the first time. Dark hair, long on top, short at the sides, glasses, headphones (one in, one out), two-day growth of facial hair.

"Is that a baseball book?" he asked again, pointing at the volume in Heart's hands. Puzzled, Lancaster turned the front cover toward his own face to get a better look.

"Oh, I get it," he replied. "The title." Heart stared at the two words on the front cover, one red, one white. *"Big Flies,"* it read. "Nope, it's actually a mystery, and not a bad one." He went back to reading it.

"Huh," Black Converse reacted. "Should've been a baseball book." Then he stuck the other earbud into his formerly empty ear. Relieved that the conversation was over, Heart tried to focus on the pages in front of him, but fatigue gained a foothold. He was asleep before they left the ground.

CHAPTER TWENTY-SIX

The alarm on Teri's phone went off at 5:00 a.m. She had already been staring at the ceiling for fifteen minutes. She thought briefly about Harper. She had left her lover hours ago, but the scent of her was still all over Teri's skin. Those thoughts quickly gave way to other ones. Harper had mentioned two types of guns that she thought would be perfect for Teri, a Smith & Wesson and another Sig Sauer. The gun club had both, Harper had said, and she was sure they'd let Teri give both a try. Excited again, she rolled out of bed, gave the sheets one last sniff, and headed for the shower.

Dressed and with hair dried, she stood at the kitchen counter finishing a note for Hank. Teri capped the Bic pen and grabbed the keys to her dad's truck, leaving her car keys in their place. As quietly as possible, she left the house and jumped in the truck. She knew her old man would hear the engine fire. It might wake him up; he might be awake already. Didn't matter. She turned on the radio, an AM country station, and pulled away from the house.

At the same time, Detective Marc Allen was having a tug-of-war with the Keurig machine at the precinct. He was a habitually early riser, always had been. Long ago he had determined he needed only three to four hours of sleep a night, so he tried to get his body to adapt to that. So far so good. *I'll sleep when I'm dead* was his mantra, and he mentally tipped his cap to Warren Zevon every time he thought or said it. Plus, he liked being the first and most times only one at the cop shop. It gave him time, undistracted, to think.

His day promised to be a busy one. He'd start it by putting in a few hours at his desk. Allen was dismayed that he hadn't made much progress in the Burns murder case, but much of that was his own doing. He had made a deal with Denise Clawsew to not go public with a request for information. He didn't regret it, but he was about to put an end to it later that morning. Two separate interviews with the woman's husband had done nothing but eliminate him from consideration as a suspect. Allen couldn't, for certain, offer up an opinion as to how much the man loved his wife, but he was convinced beyond a doubt that Teddy Burns didn't want her dead. As a cop, he had seen an entire spectrum of emotions displayed on the faces of an entire array of men, women, and children associated with both minor and major crimes. Allen felt that experience put his gut feeling on solid ground after he looked into the eyes and the broken heart of the grieving husband. He was even more positive he couldn't have killed her—or had her killed—in cold blood. But who could? Who did? Getting those answers would begin in earnest today—first with a press conference and then with a canvass of Daisy Burns's friends and colleagues. The people who, he hoped, knew her best. He drained what was left in his coffee mug and checked his watch. He had a couple of hours before his breakfast meet up with Clawsew and Lancaster Heart. Plenty of time to do what he wanted to do.

The landing gear found the runway at a slightly higher speed than the pilot's manual might recommend, and the impact jolted Heart awake. He had slept like a dead guy, and it took him a moment to figure out exactly where he was. Airplane, on the ground, home, he remembered. He also recalled he was reading when he fell asleep, but at this very moment, he couldn't find his book. Not in his lap, not on the floor. Then he glanced across the row at Mr. Black Converse. Wide awake, with earbuds still firmly in place, he was reading Lancaster Heart's novel. Heart shook his head at the audacity and then reached his hand, palm open, over the empty middle seat. Converse noticed and looked at Heart like it was no big deal that he had "borrowed" the book. It also appeared he was in no hurry to give it back.

"You're right—it's pretty good." He smiled and finished the page. "If you ask me, the whole 'These Days, Those Days' thing was a little confusing at the beginning. But once I got into the rhythm, I really dug it."

Don't remember asking, Heart thought sincerely. "Glad you like it," he said insincerely. "You can pick up your own copy at Amazon," he said sincerely. Then he leaned over and grabbed his bag from under the seat in front of him. They had landed a few minutes early, so Heart found himself with even more time before breakfast. He didn't want to go home, preferring not to wake Brodie, so he decided to go to the television station. He had a toothbrush in his desk and could use the shower there to freshen up. "Enjoy your day," he said to Converse as he got up and eased his way into the aisle, not caring one iota if the guy enjoyed his day or not.

CHAPTER TWENTY-SEVEN

It was nearly nine o'clock in the morning, and Teri, suddenly famished, found herself sitting in the driver's seat of her old man's pickup truck across the street from Big Eddie's Diner. She had never eaten there, but a number of her colleagues at the firm said it was the best breakfast place in town. "The shrimp and grits are to die for," her friend Harper had said more than once. She was thinking about going inside to find out for herself. She was also dying for a cup of coffee. But at the moment, she was focused on a bald-headed man, not bad looking, sitting down in a booth. The guy looked like a cop. He had been greeted at the door by a mountain of a man; Teri assumed it was the establishment's namesake. If he wasn't, he should have been. An elderly waitress poured the bald guy a cup of coffee. He was still sipping it when Teri noticed two more vehicles pull into the parking lot.

For reasons she couldn't even try to explain, she reached into the truck's glove compartment and pulled out the handgun she had placed there this morning. She cradled it in her right hand, finger on the trigger. It made her feel good, comforted her. She felt a weird, wild rush—a quickening of her heartbeat and a recurring desire to use the gun for something more than target practice. She ran the index finger of her left hand lovingly over the recently oiled barrel of the pistol. Then she lifted that same finger to her nose and took a deep sniff. Out of the corner of her eye, she saw a man exit one of the cars that had just pulled into the diner's parking lot. He seemed familiar, so she took a better look.

She recognized him because she had seen him a lot of nights delivering the news from the living room television set. She always thought Lancaster Heart looked pretty good on TV—handsome. From what she could see across the street, he looked even better in person. A woman emerged from the other car. Petite, all hair. Teri didn't recognize her. *Is she with the newscaster? If she is with the TV guy, is it his wife? Girlfriend? Or just some morning hookup?* While she sat wondering, some questions were answered when the two high fived in the parking lot. *Friends for sure,* thought Teri. *Fucking? Not a chance.*

But what *was* the deal? That answer came seconds later when the bald man rose to greet the two newcomers and they all started to slide into the booth by the window together. Teri looked at the gun in her lap and caressed it. While she had her eyes down, the threesome in the diner took their seats.

She saw the detective turn and look out the window, his eyes locking on the blue pickup. Her mind suddenly raced. Did he recall seeing her in that same truck earlier that morning? Could he have noticed she was behind him shortly after he left the precinct? She took a deep breath and realized there must be dozens, if not hundreds, of trucks just like Hank's on roads all across the state. Then Allen turned back and started talking to the other two, and Teri instinctively breathed a sigh of relief.

What are the possible reasons a TV guy, some girl, and another guy who is obviously a cop would be getting together this morning? she thought as she put the pistol back in the glove box. Suddenly Teri was no longer hungry. In fact, the thought of shrimp and grits turned her stomach.

The conversation inside the restaurant continued.

"Denise has given me some details, but what have you got?" Heart asked Allen, taking a sip of coffee and setting down the white ceramic mug.

"Dead woman. Shot three times, close range, execution style, then dropped by a Dumpster behind a PP." Allen was all business. Clawsew sat silent, listening.

"Clues? Initial suspects?" Heart wondered aloud, then added, "I'm guessing not because we're all sitting here at Biggie Smalls together."

"No, and no." Allen took a sip from his own mug. "And it's Big Eddie's, not Biggie Smalls. But you are right. I need your help."

Under the table, Denise placed her right foot on top of Allen's left. She hated seeing this man have to ask anyone for help. It wasn't in his nature, she knew, and she wanted to offer some support, no matter how small the gesture might be. Allen acknowledged the outreach with a small smile. Denise noticed. Heart didn't.

"What can we do? How can we help?" Heart's questions were sincere.

"Guy has the footage." Allen instinctively used the nickname he had given Denise.

At the sound of it, she cringed and sneaked a look at Heart to see if he'd react. Nothing. *Maybe he didn't hear it,* she thought.

"Maybe run a story and then a CTA," Allen continued. Heart knew a CTA was a "call to action," a fairly standard tool police used to ask viewers who might have any information to contact authorities. He was also well aware the cops hated CTAs because they usually unleashed the crackpots and attention seekers, rarely provided substantive clues, and always created headaches for law enforcement.

"You sure you want to do that?" Denise spoke up for the first time.

"Not really, but I'm not sure I have a choice." Allen was resigned.

"Is there a reward?" Heart interjected.

"Not yet. Not at first. We're hoping to attract the good Samaritans before the knuckleheads get involved."

"Do you have any suspicions or theories about how or why this went down?" It was Denise again, asking a question she was sure Heart wanted to know the answer to again.

Allen ran his hand over his bald head and let out a long slow breath. "I don't know. Maybe." Heart and Clawsew leaned in. "It was no robbery, no accident, no crime of passion. This was a cold-blooded murder, pulled off in broad daylight."

All that seems obvious, Heart thought.

"All that seems obvious," Denise said. "But who could do something like this? Who could hate somebody *that* much?" Both Allen and Heart glanced at the young woman, who suddenly looked like a sad, bewildered little girl.

"Welcome to the world today," Allen said, shaking his head.

"Could this be gang related?" Heart piped up, hoping to steer the conversation off such emotional ground. "An initiation? A badge of honor thing?"

"Gawd, I hope not!" Allen blurted out. Then he thought for a moment. "If it is, it would be unusual for around here. It's going on in parts of Charlotte and Greensboro, but so far we've been spared."

"Worth a look," Denise said, oddly hopeful, looking for any explanation more palatable than pure hate, unbridled evil.

"Why dump the body behind the PP?" It was Heart again. Allen shrugged, then said nothing. "We'll get the story and the CTA on the air tonight." Heart was suddenly more than ready to get to work. "Probably won't lead the newscast, but it should go at the top of the second block."

"Thanks." Allen sounded sincerely grateful.

"Not a problem, Marc. It's the least we can do." Heart started to slide out of the booth; Denise and the detective did the same. Across the street, the blue pickup slowly pulled away.

Once outside in the parking lot, Heart, Denise, and the detective shook hands and headed their separate ways to waiting cars. The blue pickup that Allen had noticed was long gone.

CHAPTER TWENTY-EIGHT

The next day, Teri was back at work, with little time to think about anything other than copyediting, sorting, and filing documents. Her cubicle pod was in the middle of a section of the office on the seventeenth floor. Junior partners and associates surrounded her. When she looked over the top of her computer, she could see directly into the office of Connor Clifton, one of the firm's newest and youngest associates. Teri remembered Clifton trying to make a play shortly after he moved up to the seventeenth floor. She also remembered wasting little time in putting him in his place. He was married, and she knew it, but he had failed to mention it when he approached her from behind at a filing cabinet and suggested they "grab a drink after work and get to know each other better."

"I know you well enough already," she said without turning around. Then after turning around, she added, "You're the kind of creep that thinks it's okay to lie to and cheat on both his wife *and* someone else because he thinks one woman won't know and the other won't care."

"Shit, Hickox," she remembered him snarling. "It was just a friendly drink request."

"No, it wasn't," she said, starting to walk away. Then she flipped him the bird and continued on, showing the little turd exactly what he wouldn't be enjoying.

Now she stared at Clifton, wondering if he remembered that initial exchange. Perhaps sensing her gaze, he looked up and at her. He smiled and nodded. She flipped him off again. In the corner of his office the TV was on, and Teri could see part of the screen. It looked like a picture of a woman, but she couldn't get a good look at the ten-year-old photograph of Daisy Burns. She could see some big block letters that virtually screamed "MURDER VICTIM." Beneath the picture, in smaller type, was what looked like a name and a phone number. Had Teri been able to hear the TV as well as see it, she would have heard a plea for information. For a little more than a split second, she thought about sticking her head into Clifton's office to find out what the story was all about. Then she thought better of it.

"Do you think it will help?" Brodie and Heart were on the couch in their living room, her legs across the sofa, bare feet on his lap. He rubbed them.

"What?" he asked, his mind elsewhere.

"Lobbing that grenade across the bow." She pointed at the TV screen showing the plea for help in solving the Daisy Burns murder. He just stared at her, then smiled. He turned his head toward the television and then back at Brodie.

"I think it's firing a shot across the bow, and yes, I hope it helps."

"Me too."

He lifted her feet from his lap and started to get up.

"Hey! Where do you think you're going?" she protested. He didn't answer. "You have not been dismissed!" She tried again.

"I'll be right back," was all he said as he walked away. In less than a minute, he was.

"That *was* quick," she chided.

"Didn't have far to go," he replied, leaning down and kissing her on the mouth. "I didn't go to Reno," he confessed, plopping back down on the couch.

"I know," she confessed.

"I know you know," he admitted.

"So where did you go?" She very much wanted to know.

"Denver," he said truthfully, "and then Aspen." Brodie pulled her legs up underneath her.

"What in the world for?"

"I needed to speak with Claire and Park."

"Did you now?" She looked suspiciously at him; he looked down at his stocking feet.

"Brodie," he started, still looking down, "maybe my biggest regret is that you never really got to know my mom and dad, especially my dad." He stopped, cleared his throat, and looked up and at her. "In the short time he did get to spend with you, he gained a tremendous amount of respect for you and came to love you. You would have been great friends." He shifted his weight slightly and reached into a front pocket.

"Oh God, you're not going to do this right here, right now?" She had been steeling herself for this, actually hoping it would happen, but all of a sudden, she felt amazingly ill prepared.

"I know once upon a time you probably had a different set of circumstances, another outcome in mind, when you thought about your future." Heart started to get choked up, and she wondered if he was going to be able to get through his proposal. A tear left her left eye and lazily rolled down her cheek. "I love you, Brodie Murdoch. I don't want to imagine, can't imagine, living my life without you in it." She couldn't help but notice his eyes filling with tears as well. "I went to Aspen to ask your parents to give me—us—their blessing." Brodie's first tear was joined by others, the wet, salty expressions of joy running down her face and over her smiling lips.

"What did they say?" she half said, half spit.

"Your mom was thrilled. Your dad took a little more convincing," he answered, opening his right hand to reveal the diamond ring they had looked at months before. Brodie laughed out loud, snot, tears, and spit spraying in Heart's direction. "Brodie, will you marry me?" She pulled the sleeve of her shirt over her right hand and rubbed it across her nose and mouth. Then she nodded happily.

"I can't think of anything I'd rather do," she blubbered. He slid the diamond onto the ring finger of her left hand. It was a little big. She held it up, inches from her face, and sobbed.

"I hope those are happy tears," he said facetiously. She nodded again. "I was going to wait until Friday night, at Revolution," he admitted, "but I just couldn't wait."

"Decided to grab the bull by the tail?" she said, gaining a modicum of composure.

"Something like that." He smiled and leaned in for a sloppy celebratory kiss.

Blanche Avery was getting ready to enjoy her favorite snack. Celery sticks, filled with crunchy peanut butter and topped with juicy raisins. "Bugs on a log," she remembered her childhood best friend Martha calling it. Thanks to her brand-new teeth, she was able to savor the crunchy, rather pedestrian delicacy once again. She was at home on her lunch break, just a little more than a block away from the place she had worked for more than half a century. It was a woman's shelter now, but once upon a time it had been a convalescent home for young mothers who were unprepared, ill equipped, or unwilling to care for their newborn babies. The home and the women like Blanche who worked there took that burden off their hands. The babies were entered into the system while the mothers were nurtured back to physical and mental health.

Blanche carried her meal, the "bugs on a log," on a plate and a glass of cold whole milk from the kitchen counter to the portable tray that occupied a space between the upholstered couch and the television set in the living room of her one-bedroom, first-floor apartment. Her son, during his last visit, had purchased and set up a new flat-screen TV. It replaced the bulky Zenith Space Command nineteen-inch walnut box that she had won in a church raffle. Her boy programmed the remote and walked her through all of the amazing things it could do and the multitude of channels she could now watch. He paid the cable bill, so she never knew how much the privilege of having so many options cost. She pretended to listen, then thanked him, but in truth she didn't care, actually didn't have the heart to tell him she planned on turning it to and leaving it on channel seven the entire time. The programs on that station were just fine, but most of all she liked the young man Lancaster Heart, who delivered the local news. She thought he was handsome. If she had a daughter, he was the exact type of man she would have wanted her girl to marry.

But a different young man was currently in her home, delivering the news. A young man she didn't like nearly as much. She took a bite of her celery and paid attention anyway. Suddenly she couldn't chew, could barely breathe. She just stared at an image from the past on her futuristic color TV screen. The woman in the picture was older, but Blanche knew her all the same. She recognized the sadness in the eyes, even in a photograph on the television. She also recalled the name—Daisy. It wasn't Burns back then; she couldn't remember what it was, but it didn't matter. The first name was the same. She had never forgotten it, would never forget it. A daisy was such a delicate, beautiful flower, and this Daisy, *her* Daisy, was a delicate, beautiful young woman, just a girl really.

She also remembered the baby, a bundled-up baby girl who seemed to stare right through Blanche whenever she held her. She could suddenly still feel the weight of the baby in her arms. She was transported back to that time. Trying to comfort the mother who couldn't stop crying and care for the child who never did. Blanche kept a pad and pencil on her TV tray in case the news brought up something she wanted to discuss with her weekly church group or advertised a product that she couldn't resist. There seemed always to be something concerning the former, rarely anything with the latter. With a trembling hand, she wrote down the telephone number.

CHAPTER TWENTY-NINE

Detective Marc Allen sat in the precinct; uncharacteristically his feet were up on his desk. His left hand repeatedly squeezed an orange foam ball, an exercise that was supposed to strengthen his grip. His right hand held a pencil, which he twirled back and forth between his fingers. The ability to perform both tasks simultaneously was a credit to his dexterity and his concentration or, more aptly, lack thereof. He thought it was a lot like rubbing his stomach and patting his head at the same time. It took practice, and over the years Allen had perfected these particular tasks by getting into a rhythm. He also found that if he thought about either hand, neither worked, so this stunt helped him think about something else entirely. He was contemplating the confounding case that was the murder of Daisy Burns. He was still formulating themes about how and why it happened, but he had been convinced from the instant he laid eyes on her lifeless body that it was a cold-blooded killing. He had investigated and solved murder cases before, not many but enough, and his experience had taught him that killers were motivated by all sorts of reasons. But usually the people on the wrong end of the lead, the knife, or the poison had enemies, knew someone out there who felt this world would be a better place without them in it, someone who felt responsible for wrongs that needed righting. He also knew the recent rise in gang-related killings meant someone could have committed this crime as part of an initiation, a dare, or, as sick as it sounded to Allen, "just because." As sad as that sounded, some small part of Marc Allen actually hoped that was the case because that type of crime, committed by that kind of criminal, was among the easiest of all to solve.

He felt, for a second, that explanation might apply to Daisy Burns. Why would anybody *want* her dead? *Whom* did she piss off? It didn't add up. Her husband couldn't answer those questions. In fact, he was the one asking them of Marc Allen over and over and over again. As hard as Allen tried, he couldn't find one solitary soul who had a disparaging thought or anything remotely negative to say about this poor woman. Her friends spoke glowingly about her. Her kids—step kids, Allen reminded himself—adored her. Her husband clearly loved her and didn't just appear distraught and heartbroken; he *was* more heartbroken and distraught every time Allen spoke with him. Daisy Burns didn't owe anybody anything, at least according to her credit-card statements. She paid all three off every month. Her bank statements shed zero light on her dark, diabolical murder. No interesting deposits or withdrawals; Allen couldn't find any out-of-the-ordinary transactions at all. The woman had no social-media presence—not a Facebook, Instagram, or Twitter account in sight. She did belong to a book club that read mostly romance novels, went to church almost every Sunday, and volunteered at her kids'—step kids'—private school whenever she was needed. *Why in the world was she murdered? Who in the hell wanted her dead?*

Allen's thoughts drifted back to the bullet holes in her body. The three reasons he was certain this was no accident, suicide, or random act. One shot, the first one according to the medical examiner, to the heart. A second shot, point-blank right between the eyes, and a third, apparently just for good measure, *after* she was already dead, to her crotch. Allen's pencil traveled from the pinky finger to the index finger and back again. The orange ball squeezed four times while the pencil left, then returned. *Why three separate shots? Why in these particular spots? Wouldn't one to the heart or two to the head do the trick?* Of course they would have been enough, but it clearly wouldn't have been enough to send whatever message the killer wanted to send. A message Marc Allen was having a devil of a time trying to decipher. His phone buzzed.

"Hey, Allen," the voice of desk sergeant Jimmy Esposito boomed through the speaker. Marc suddenly thought about the squeeze ball in his left hand and dropped the pencil.

"Yeah, Espo," he answered, picking up the number two Adirondack off the ground.

"You got another call about your flower-girl murder." The cops in the shop, as well as one of the local newspapers, had started referring to the Daisy Burns case that way.

"Thanks, I got it." He punched the button above the blinking light on his phone, ready to speak with another crackpot, fame seeker, or gold digger. "Detective Allen." He steeled himself.

"Are you the cop I need to talk to about the dead lady?"

"Depends, sir, on which dead lady and whether or not you have usable, verifiable information."

"The dead lady on the TV, and you bet your ass I have useifiable information!" the caller practically shouted. "But before I give it to *you*, I need to know what's in it for *me*." Allen shook his head slowly.

"You'll be doing your civic duty, sir. What's in it for you is serving your community by helping local law enforcement solve a terrible crime." Allen was so sick of people who thought so little of themselves or their fellow human beings. It was a constant stream of "What's in it for me?" or "What do I get out of it?" It's why he hated having to resort to this CTA method in the first place.

"Fuck that!" Now the man on the other end of the phone actually was shouting. "I got what you need, and you need to pony up before you get it." Disappointed in humanity for the umpteenth time just that day, Allen took a deep, calming breath.

"What I *need* to do is get back to work," he said and hung up. He got up and grabbed the jacket from the back of his chair. As he slipped it on, Jimmy Esposito buzzed again.

"Allen, you got another one." Marc sighed, unable to deal with whatever "use-ifiable information" the person on the other end of the line "surely" had to offer.

"Take a name and number, will ya, Espo? I'm outta here."

"You're the boss," Jimmy said unconvincingly. Then he took the caller off hold. "Ma'am, the detective handling the case isn't available right now. He would like your name and number so as to call you back when he becomes available again." Jimmy prided himself on being such a smooth talker.

"Oh, I don't know." On the other end of the line, the woman was nonplussed. "I'm not sure it's worth troubling him."

"Suit yourself, ma'am, but I don't see how leaving your name and number is any trouble at all." Jimmy reckoned it was the perfect thing to say, but Blanche Avery had already hung up.

CHAPTER THIRTY

"Where's Cody?" Hank Hickox stood in the doorway; Tanner Goochly Jr. was on the porch. The screen door let the air and the hint of hard feelings pass between them.

"Day off." Tanner turned his head and let loose a stream of tobacco juice; none of it missed the porch. "Teri home?" Hank, unable and unwilling to hide his disgust, shook his head. "Too bad." The Goochly kid continued his two-word dialogue and then pulled open the screen door and pushed past his host. Before turning and following, Hank stuck his head outside and looked for the dog. The Rottweiler was nowhere to be found.

"Come on in, son," Hank said sarcastically as he headed inside. He found Goochly in the kitchen. He noticed the brown paper bag the young punk held in his right hand, as well as the butt of the firearm tucked into the back of his blue jeans.

"Playing delivery boy today?" Hank wondered aloud as Goochly lifted and then dropped the bag, filled with money, on the counter. He kept his back to Teri's father.

"Like I said, Cody's day off." Something in his delivery made Hank wonder if Cody had a number of days off in his future. "Don't worry about it, old man. The kid is alive and kicking." Tanner chuckled. Hank wondered how he knew what he was thinking. Goochly was already thinking about something else.

"Ever look at all this money and think nobody will miss a few bills here and a few bills there?" Hank Hickox instinctively held his breath, eyes moving from the back of Goochly's head to the pistol in his pants. "Do you, old man? Ever think that?" Tanner turned slowly until he was facing Hank. Hickox slowly, deliberately, shook his head from side to side.

"Not once. Never," he said matter-of-factly.

"Really? Never? Not Once?" Tanner questioned Hank's sincerity.

Hank stood stock still and shook his head again. "I have everything I need."

"Huh." Goochly smiled a slender, sinister smile. "'Cause I do. All the time." Then he opened the paper bag and stuffed his right hand in all the way up to the elbow. When he pulled it out, his hand crushed bills of varying denominations. Hank could see several hundreds as well as a number of fifties. "What would you do if I took all of this money and stuffed it into my pocket?" The young man stared at the older one. "Who would you tell?"

"Wouldn't do nothin'." Hank stared back. "Wouldn't tell no one." Goochly blinked. "That's between you, your God, and your father."

"Good answer, old man." Goochly smiled again, less sinister this time, and he stuffed the money into his pocket. As he headed back the way he had come, he stopped at Hank's side. "Tell Teri I was asking for her." He patted Hank on the cheek, then resumed walking.

"Asshole," Hank muttered under his breath.

"You better believe it, old man," Goochly called just before the screen door slammed.

Detective Marc Allen sat in his Charger, nestled in a small grove of trees just off the two-lane road. A wooden gate marked the entrance to a homestead a couple of hundred yards down the way. Allen needed to clear his head, leave the office, get away from the unanswered questions about the flower-girl murder. He needed a break from the useless leads, the empty exclamations of assistance. Allen was a proud owner of a long history with the Goochly family. They had been up to no good when he busted them the first time; figured they were probably still up to no good now. So he figured, why not check in on their enterprise?

He couldn't believe his timing, not to mention his luck, when he noticed Tanner Goochly Jr.'s race-red Ford F-150 Raptor pull out onto the highway in front of him. Allen knew the color was race red because he had looked at the prospect of purchasing one himself but ultimately found it a little too ostentatious, not to mention rich, for his blood. He knew it was Goochly's because he had seen him in it around town more than once. With a handful of vehicles providing cover, Allen followed. He kept the shiny red truck in sight until it turned through a gate and down the dirt road he could see from his current perch. As he continued past it the first time, he noticed an unmarked mailbox in need of a coat of paint, but no house in sight. After a few hundred yards, Allen circled back, passed the dirt road again, and found his hiding place.

Where was Goochly going? Allen wondered. *What was he up to?* Knowing more than a little about the delinquent, he figured it could be anything from a little midafternoon target practice to a hookup with a married woman. He couldn't be sure, but it was safe to assume that whatever he was doing was either illegal or immoral.

"Hey, Marc, you there?" It was master officer Kelly Ann Bynum calling on the radio. They had worked together on a handful of cases, and now Marc turned to her when he needed a question answered without anybody else knowing he was asking.

"I'm here, KAB." Allen smiled. "Thanks for getting back to me so quickly."

"No worries," she shot back. "You know I just sit around here all day long waiting for your call. *Praying* it will come sooner rather than later."

"What have you got for me?" he asked, ignoring the jab.

"Looks like a pretty decent spread. Good-sized piece of property." As Allen listened, he drummed his fingers on the steering wheel. "Lots of trees. Deed says it's zoned for residential, crops, and livestock. Two structures. Looks like a home and a barn."

"All very useful information," Allen remarked sarcastically, "but not exactly what I'm after."

"Hmm." Bynum pretended to think. "No pool."

"Come on, KAB! Who owns it?"

"Oh, that?" She paused for dramatic effect. "Looks like it all belongs to somebody named Henry Lodge Hickox."

"Huh." Allen reacted the way anyone would react when the name didn't ring a bell. "Can you run him through the system?"

"Already did," Bynum said smugly. "Widower, one kid, a daughter named Teri with an *i*. No priors, just your run-of-the-mill, law-abiding North Carolina farmer."

So, what's the connection to Tanner Goochly? Allen thought. "Thanks, Kelly Ann. I owe you one."

"That's Master Officer Bynum to you, Detective, and I think you mean you owe me *another* one." Then she was gone.

"Maybe a hookup after all," Allen wondered aloud, "but with a daughter instead of a lonely housewife." As he contemplated that thought, he saw Goochly's truck exit the dirt road and hit the highway again. "Well, that gives new meaning to a quickie," Allen said under his breath as he fired up the engine of his own car.

Hank sat in silence. Snug in his favorite chair, he discontentedly stewed in his own juices. He was not a fan of Tanner Goochly

Jr. Senior was bad enough, but the kid was exponentially worse. No respect, no manners, no morals, no redeeming qualities. And then the little puke had had the gumption to ask about Teri. Hank hadn't seen his daughter in more than forty-eight hours. That wasn't unheard of, but it was unusual. He knew she had borrowed the truck and then brought it back, both while he was sleeping, working out back, or running errands himself. Her using the pick-up wasn't out of character either. His thoughts returned to Tanner Goochly Jr. His stomach turned thinking about his only daughter spending any time at all around that ne'er-do-well, not to mention *that* kind of time. It wasn't that he imagined she couldn't take care of herself; he knew better. It was just that his daughter was smart, sometimes too much so for her own good. In fact, he reckoned that his Teri was the smartest person he had ever known. That thought made him chuckle to himself with the realization that that particular pool of people wasn't very deep. But Teri was smart, a straight-A student, at or near the top of her class every step of the way, including law school. If she was messing around with Tanner Goochly, in the biblical sense, it could mean one of several things.

One, she didn't care about the implications of having that kind of relationship with a blood relative. Two, she did, in fact, care, but her emotions outpaced her intellect. Having already conceded how smart his only child was, Hank, shifting in his chair, decided to dismiss both of those possibilities. Teri wasn't the kind of girl to risk her reputation and threaten her personal and professional future. She also wasn't the type to let her heart run roughshod over her head. Hank put the brakes on the runaway train that was his thoughts. He let out a deep breath, closed his eyes, and ran his hand over his face, from his forehead to his chin. He needed a shave. After a few more seconds of contemplation, Hank came to the only logical conclusion. Teri was carrying on with Tanner Goochly Jr., most likely having sex, because she knew he wasn't blood. She had figured out there was no earthly way the two of them were actually related. At that moment, he wasn't exactly sure how to wrap his head around the realization that Teri knew much of her life, a good part of her childhood, was a lie. How could she not blame him?

Hank had to shut off his brain before his thoughts drove him to the Evan Williams bottle. The sun was still way too high in the sky for that. He looked left and right for the remote, hoping that turning on the TV might help him change the conversation happening inside his head. He quickly stopped his search, thinking additional voices would only make matters worse. Instead, he lifted himself out of his favorite chair and headed to the big safe in the barn.

Hard as she tried, Blanche Avery couldn't shed the image of Daisy Burns. She cleaned the house, did a load of recently washed laundry, and ultimately dropped down on her knees, bowed her head, and prayed. None of it helped. She continued to see the image on the TV screen one second and the distraught young, petrified woman she had assisted and comforted decades ago.

"Lord, Lord, that poor child," she whispered as she reached for the phone again. This time she punched out a different number than the one she had reached hours before.

Denise Clawsew sat at Lancaster Heart's desk. She always enjoyed plopping down in the lead anchor's chair, but not because she harbored any fantasies about having his job; she just thought his chair was the most comfortable seat in the building. She had sat her butt in this very same seat on hundreds of occasions, but this time it felt oddly unfamiliar. It took her less than thirty seconds to figure out why. Her surroundings seemed so much less cluttered. He appeared to be slowly but surely cleaning up his desk, or was he cleaning it *out*? She sucked on the chocolate Tootsie Pop she had purchased earlier in the day. Her eyes scanned the desk and lit on the picture of Lancaster and his girl, Brodie. *I always liked that girl,* she thought as she realized there was only one framed photo where there used to be three, or was it four? The various notepads and file folders were gone too. Had Caster put those *in* his desk as opposed to *on* it? There was only one way to find out for sure, and she had no intention of taking the unprecedented step of actually opening any of the desk drawers without the man's permission. Instead, she surmised he hadn't, because she had never seen him put anything in his desk before. She took another long suck on the lollipop and then aggressively chomped down quickly, reaching the candy's Tootsie Roll center.

"What's up, superstar?" she asked the photograph. Before she could get an answer, the phone on the desk rang, scaring the crap out of her and making her jump, just a little, in his chair. Curiosity sizzled through her veins, but as badly as she wanted to answer his phone, she couldn't bring herself to commit that minor act of faithlessness either. So she decided to play a little game and with each ring wondered who might be on the other end of the line. *Brodie?* Probably. *Detective Allen?* Maybe. She could always ask the cop later if he had called, and she made a mental note to do just that. *Somebody wanting Heart to appear at a charity fundraiser or MC a gala?* Could be. According to him, that happened occasionally. *The cochair of his fortieth high-school reunion?* Wouldn't that be a gas? *Some random viewer?* Possibly, but she knew the woman at the front desk—was it Chelsea?—rarely let random viewers directly through to the on-air talent. It was most likely someone he knew, which made it even more likely that she would never answer it. Before she could further consider taking the chance, the phone stopped ringing. Denise knew that meant the call now had gone to his voice mail or been kicked back to the front desk. All the talent had the option to pick one way or the other, and she had no idea which preference Lancaster had selected; she always called him on his mobile.

"Hello, this is Lancaster Heart. Thanks for taking the time to call Channel Seven news. I'm sorry that I'm unavailable to take your call right now, but what you have to say is very important to us." Blanche felt herself blush. The newsman was so handsome on TV and sounded so sincere on the phone. She had been nervous about calling, and while his reassuring voice calmed her some, she found herself more than ever wanting to leave the right message. "So please leave your name, a number, and a message, and I'll make sure somebody gets back to you as soon as possible. If what you have to say can't wait, just press zero, and that will get you back to the front desk, and they'll take it from there. Have a great day, and thanks again for being a Channel Seven viewer." She found herself half listening to Heart's message and half formulating the exact words she wanted to say. She lamented that she hadn't had the foresight to write them down so as to avoid this very situation. Then she heard the beep, and the phone suddenly felt like a stick of dynamite, fuse lit, spitting sparks and smoke, in her hand. Blanche tried to gather her thoughts but felt only panic. She tried to clear her throat, but it had dried up. She felt the pressure of trying not to waste the man's time but to say the right words, which in an instant came tumbling out.

"I knew that girl, that murdered girl. Lord have mercy on my soul, I knew that girl." She stopped for a split second and then released the next batch of syllables with a sudden sob. "As the Lord is my witness, I *knew* that poor girl." Then Blanche Avery dropped her phone back in its cradle. She was suddenly exhausted. She put her head back and closed her eyes, never realizing she had failed to leave either her name or her number.

CHAPTER THIRTY-ONE

"Hi, Mom." Brodie really didn't have time to answer her mobile phone, but she felt guilty because she hadn't spoken to her mother in more than two days.

"Hi, honey. I know you're busy, so I won't keep you," Claire said. Brodie thought her mother sounded a little guilty herself.

"It's no problem at all. I miss you. What's up?"

"Not much, really. We just hadn't talked in a while, and I wanted to catch up. Dad is out in the garage, and I'm getting ready to go to the store to get stuff for dinner."

Brodie smiled. There really *wasn't* anything up, but she didn't care. She loved her mom and never tired of talking to her. She loved her dad too, but she and her mother had a special connection. Claire Hooper Murdoch was her mentor, her role model, her rudder. Her hero. They usually talked, at least briefly, every day, so it didn't strike her as odd that her mom labeled this more-than-two-day hiatus as "a while." She thought about Heart, her boyfriend, now her fiancé. His parents had both passed away, but even when they were alive, he had spoken to them only occasionally by phone. She had joined his friends and colleagues in a chorus imploring him to check in more often. Now that they were gone, she knew that lack of communication weighed heavy on his heart. She never doubted they were a loving family; he worshipped his parents, especially his dad, and loved them both unconditionally, especially his mom. But she couldn't imagine he had said everything he wanted to say to them. In fact, she knew he hadn't.

She knew she didn't have that problem with Claire and Park. She also knew her mother well enough to know this was more than a catch-up call. This was a fishing expedition. Unable to contain his excitement, Heart had popped the question. She was aware that Claire knew he had been going to, but she clearly believed he hadn't done it yet.

"What are you planning to make?"

"I found a recipe for cauliflower risotto, and I'm going to make your dad eat it." She chuckled.

"I'm sure it will be delicious. You don't know how to make anything that isn't." Brodie meant every word. Claire Murdoch was the best cook she had ever known.

"That's sweet of you to say, but I've made my share of inedible meals in my life."

"Hey, Mom?" Brodie shifted the conversation down a road Claire had no idea was coming.

"Yes, dear?"

"Can we plan a trip to New York? I need a wedding dress." Her words hung between them for several seconds. Claire fought back tears.

"Nothing would make me happier!" Claire finally exclaimed. Then she added, "Wait a minute, I thought he was going to propose on Friday night?"

"Well, he spilled the cat out of the bag. Just couldn't wait," Brodie said, and suddenly they were both in tears.

"Name the date." That was how Claire ended the conversation.

Teri Hickox grabbed a cold beer from the fridge, shut the door, twisted off the cap, and took a long, slow pull. She turned without looking and, using a technique learned around some campfire on some beach during a much less complicated time, snapped her thumb and middle finger, sending the bottle cap spinning toward the trash can. It hit Hank Hickox smack dab in the chest. After bouncing off, the bottle cap rattled around on the floor before coming to rest at Hank's feet. The sound made Teri look up.

"Holy crap!" The surprising sight of her dad standing in the kitchen almost made her drop the bottle. "You scared the bejesus out of me." Knowing her father's disdain for the use of what he called "blue language," Teri chose "bejesus" over the much more appropriate "shit," but even that tested her old man's moral compass. "How long you been standing there?"

"Not long." Hank bent over and plucked the bottle cap off the hardwood floor. "Watch your language, please," he remarked as he dropped the cap in the trash can. "Where have you been?"

Teri thought about the question. Since her twenty-first birthday, she and Hank had an understanding that she was a grown woman, capable of making and being responsible for her own decisions. But that understanding came with a caveat that she was still living in her childhood home, Hank's home. As long as that was the case, she owed Hank answers to reasonable questions, and at the moment this one sounded reasonable.

"Working my a—uh, tail—off," she lied. "Big case, and they've given me a ton of responsibility." Hank nodded, and she kept going. "Spent the past two nights in the office working late and spending the night at Harper's." It amazed her how easily her lies went from her brain to her mouth to her father's ears.

Hank nodded again. Teri knew Hank would find all of that plausible. She also knew her dad loved his little girl and would want more than anything to believe her. She figured he decided to.

"Wanna beer?" Teri asked, motioning to the fridge with her eyes. Hank looked past her to the cuckoo clock on the wall. He remembered the day his late wife had brought it home and asked him to mount it. For a split second, his eyes misted over as he read the time.

"Sure, why not." A warm smile formed on his lips. "Can we talk?"

Lancaster Heart drummed his fingers on his desk. *So much to do, so little time,* he thought as he reached for the phone. For the first time since sitting down, he noticed the message light blinking and gave some serious thought to pressing play. He used to listen all the time, actually enjoyed hearing what the viewers had to say. He even called a few back. But not anymore. The dialogue had become mostly a one-way street of criticism and complaints. He remembered the station's PR person sarcastically telling him they had an entire department ready to assist him with that particular constituency, and then she showed him, by pressing a series of buttons, how to send all the correspondence over to the aforementioned department without having to go through the trouble of "engaging with the proletariat." The way she said it almost made him change his mind. Then she wondered aloud if maybe he'd like to meet her for a drink after work. He graciously thanked her for the phone tip and then with equal finesse declined her offer. "Maybe next time," she had said, leaving. "Maybe never," he had replied after she had left.

He not only recalled the transfer trick but put it to good use on a weekly basis, sending the chorus of "Get off the air," and "How did you get this job?" and "You mispronounced Ne-vah-duh" to some unsuspecting intern or minimum-wage employee down the hall. This time around, the usual reproaches also included Blanche Avery's heartbreaking admission.

Having accomplished one task, Heart set his sights on the next and punched in ten new numbers. After a couple of rings, the connection was successful.

"Pierce Edwards."

"Pierce, hi. It's Lancaster Heart. Got a minute to talk?"

"Is this a good time?" Brodie couldn't put the call off any longer. She loved her house, hers and Heart's house, had loved it from the first minute her realtor friend Dana Sutton had shown it to her. Now, with mixed emotions, she faced the fact that it was time to let it go.

"Of course. What's up?" The realtor, no matter how busy, always sounded like she had nothing but time for Brodie. She was smart enough to know that it was a good business tactic, and Sutton was good at her business, but it still made Brodie feel special all the same.

"So many things."

"Do tell."

"Well, first and foremost, Heart proposed." The scream from the other end of the line lasted a good thirty seconds before the words came out.

"Oh my goodness gracious, Brodie, that's *so* fabulous. I am so, so happy for you." Brodie smiled but said nothing. "Oh wait, oh Lord." Sutton stopped in her tracks. "Did you say yes?"

"Of course I said yes!" The scream, from an office miles away, hit her ears again.

"You said 'so many things,' so what else?" The realtor had regained her composure and was back to business.

"We're moving to Reno."

"Ne-vah-duh?"

"Yep, Nevada," Brodie answered, pronouncing the name of the state correctly, "and I'm coming to grips with the fact that that means I have to sell the house."

"Ooh." Brodie could hear the word through a sip of something. Knowing Sutton, it was probably Earl Grey tea. "Not a great idea right now. The market, while on the way back, is nowhere near where you need it or want it to be."

"How bad?" Brodie asked, having done some research on her own. She knew that the real estate market in and around Raleigh had been hard hit, but the house was fairly new and in great shape. She harbored hopes of getting close to top dollar for the three-bedroom, two-and-a-half-bath house.

"Off the top of my head?" Sutton asked a rhetorical question and then kept going. "We could probably put it on the market for four hundred, four twenty tops."

"Ouch." The number was less than Brodie had expected and much less than she had hoped.

"Hey." The realtor sounded suddenly hopeful. "Have you thought about renting?" Brodie hadn't until now.

CHAPTER THIRTY-TWO

Hank was surrounded by darkness. Whatever natural light had been coming through the picture window in the living room was long gone, and so was Teri. He didn't know what had possessed him to pick that particular time to confess, but he had told his daughter everything he thought she should know. Everything he could remember. Once he started telling his story, *her* story, he couldn't stop. The lies, the justifications, the guilt all came pouring out, and Teri just sat there, unmoved. Hank now knew it was because she had already figured all or most of it out, at least the important parts. He didn't, wouldn't, call Daisy Burns her "birth" mother. Instead, he referred to her as the woman who "had" her. He told her why it was impossible for Betty Lou, his wife, her mother, to have children of her own. He laid bare the heartbreaking admission that they kept the true facts about Daisy Burns, and the details of Teri's birth, a secret. The whole time he spoke, he had no way of knowing Teri had already heard the whole story. He was too embarrassed to look his daughter in the eye, but he told her about another woman, the one Betty Lou had met at church. She volunteered at the shelter that cared for young mothers who didn't want or didn't have the means to keep their babies. The wonderful woman who knew of a newborn that was unwanted and awaiting a loving home. The angel who brought Teri into their lives.

Then Hank cried. He told Teri how much he loved her, how much they both loved her. He hoped she could understand. He wouldn't pretend he did it for her, and he thought he perceived a nod of appreciation from Teri about that. He admitted that they did it for themselves. Finally, he begged her forgiveness. During it all Teri never spoke, never tried to stop Hank's confession from flowing. Maybe it was because the words Hank offered up matched, almost exactly, the ones she had heard from Betty Lou's mouth. When her father was spent of consonants and vowels, drained of emotion, they both sat in silence as the darkness descended around them. After several more minutes Teri had stood up, walked over, kissed Hank on the top of his head, and walked out the door.

Teri drove. She had already forgiven Hank long before he begged for absolution. She spent much of the time between the darkness and the dawn trying to figure out why it was so much more important to find and confront her birth mother than it was to do the same to the man who had planted his seed inside Daisy Burns. She never could come to a sufficient conclusion. Hank was simply her dad, even though he wasn't. She loved him, always had, always would. She realized that until just a few hours ago, she had never seen Hank cry, and she decided she never wanted to see it again, ever. But she also knew she wanted to find two things: a place of her own and the woman who brought her to Hank and Betty Lou, the "angel," as Hank described her, who made her a Hickox.

She continued to drive, adrenaline, anger, and determination fueling her aimless excursion. Much of what Hank had told her she already knew, or suspected, but finally hearing it from him still stung. She had deduced the who and surmised the why, but now she had something else: the where. Without realizing it, she ended up at Tanner Goochly's place. He greeted her at the door, pissed because she had pressed the buzzer instead of simply using the key he had given her. After letting her in, he let go a grunt, then turned on his heels and headed straight back to bed. *Bastard*, she thought as she followed him only as far as the couch, plopped down, and stayed there, fully clothed, not sleeping, until the sun came up in the east.

At the moment, they were four feet apart, facing each other in a booth at the IHOP. Teri had her hands around a cup of steaming coffee; Tanner was shoveling something called a Rooty Tooty Fresh 'N Fruity down his throat. Everything he did so far that morning aggravated her, from blowing his nose to leaving the toilet seat up, to noisy open-mouthed chewing, to the speck of pancake and whipped cream that had lingered at the corner of his upper lip since he took his very first bite. Teri's eyes scanned the restaurant. As far as she could tell, they were suddenly alone. Even the greasy-haired waitress had disappeared, probably, Teri figured, out back to share a smoke with a busboy. Teri took her right hand off the mug and slipped it into her handbag. When she pulled it out, she was holding her brand-new gun, the Smith & Wesson Bodyguard. She had bought it because she liked the name and the way the gun looked and felt. She also liked the fact that it was a different model from the Sig Sauer. It had a different yet still comfortable feel, and she figured it wasn't a bad thing to have more than one. She raised the gun and leveled it at Tanner. Then, midchew, she put a bullet in his brain.

"Order up, Brenda!" The short-order cook shook her from her fantasy.

"You want a bite?" Tanner asked, mouth mostly full, waving his fork over the plate. Teri couldn't decipher whether what was left was the Rooty Tooty or the Fresh and Fruity. Regardless, she didn't want any. What she really wanted at the moment was to shoot Tanner Goochly Jr. right between the eyes.

CHAPTER THIRTY-THREE

Dawn broke warm but with an easy breeze rustling the decades-old curtains that covered Hank's slightly open bedroom window. Duke, more and more spoiled every day, lay on his back, hind legs spread, on the floor at Hank's side of the bed. A light snore emanated from the Rottweiler's slightly open mouth. Other than that, the morning was quiet. Hank knew immediately that another night had come and gone without Teri in the house. He remembered, and in a strange way still thought he could feel, the weight of her lips on the top of his head. A parting gesture that gave Hank hope. He knew for a fact things between him and his only child would never be the same, but the tenderness of that simple signal put a brick in the dam that had burst inside Hank's heart. It made him think that maybe he could keep all the happiness from escaping, prevent all the sadness from filling the void. Just maybe.

The previous night, he had started to pray that it was true just before he closed his eyes, then stopped almost as quickly as he had started. Hank wasn't a religious man, never had been, and he knew the reason was that he thought people all too often only turned to it when there was something they wanted or thought they needed. As far as he could determine, that wasn't the point of it—or at least wasn't supposed to be the point of it. He lay in bed, admonished himself with a shake of his head, and then closed his eyes, inviting sleep. As he drifted off, he had held on tight to his hope, to the possible promise of a new, yet no doubt uncertain, road for their father-daughter relationship.

Hank awoke no more hopeful, but he took encouragement from the fact that he was no less hopeful either. Things were going to work out one way or another, he correctly assumed.

"C'mon, Duke," he called over the edge of the bed. "Let's you and me go pee."

Marc Allen greeted the same dawn knowing he needed a break. Every day that he didn't make progress in the flower-girl murder was a disappointment. He realized that noun would seem cavalier and inadequate to the ill informed and uninitiated. Worse, it would come across as callous and uncaring to the friends and family of Daisy Burns. When Allen was a younger man, a less experienced cop, he would have felt the same way, wouldn't even have considered using such a word, but then he grew up. He came face to face with hundreds of questions that remained unanswered.

The detective knew all about the statistics. In the last half century alone, there were close to a quarter of a million unsolved murders in the United States. There were dozens in Raleigh, hundreds more in nearby Durham. Daisy Burns had become one of those numbers. Allen knew the possibility of never finding the killer was very real in the initial hours after catching the case. Little things piled up and added up to trouble. Her car was on the street where she had parked it; her phone, an early generation Apple product, was in the glove compartment where she had left it. He had asked her husband about that and had been told, without hesitation, she did that all the time.

"That was Daisy." Allen remembered Teddy fighting back tears. "She never wanted to appear distracted or rude in public," he announced with a sniff. "She always left her phone in the glove box."

So, a middle-aged woman, polite, respected, loved, had done, that day, what she did on more than a hundred different days, with one exception. On this one of more than a hundred days, she didn't go home. The detective, with a couple of uniformed cops, had canvassed several city blocks. Questions were asked, cards with contact information left. Promises to get in touch if anything changed. So far nothing had come of any of it. During his time as a cop, Allen had walked away, or had to be pulled away, from dozens of cases that would remain unsolved. Some of them murders. He was determined not to let that happen this time. Disappointed, he once again took stock of what he knew.

A woman with no known enemies, no perceived problems, was murdered with apparent premeditation, somewhere, sometime, between her hair appointment and her next obligation. Her body was then physically moved and dumped behind a Planned Parenthood office. Allen had three 9mm slugs, or in a couple of cases remains of slugs, each probably enough to achieve the ultimate and desired result, as well as blood, hair, and clothing samples, sitting in evidence bags down at the precinct. He knew the bullet to the heart was the official cause of death; the coroner had told him so. She had determined it had been the first shot fired and had done the lion's share of the damage to Daisy Burns's life. The bullet to the head was unnecessary, but next, and then the killer fired a third shot between the woman's legs for good measure, or giggles, or to send a message. For a little while, Allen had had a bitch of a time figuring out which, but now he was almost positive none of the shots was an afterthought, fired for insurance or administered to create a diversion. His experience told him each was a separate message, a savage story told in three short chapters.

The three slugs by themselves weren't a whole lot of help. Allen knew there were dozens of manufacturers making various types of 9mm weapons, and hundreds of thousands of those weapons—most obtained, carried, and put to use legally—were in the United States. The slugs, which went from inside the gun to inside Daisy Burns's body to inside the evidence bag, were of little or no use to him unless he could find the exact firearm from which they had been unleashed. Sadly, for Marc Allen and everyone involved at the moment, the killer had proved too smart to leave the smoking gun sitting next to the lifeless body.

The detective went back to the question he had been asking himself and others since those very first moments: *Who would want this woman dead?* Her husband, still suffering, had managed to raise more money for the reward fund, making any information leading to the apprehension of Daisy Burns's murder very valuable. Allen didn't have the heart to tell him that, while more money sometimes had better memory-restorative powers than *Ginkgo biloba*, it mostly just encouraged a new and more determined group of charlatans, grifters, and goofballs to waste Detective Marc Allen's time. Instead, he thanked the man, told him his efforts would help a great deal in the investigation, and assured him they were doing everything possible to solve the case. Maybe subconsciously he figured if he said it enough times out loud he might convince himself it was true. So far, no luck. It was time to head in and listen to what the fine folks in the Research Triangle had to say.

Brodie and Lancaster had decided before they went to bed that they'd get up early and play golf. Heart's favorite time to play was late afternoon into early evening, but first thing in the morning was pretty high up the list. Plus, Brodie was a morning person. She enjoyed golf—and for that matter a whole host of other things—before an invasion of thoughts and the onslaught of comings and goings engaged her brain and overtook her day. He had tried to tell her on numerous occasions that golf was a game best played with a modicum of outside influences, which included random thoughts, unrelated to the game, rattling around one's head. It was a concept much easier to put into practice for him than her. But he felt like she was getting the hang of it, especially this particular morning, which found him standing on the sixth tee, two down with four holes to play. To add insult to injury, that was also the moment the club's head pro, David Gerald, decided to pay them a visit.

"Hello, Pro." Brodie shrugged her bag off her shoulders and engaged the kickstand that kept it off the ground. Heart, driver in hand, was already on the teeing ground.

"Morning, Mayor," he said as he stuck a tee in the turf.

"Hi, kids," the golf pro said with a smile as he punched the brake pedal on his golf cart. "How's the match stand?"

"Two up." Brodie beamed.

"I've got her exactly where I want her." Heart smiled too but sounded much less convincing. "What brings you out for a chat?"

"Can't I come out and say hello to my two favorite members?" Gerald feigned hurt feelings.

"Of course," said Brodie.

"Absolutely not," offered Heart at almost the exact same time.

"That hurts." The pro shrugged. "But the good news is I now have one less favorite member." Brodie offered up her best curtsy. Heart smiled—at her, not him.

"Now I'm hurt," he said.

"Seriously," the pro said, quickly changing the subject. "Are you guys still leaving?"

"We are," they answered in unison.

"What did you decide to do about the house?"

"We decided to rent it," Brodie responded before Heart could. "Why?" Gerald looked at Heart, who looked back and shrugged.

"I was telling your boyfriend here—"

"Fiancé!" Brodie interrupted.

"What!" The pro sounded both pleased and surprised.

"Yep." Brodie flashed the diamond on the ring finger of her left hand. "He asked, and I answered."

"Well, then congratulations are in order. When's the big day?"

"August," Heart offered.

"So there's still time for you to come to your senses." The pro nodded toward Brodie.

"No time needed." Brodie looked at Heart. "I've been all in for a while. His asking was just the last straw to fall."

"Domino to fall," Heart said under his breath. The pro couldn't hear him either, but judging by the look on his face, Caster figured David Gerald understood exactly what Brodie meant. Most people usually did.

"Anyway, as I was saying…" The head pro picked up the thread that Brodie had interrupted with her news. "A while back I told your fiancé that my sister has a friend at the law firm who might be looking for a place to rent. I'm telling both of you now that she's more serious than ever."

"Great news," Brodie said. "We're going through the Oakwood Agency. Have your sister tell her friend to go over there and see Andie or Dana and fill out an application."

"Will do," the pro answered and then looked back up at Heart. "Let's see what you got." Caster took half a practice swing and then ripped one right down the middle of the fairway.

"Nice," Gerald said with pride. "You're clearly getting good advice." Then he hit the gas pedal and drove away.

"I'll tell the teaching pro up at the Governor's Club you think so!" Heart called after him. The pro's response was the middle finger of his right hand, but Heart knew there was a smile on his face that he couldn't see. Neither of them saw Brodie stand up and blast her tee shot twenty yards past Heart's.

CHAPTER THIRTY-FOUR

Hank decided to clean his firearms. He did that after each use or when he felt like he needed to take his mind off less pleasant things. He owned several weapons, including several handguns, two Remington rifles for hunting both small and large game, a Mossberg 500 tactical pump shotgun that he kept in a special easy-access casing attached to the underside of his bedframe, and an AK-47. Hank had been shooting guns since he was six years old and his grandpap, against the wishes of his mother, introduced him to firearms. The old man plopped young Hank onto his lap and told him tales about how members of the Hickox family tree, with the help of their sidearms, helped settle the "wild, wild West." Grandpap Wylie told a wide-eyed Hank that *his* grandpap James Butler Hickox was a soldier, a spy, a scout, a lawman, a gunfighter, *and* a gambler who was one of the most famous figures to "ever walk the face of God's green earth!"

"Don't you go filling that little boy's head with your tall tales," Hank's mother would say to her father whenever Wylie got to expounding on their family history, but it was too late. Six-year-old

Hank swallowed it hook, line, and sinker. Believed it all until he visited the county library during a grade-school field trip. He wandered off into the section that included several shelves of *Encyclopedia Britannica*, so he excitedly looked up his great-great-grandpap James Butler Hickox. Even after disappointedly reading about James Butler "Wild Bill" Hicko*ck*, Hank stubbornly clung to the hope that someone at the encyclopedia company had made a typing error. The bitter pill didn't dampen his enthusiasm for guns.

But Hank never taught Teri the things his grandpap had taught him. Like his own mother, Betty Lou would have none of it. For reasons that eventually made sense to him, she wouldn't let Hank keep any of his guns in the house. She understood why he had them, even appreciated, in her own way, how much they meant to him, but she would be damned if they would end up anywhere near their precious Teri. The guns, all of them, stayed safely locked up inside a large metal safe, covered by a tarp, in the corner of the barn.

Hank never argued, didn't even put up a contrary fuss. He would sometimes think, before a hunting trip or a day of target practice, that he had become his mother when it came to the subject of his child and guns. And since Hank's father was long gone, having run off when times turned the toughest, there was no Grandpap Wylie to intercede and offer an opposing opinion. So as far as Hank knew, Teri had never held a gun in her life, let alone fired one for fun. Or in anger.

CHAPTER THIRTY-FIVE

It was another night of disquieted sleep for Blanche Avery. The visage of the murdered woman seemed to take up permanent residence on the inside of her eyelids, staring sadly back at her whenever the old woman climbed in bed and closed her eyes. Daisy Burns's death weighed heavily on her mind and even more so on her heart. Blanche was no fool; she knew the world was an unkind place, but she always tried (and sometimes felt she succeeded) to keep the anger, arguments, indignities, and outright violence at arm's length. Most of it was confined inside the electronic box, and she could watch from the comfort of her favorite living room chair. Her real world was full of sadness; she witnessed it every day. Homeless men and women on the streets, having lost their way and fallen through society's cracks. Children, some in groups, others alone, on corners or at playgrounds during the time of day when Blanche was certain they should be seated at desks, facing teachers writing on blackboards, in school. Even the dogs and cats she visited on a weekly basis at the shelter near her home. She always stopped in with a smile or a treat, hoping the beagle or the mutt or the calico kitty would be gone, off to a for-real home with loving masters, but it rarely was.

But Blanche also knew sadness and strife were not murder. Hardship didn't have to be permanent. She felt, deep in her heart, there was always hope to be found in life. An opportunity to make the next day better than the last one. But there was no hope in death, no next day for the sorry soul whose life had been stolen. When Blanche prayed, she occasionally even said a prayer for the executioner, but mostly she just wondered how anyone could do such a thing to another living soul. She knew it happened, but having it happen to someone she knew broke her heart.

She turned her head to look at the small clock on the bedside table: 3:40 a.m. She knew sleep would not return, but it seemed too early to get up. She got up anyway. After sliding her feet into the new slippers her son had given her for her birthday, she eased into her robe and headed for the kitchen. She flipped on the light and sat down at the small wooden table in the center of the room. A pen and pad of paper, a recent addition, rested on one corner. With a slightly trembling hand, Blanche reached for them both. In the weeks since learning of the young woman's murder, she had taken to putting pen to paper, finding a place to transfer the jumble of thoughts that disrupted her sleep in the middle of an increasing number of nights. She was surprised, at first, at the sharpness of her mind when it came to recalling the details that were now decades old. She relived the heartbreak of that poor young woman. She harkened back with specific detail to the joy on the faces of the man and especially the woman who would become new parents. And she remembered the child. She could close her eyes and feel the newborn's soft skin on her cheek, sense the tiny fingers gripping the first two of her left hand. The smell of powder and preciousness invaded her nostrils. Sitting at the kitchen table with hours until sunrise, Blanche Avery cried, and Blanche Avery wrote the words she hoped would explain, then justify, her life while retelling the story of theirs.

NINE MONTHS LATER

CHAPTER THIRTY-SIX

Hank stood at the sink hand washing the two dishes and the decades-old pot he had used to cook and consume his dinner. Duke sat at attention by his master's side, perhaps thinking, more likely hoping, that a leftover morsel might come his way. The dog did this every night despite the fact that, while in the house, Hank had never fed him anything anywhere other than in his dog dish. With a still-wet hand, Hank patted the Rottweiler on the top of its head. The old farmer realized his constant companion had long since stopped lying in wait, staring out the window, longing for Teri to return home. It actually only took a few weeks. For Hank, on the other hand, it seemed to be taking a bit longer.

He professed his support when she came to him with the news that she was moving out, having found a place of her own. She told him, and she meant it, that it had nothing to do with the recent revelations or any awkwardness, perceived or otherwise, that may have come between them.

"It's just time, Daddy," he could still hear her saying during an extralong embrace. "I still love you, always will." He clung to that memory too.

So Hank decided he'd help. He loaded up the pickup during the move out and was right there to unload it when it came time to move in. He also found time, on many days, to solve any and every problem that arose. It didn't matter how small. And even now he spent at least some part of every day hoping the phone would ring and he'd answer it to find Teri on the other end of the line decrying a clogged drain or bemoaning a squeaky door hinge. Hank was always happy to oblige, to be his daughter's personal handyman, fixing the things *she* said needed fixing and mending the things *he* knew needed mending. But as much as Hank enjoyed being both needed and wanted, he made sure Teri felt he was always cognizant of her personal space, her privacy. As much as he occasionally wanted to, he never dropped by unannounced, hadn't yet taken it upon himself to drive down her street to see what car, or truck, was parked outside.

Hank knew how much Teri liked her new home—loved it, actually. She had told him so more than once. She said she felt safe there, enjoyed the neighborhood, and got a kick out of the neighbors, especially the "delightful older gentleman" next door—her words, not his. Hank's after-dinner contemplation was interrupted by a knock on the front door. Duke had already made a beeline for the sound, but the fact that no bark emanated from the beast told Hank the person doing the knocking was a known quantity, at least to the Rottweiler. He finished drying his hands and left the kitchen to find out just who had come calling.

CHAPTER THIRTY-SEVEN

Teri was in a rocking chair on her front porch, sipping a glass of chardonnay. She was also watching her next-door neighbor Mr. Rosenberg water the plants in his window boxes.

"Hey, Rosie," she called out, raising her glass as if to toast the man.

"Hello, dear," he returned. He hated the moniker but was too polite to tell Teri that. She loved the fact that he always called her "dear," even though she knew he probably used the term for every woman younger than he. In the months since moving in, Teri had learned that Mr. Rosenberg lived alone, having lost his partner more than fifteen years before. He was a retired school teacher and part-time movie critic, offering up his reviews on one of the local television stations that Teri never watched. He also critiqued films in a monthly entertainment magazine as well as on a national radio program. Teri realized he was marginally famous, although he would never cop to that. He was, she thought in no uncertain terms, a hoot, and that's exactly how Teri described him to her colleagues, family, and friends.

She had had him over for dinner a few times, and he had returned the favor. As far as Teri could tell, he was all alone; she never saw another soul come or go, had yet to see a strange car parked in front of his house. She neither felt sorry for him nor envied him. In fact, she didn't really care about his personal life, or lack thereof, all that much. He was kind and funny; he was friendly to her; and he never once made a peep about the people who entered and exited her orbit, sometimes at odd hours. Teri took a sip from her glass and thought about how lucky she felt. She had just finished law school and still had a job she enjoyed, working with people she mostly liked. She also lived in a house she adored. The place was actually a little big, more than she needed, but she appreciated the fact that there were extra bedrooms for Harper or Tanner or anyone else who might need a place to crash.

"Room to grow," her old man had said with a wink. She knew he was looking forward to the day when Teri met a "marrying kind of guy" and perhaps even delivered him a grandbaby. The kitchen in the place was wonderful, the perfect size whether cooking for one or half a dozen. The fact that the landlord had left a fifty-five-inch wall-mounted flat-screen TV in the living room above the fireplace didn't hurt either. She knew having a big—for her—house wasn't without issues, and she was extremely grateful and fortunate to have her dad around to fix the occasional broken thing or replace the filters, alarms, and carbon monoxide detectors. She finished her wine, gave one final wave to Herschel Rosenberg, and headed inside. She smiled to herself, knowing there were many times during the last year that she felt as if she had gotten away with murder.

Several miles away, Hank opened the front door to find Cody Switzer, cowboy hat on his head, warm smile on his face, and a chock-full-of-cash paper Winn-Dixie grocery-store bag in each hand.

"Cody," Hank addressed the young man through the screen door. Duke whimpered as his stubby tail wagged a mile a minute.

"Mr. Hank." Cody raised his right hand to tip his hat, and the bag, full of money, hit him on the nose.

"What brings you by?" Hank asked, knowing the answer. This time Cody raised both bags. "Didn't you just make a delivery?" Hank opened the screen door to let Cody in. Duke, after a couple of thorough sniffs, attached himself to Switzer's side. "How was the traffic?" Hank added.

"Yes, sir. On Tuesday." The boy answered the first question and then walked by Hank toward the kitchen.

And today is Thursday, thought Hank as he followed. "Been a while since deliveries came twice a week," he said out loud.

"Wouldn't know," the boy answered honestly. Hank knew he was correct but couldn't for the life of him remember the name of the kid who had dropped off the cash before Cody. "I don't pretend to know anything," Cody said, turning to face Hank, "but *something's* going on." They both let that hang in the air for several seconds, and then Cody spoke again. "There just seems to be a whole lot more money changing hands lately." The deliverer nodded in the general direction of the delivery. "And Mr. Goochly has been in a lot better mood." Hank still said nothing, but he nodded. "Is there anything you need?" Cody asked hopefully. "Anything I can do for you?"

Just keep bringing me bags full of money, Hank thought. "Not that I can think of, son, but thank you," he said.

"Well, then I'll just be heading home." This time Cody successfully executed a tip of his cowboy hat. Then he scratched the dog behind its right ear, then the left. "See ya, Duke," he said on the way out.

With the kid long gone, Hank opened one of the bags. The good look and long whiff of an assortment of bills brought a smile to his face.

CHAPTER THIRTY-EIGHT

Detective Marc Allen ran his hand over his clean-shaven head and exhaled the breath he had been holding since he exited his Charger. A quick look at the watch on his left wrist told him it was far too late, or way too early, depending on the frame of mind. He had been hanging out with Denise Clawsew, playing something called Cards Against Humanity, with her and a couple of other folks in her apartment. He split his time, giving minimal thought to which card to play and much more consideration to spending the night. The current question in front of those assembled was, "The blind date was going horribly until we discovered our mutual interest in _____." He perused the options in his hand and plopped down "Throwing a virgin into a volcano." He knew it wouldn't be chosen. Forty-five minutes of playing and no winning cards in his possession had proved his thought process and sense of humor were incongruent with those of the rest of the group, including Denise. Having long stopped giving a shit whether his card was chosen, he excused himself and headed for the kitchen to grab another Diet Coke. Denise had followed him, so they both heard the scanner squawk. Rapid fire codes, 10-37, 10-32, and 10-52, got his adrenaline going, and suddenly Marc Allen was no longer thinking about Cards Against Humanity or a chance of sleeping with Denise Clawsew.

"Gotta go," he said, kissing her on the forehead.

"Understood," she said. "Keep me posted." He promised he would.

The city was mostly deserted and, thanks to an occasionally broken or malfunctioning streetlamp, intermittently dark. He made a mental note to lob a call into Public Works. When he finally rolled up on the 6500 block of Creedmore Road, he found several black and whites, lights flashing, circling a Toyota Prius. *Unlikely getaway vehicle*, thought Allen as he spotted two uniformed officers standing off to one side. He knew one.

"What have we got, Boone?" he asked. The tag on the right side of his chest read "Grant," but Allen addressed the officer by his given name.

"Hard to tell, Detective." Boone Grant showed the proper respect by addressing Allen by his rank. "One victim, single gunshot to the head, appears to be the car's driver."

"Suicide?" That was where Allen's mind went first. "Something else?"

"Like I said, hard to tell," Grant repeated.

Do I detect condescension? Allen thought. "I *know* that!" he said condescendingly.

"I meant no disrespect, Detective." The cop seemed to realize his reply may have contained a certain amount of snark. "My personal opinion?" he offered. Allen nodded. "Looks like a self-inflicted wound to me."

"Thanks." Allen appreciated the on-the-spot analysis but knew "self-inflicted" only told part of the story. "I'll take a look for myself." And he did.

What he saw was a middle-aged, mostly healthy-looking white male, half in and half out of the driver's side of a blue Toyota Prius.

He found a bullet hole, blood, and some bone and brain matter near the ear on the right side of the victim's head. He also noticed a handgun, half hidden, between the seat and the center console. He knew the automobile and the firearm would be given a thorough examination; he felt his brethren were among the best in the business at that. The medical examiner would also go over the body with a fine-tooth comb, but Allen already had a good idea what conclusion they'd reach. This was no gun-related suicide. He had seen the aftermath of a few of those, and without exception the victim's position in death always made perfect sense. This one didn't. It looked to Allen like this guy was trying to get out of the car, which meant either he shot himself accidentally or someone shot him on purpose. He wasn't about to make a final judgment on which one of those was fact.

He did know for a fact that the weapon was a 9mm; he could tell that by the exposed barrel pointing in his direction from its spot usually reserved for gobbling up dropped keys or loose french fries. He also knew for a fact that the entire team would figure this one out, unlike the flower-girl murder case that had haunted him for close to a year. He recalled the first weeks that turned into first months immediately after finding the body of Daisy Burns behind a Planned Parenthood. It was a brutal act perpetrated by an evil person, and he still hadn't solved it. In different bars, over a number of cocktails with friends on the force, Denise, and even Teddy Burns, the husband of the murder victim, Allen had confessed what dug deepest was the fact that he couldn't make any forward progress. Despite escalating rewards, persuasive pleas, and good solid detective work, he couldn't come up with more than a handful of clues, let alone an honest-to-goodness suspect.

Now he had another dead body and another 9mm weapon. But Detective Marc Allen knew the two crimes were unrelated. All of his experience, every gut indicator, told him this guy—his driver's license identified him as Michael Jonathan Miller—was just another dipshit who had accidentally shot himself in the head with his own gun as he tried to get out of his hybrid car. He turned and walked away, flipping the dead man's wallet to Officer Grant.

"My personal opinion?" he said to Boone. "This is nothing more than a tragic accident." *As opposed to a heartbreaking murder,* he thought as he headed to his car, sadder than ever.

CHAPTER THIRTY-NINE

Heart took a sip of his midday scotch. He didn't make a habit of imbibing before the sun went down, but this lunch gathering was worthy of an exception. He looked around the table at Louis' Basque Corner, an iconic Reno dining establishment that wore its close to fifty years proudly. A tradition in his old, now new again, hometown. He had assembled his dream team, a group of professionals and friends for whom Heart had the highest esteem and in whom he held the ultimate confidence. To his left sat Pierce Edwards, Joe Beckett, and Chris Haley; on his right were Brice Breslow, Peggy Witchman, and Frank Buddings. This was the band of brothers and sister, thought Heart as he looked and smiled at his newly hired assignment editor. Including the entire group in his gaze, Heart felt a surge of something: Pride? Responsibility? He lamented the fact that his profession, *their* business, had become far too populated with thirty-something pretty faces. Nobodies with little seasoning and less knowledge getting first jobs on national networks. Sons, daughters, nephews, and nieces of somebodies who were doing more to damage the institutions for whom they worked than to elevate them. Long gone were Edward R. Murrow and Walter Cronkite. *Heck,* Heart thought, *I'd even settle for Peter Jennings at this point.* But Lancaster Heart was determined to right the listing ship, one reporter or anchor at a time. His mission was to restore some sanity to the business of gathering and reporting the news, put some professionalism back into the profession. This motley crew he had assembled was going to help him train, teach, and turn out a new generation of newsmen and newswomen into the world and onto the networks. *At least one,* he thought as he looked from face to face. First Beckett's, then Buddings's, then Haley's, Breslow's, and Witchman's.

"Who am I kidding?" he asked so softly he wasn't sure if he had said it or thought it. "What am I smoking?" Then he turned his head and found Pierce looking right at him. It didn't matter if he had said it aloud or not; the look on his mentor's face was proof positive that they were on the same page. Then Edwards dipped his head in a conspiratorial nod and, as an affirmative exclamation point, drained his Pincon Punch in one manly gulp.

"Here's to covering the news, not making it," Heart, knowing his mentor was dry, said, raising his glass.

"Hear, hear," said the group as one.

"Hear. Fucking. Hear!" repeated Pierce Edwards.

The waitress approached with dishes filled with sweetbreads, roast leg of lamb, beans, and porrusalda, the traditional Basque vegetable soup with chunks of potatoes that Heart remembered loving as a kid. The wonderful aromas reached the corner table in advance of the food. Before all of it arrived, Heart's phone buzzed in his pocket. Retrieving it, he noticed the call was from Brodie, so he excused himself from the gaggle and headed outside, answering on the way.

"Hey, doll," he said happily.

"Hi, babe," she answered.

"What's up?" They had been back in Reno for months, and everything seemed to be going smoothly. At least that's what Heart believed, and so far, Brodie hadn't given him any reason to alter that opinion. "Everything okay?" He hoped no kernel of doubt had slipped into the question.

"Couldn't be better." Brodie spoke the only way she knew how: honestly. She loved living in Heart's childhood hometown almost as much as he did. Heart exhaled. "Are you having tripe?" she asked, knowing about his lunch meeting at Louis'.

"Not today," he said as his stomach growled. "Sweetbreads."

"Oh, gross." He actually thought he could hear her stick her tongue out. "That's worse!"

A sheep's thymus gland or the lining of the same animal's stomach? Heart did the calculation in his mind. "I'm guessing what's on the lunch menu isn't the reason you called."

"Once again, you've hit the hammer in the head, my love," she said proudly. Heart succeeded in stifling a laugh. "I just got a call from Dana in Raleigh." It took Heart a second, but he put the name and town together and came up with their real estate agent.

"Everything okay?" Heart asked the question again, this time expressing a different concern. Teri Hickox had turned out to be a model tenant. The rent check always arrived on time; the initial worry of being long-distance landlords dissolved because of desuetude. If anything in the home needed repairing, Teri, or someone Teri trusted, seemed perfectly comfortable repairing it without their help. Brodie still meticulously examined the monthly homeowner's newsletter and never once came across an incident, good, bad, or indifferent, about their address. In addition to all of that, she had her ace in the hole, Mr. Rosenberg, next door.

"I think so," she replied, unconcerned. "Apparently, our tenant's father would like a face to face. Something about buying our little house for his little girl."

"That sounds like good news and bad news."

"Bad news?" Brodie wondered. "For whom?"

"For me," Heart answered quickly. "'Cause it sounds like you're headed to Raleigh for a few days."

"You're sweet," she said, "but I think you can handle it."

"I know I can, but it doesn't mean I have to like it."

"I'm thrilled you don't," she said with love. "Why don't you come with me?"

"No can do, doll. As good as that sounds, the very fate of journalism rests on my shoulders." He may have said it tongue in cheek, but he actually meant it. "You should give Becky and Kim a jingle, see if they can meet you there. You can make a real girls' weekend out of it." He knew his bride-to-be missed her friends, and he welcomed any chance for them to get together. The fact that she stayed close with friends she first met in middle school was a constant source of amazement for Heart. He had no idea where most of his best friends through the years hung their shingles these days. He also knew it meant a couple of nights of Honey Nut Cheerios or Frosted Flakes for dinner, so he made a mental note to get fresh milk.

"What a fabulous idea! That's why I love you."

"So *that's* the reason." Heart knew the conversation was coming to an end, and his food, cooling at the table, was waiting inside.

"Just one of the many reasons," she added. "See you tonight."

"Yes, you will." Heart told Brodie he loved her and headed back into the restaurant.

Tanner Goochly Jr. sat at the desk in his office and looked out the dirty window. A bright sun filled a huge section of the blue Carolina sky, but Goochly's outlook on life, as he looked out on it, was considerably less sunny. He was pissed, he was frustrated, and he told himself he was sick and tired of filling up bags full of money for his old man and not coming away with his fair share of it. From where he sat, it looked like he was doing the lion's share of the work and getting a mouse's share of the profit. And, of course, that little puke Switzer was paid too much for whatever it was he did, as far as Tanner was concerned. The incredible lack of perspective was lost on Goochly as he stewed in his own juices. He wasn't great at math, remembering his heroic efforts to *not* pay attention during his high-school classes. Instead, he spent the time on more worthwhile (in his mind) pursuits, like wondering how any of this was going to be useful after graduation or figuring out the various ways he could try to get into Hannah Jane Witterson's pants. In spite of his success at not paying attention in school, he knew he was a whole lot smarter than his seventh-grade-educated dad. He also was well aware that Tanner Goochly Sr. was a whole lot meaner, so Tanner was going to have to be extra sneaky about putting his hand in the cookie jar.

Business at Goochly Music and More, the family-owned establishment that derived a much greater chunk of revenue from the "More" than the "Music," was booming. Tanner didn't know if the joints he and his dad co-opted were merely busier lately or if the clientele simply had more money to spend and lose. He spent a couple of seconds figuring he could ask somebody, then an equal amount of time deciding not to bother because, after all, he couldn't determine that it would make any difference. The machines were internally adjusted to produce favorable results for the Goochlys, and recently Tanner, through a series of conversations with his old man, had suggested an additional tweak or two to make that advantage even greater. Goochly Sr. shot the ideas down every time, saying things like "There ain't no need to rock the boat." The customers either didn't know the machines had been fiddled with or didn't care, and both worked equally well. He dismissed his son's ideas as greedy and stupid. Tanner couldn't care less about being labeled the former, but he seethed every time he thought about being called the latter. *If I can't get his blessing,* Tanner remembered thinking, *I'll just take his money,* my *money*. And that's exactly what he planned to do.

A beautiful Cooper's hawk soared through his field of vision, probably on the lookout for a pheasant, a grouse, or an unsuspecting mourning dove. For some reason, the bird of prey made him turn his attention to his cousin Teri. She was another person who mostly pissed him off, but man, that body! Sex with Teri Hickox was worth the irritation of having her tease him constantly. If he could just tape her mouth shut, it would be even better. He could ask her if that would be okay, but he knew the answer. The thought of his "cuz" stripped down naked in front of him with a strip of duct tape covering her pouty lips made Tanner smile and get a little hard. He thought about giving her a call, but then he pivoted back to thinking about robbing his father.

Teri instinctively closed her left eye, then, remembering what both Harper and Tanner had told her, opened it wide. Seconds later the gun went off in her hand, three quick shots, bullets exploding out of the short round barrel, traveling at more than a thousand feet per second. The gun, a Ruger 101, wasn't hers. It belonged to her girlfriend who was in the next stall firing away with a Smith & Wesson 642 Lady Smith revolver. Teri thought the firearm she held in her hand was cute, mostly because Harper had modified it with a hot-pink grip. Except for that grip, it looked to Teri like the guns every cop used in the old TV shows she sometimes caught Hank watching when he thought she had gone to bed. But the gun was heavy in her hand, more than half a pound heavier than her Sig Sauer, and the trigger was a lot tougher to pull. She also felt something she could only describe as a growl when she fired it, an angrier gun eager to show off its deadly potential. Maybe she'd try the Lady Smith next. Its appearance was similar to the Ruger's, except for the grip, and Teri wondered if it carried with it the same slight kick.

She hadn't shot at anything, animate or inanimate, in a while, and she missed the feeling. When she and Harper first arrived at the range, it showed. The first targets slid back clean of anything worth boasting about, and Teri, blaming it on rust, tried valiantly to laugh it off. But on the inside, she was annoyed—no, more than annoyed, she was incensed and embarrassed, and more than thankful it was Harper watching her and not Tanner. But that was the only thing she was happy about. Then, after a few deep breaths and a few more loads and reloads, she got into a groove and found the peace that came with confidence. Fuller of herself, she put down her pistol and picked up her friend's—after asking permission, of course—and found firing the strange new weapon both a little frustrating and more than a little erotic. Not erotic enough to want to go out and buy one, though. Firing brought her back to the realization of how much she enjoyed holding a gun, pulling the trigger, hearing the report, and judging her competence against past results.

She also remembered just how good using the firearm made her feel inside. Empowered, impressive, safe, and yes, sexy. She knew she was in control of her life most of the time, but when she held the Sig Sauer or the Bodyguard, she felt in command of her life. It was her world, and everyone else was just living in it. She was smart enough to know it didn't make her indestructible, but it sure helped her feel indomitable. Shooting something, or someone, was the activity but not the cause of this surge of exhilaration. That came with being the shooter, embracing the gun and what it pushed through her veins. Emboldened, she reloaded the Ruger with five more .357 Magnum cartridges and fired at the target twenty feet in the distance. A target that she saw, with both eyes wide open, as Tanner Goochly Jr.

Cody Switzer strained under the weight of the two seventy-five-pound disks attached to either end of the bar. He was on his back on a bench, sweating as he pressed the two hundred pounds over his chest five more times.

"Nice, kid." Cody's older brother, Clint, serving as his spotter, offered encouragement. "Go grab some water, take a break."

Cody nodded, sat up, wiped the sweat from his face and neck, then did what he was told. As he walked away, Clint, five years Cody's senior, saw a kid growing into adulthood. He smiled to himself, remembering his role as the tough big brother encouraging the kid to join in when Cody, aged nine or ten, whined about not being able to play in a front-yard football game with Clint and his not-quite-yet-high-school-freshmen buddies. Instantly delighted, Cody embraced the challenge with gusto and almost immediately found himself with the ball—under a pile of rougher-than-need-be, sweatier-than-normal teenagers—screaming in pain with what turned out to be a broken collarbone. They all accused him of faking. Clint felt bad about that for about five seconds and then joined in on the mocking. He had felt even worse minutes later as they all sat and waited for the ambulance. For some reason, he felt even more guilt on this day than he had on that one.

He'd known for some time that the world was always going to be a little harder for his kid brother than it was for him. Clint was blessed with more than his fair share of smarts and looks. He was a varsity-letter-earning wrestler all through high school and parlayed that, with hard work and a report card filled with mostly As, into full-ride-scholarship offers to a number of schools, including nearby Davidson. He continued to compete and continued to get excellent grades, graduating with honors and landing a six-figure job with the North Carolina state government in Raleigh. He also never stopped training and had recently agreed to help his little brother add some discipline to his life and muscle to his frame. He hadn't asked Cody why he wanted a little more bulk and honestly didn't care. He just wanted to help the kid, to finally be the best big brother and friend he could be.

As Cody turned from the water cooler and started to walk back, paper cup in his right hand, Clint saw a human being with better-than-average bones that weren't quite put together in exactly the right way. His brother's head was maybe one size too small, and it was sitting, held by an average neck, on shoulders that rode a tad high. They still appeared, maybe thanks to a poorly set collar-bone break, just a bit askew. His arms looked fine, hands nice and strong, but his torso was maybe an inch too long and his legs an inch too short. In all, Cody Switzer, as observed by Clint Switzer, wasn't a bad-looking guy at all, but he was imperfect in so many little ways, *too many ways*, thought Clint.

Cody had made it through high school, mostly on the shoulders of an odd sort of charm and an abundance of Cs. But he had no interest in college, which was a good thing, according to Clint, because he knew very few colleges and universities would be interested back. His folks would have had no trouble paying for it, and Clint would have contributed if they couldn't, but that bridge never needed to be crossed. Instead, the runt of the family got a job with a family from the outskirts of town that owned and operated, Clint strained to recall, some kind of music store. The job paid him decent money, it helped that Cody still lived at home, and the kid seemed to enjoy the work. It was all good, until recently, when little brother came to big brother asking if he'd help him muscle up and maybe even teach him a few go-to wrestling moves. Clint always thought Cody was more than comfortable in his God-given, while uneven, skin, but that seemed to have changed too. Maybe it was growing up, or growing pains. Maybe Cody had met a girl. Or maybe, Clint worried just a little, his kid brother was suddenly looking for a fight.

"Ready to get after it some more?" Cody's words steamrolled right through Clint's train of thought.

"Ready," the big brother said.

CHAPTER FORTY

Heart was in a sour mood. After a fitful night, he had finally fallen into a deep sleep only to be awakened, what felt like seconds later, by the sound of an alarm clock that seemed to come out of nowhere. He heard the shower, felt the absence of Brodie in the bed, and after a moment, remembered he was chauffeuring her to the airport. After dropping her off, kissing her good-bye, and watching her backside enter the departures building, he decided to head for the station with a stop at Starbucks along the way. Far too late he realized the barista had forgotten to put the vanilla syrup in his latte. Now he was standing in front of more than a dozen reporters, producers, and anchors in the studio, preparing to deliver a teaching-moment speech. On a normal day, none of those things individually, maybe not even all of them collectively, would have set Heart off, but maybe the notion of being on his own for a few days had a more profound effect.

Kelly Sands and Mitchell Knapp were the anchors, the two who would, from in front of the camera, deliver the good, the bad, and the mundane news of the day to northern Nevadans who happened to be watching. Sands was a recent graduate of the highly respected University of Missouri School of Journalism. Upon graduating, she was offered and accepted a job as a reporter in Billings, Montana. After a couple of years there, she applied for the same job at Heart's station, and it didn't take long for her to distinguish herself, moving into the anchor chair at noon and five thirty.

Mitchell Knapp III went by the ostentatious nickname "Tripp," short for the third. "Get it? *Triple?* The *third!*" the little prick had queried Heart while poking his elbow into Lancaster's ribs. He *got* it all right. Tripp Knapp, by all accounts except his own, made his way through Syracuse on his looks and his family's connections. He grew up in Baltimore and had a brother in the business delivering sports on a top-twenty-five market station. His dad was the publisher of one of the city's most prestigious daily newspapers. Syracuse University managed to get a nice chunk of change for its journalism school, and Mitchell—not yet "Tripp"—Knapp managed to get a diploma. Reno was his first job in television, and based on the work ethic he had seen so far, Heart figured it should be his last. Tripp, on the other hand, felt from the beginning this job was beneath him, knew he was destined for bigger and better things, and was biding his time, sending tapes and résumés, until a major broadcast or cable network came calling. Both Sands and Knapp had been hired by Heart's predecessor. For the time being, he couldn't wait to get rid of one and to mentor the other.

"I'm sure you're all wondering why I called you together today," Heart said, starting the meeting. Sands sat up and moved to the edge of her chair while Tripp slunk back in his and plopped his newly polished shoes on the desk.

"Get your feet off the desk!" From the back of the studio, Pierce Edwards's voice got everyone's attention.

"Thanks, Pierce." Heart held up his right hand and then used his index finger to point at Knapp's Ferragamo loafers. Reluctantly the future superstar put his feet back on the floor. Next Heart grabbed one of the headsets hanging from a studio camera and spoke into the microphone. "Marty," he barked, "can you put what we talked about earlier on the monitor." It was a command, not a question. Marty Mabry, the longtime station director, sitting across the hall in the control room, did as he was told. Everybody but Tripp positioned him- or herself for a better look. It wasn't that Knapp knew what was coming; he just didn't give a rat's ass. What appeared was an article that had clearly come from the station's website dated that morning.

"Reno Mayor DEFIES Nevada Governor and the President!" The headline topped a multiparagraph article.

"Which one of you is responsible for this?" Heart asked, even though he already knew. This time Tripp Knapp leaned in as well.

"That would be me, Capo," he said smugly, raising his hand. The first time Heart heard Knapp call him "Capo," he thought he heard "Captain." It didn't matter because he hated both.

"It's Lancaster, remember, Mitch?" Heart returned the insult by using the kid's abbreviated given name.

"Yes sir, Lancaster." Mitch settled back into his seat.

"You need to rewrite this." Heart addressed the monitor.

"Why?" Knapp asked

"Because it's incorrect. Worse, it's misleading."

"Well, with all due respect"—Heart hated that saying as well because he knew whoever said it conveyed *no* respect whatsoever—"it's not *not* true."

So, it's going to be like this, thought Heart. "There is not one shred of evidence outside your article, or *in* it, that suggests the mayor of Reno defied the governor, let alone the president of the United States," he countered matter of factly.

"She told me, off the record, that she was considering taking a stance contrary to the position held by both." Knapp attempted to defend his work.

Heart shook his head. "Can someone please explain to Mister Knapp the meaning of 'off the record' *and* the difference between considering a different point of view and defiance." He looked around the room. He knew nobody liked the guy, but his colleagues weren't about to throw him under the bus in such a public setting. They didn't have to.

"So you're saying I should have written 'Reno Mayor Contemplates Defying Nevada Governor and the President'?" Knapp was trying to play defense.

"What I'm saying is you should have written the truth."

"Who the heck is going to click on that?" Tripp looked to his colleagues for support. He found none. "It's all about the clicks, Capo," he added, looking at Heart.

"Not any longer," he said to Knapp, and then he addressed the entire group. "You are journalists, not gossip columnists. This is a news organization, not TMZ." Heart paused. "If you want to work for Harvey Levin, let me know, and I'll put you in touch, but from now on, around here you write a headline commensurate with the facts of the story above which it sits." Heart took the time to look at each and every face. "No more canards." He noticed a few nods, a couple of smiles, and one very quizzical look. From his perch in the back of the room, Pierce Edwards had noticed too.

"Look it up!" he said loud enough for everyone to hear despite the fact that it was directed at one person.

"That's not how it works." Unfazed, Knapp plowed ahead, attempting to educate his boss about the ways of the digital world. "The headline pulls 'em in." He used both hands to illustrate his point. "It's called clickbait." And with that pronouncement, his hands ended up behind his head.

"It's called bullshit," Heart shot back, "and it ends now."

"So why would anyone ever go to our website?" Knapp wasn't quite finished.

"They'll go to our website because they'll know they can trust our reporters and our reporting. They'll go to our website because it will be a place where they can get the whole story, the best information, and a fair, honest, and objective examination of the issues." Heart stopped, realizing he had raised his voice to the point of preaching. From over his shoulder, he heard clapping, starting with Pierce Edwards and then getting picked up by everyone in the studio. Everyone with the exception of Mitchell "Tripp" Knapp.

CHAPTER FORTY-ONE

Blanche Avery's son Nick was devastated but determined. It had been a few days more than a week since his mother had passed away, silently, suddenly, in her sleep. He had spoken with her on the phone that day, and he remembered thinking she sounded a little sad but not at all sick. In hindsight, he couldn't help but wonder if that was how she really sounded or how he *wanted* her to sound. He racked his brain, stretched his memory to see if he had missed any signs, any indication, that that one day would be the last day he'd ever get the chance to speak with his mom. He couldn't come up with a thing but did recall that, lately, she had occasionally been preoccupied or distracted, but he wasn't ever troubled by it. She certainly wasn't addled or confused. It was true that it had been a while since he had come by for a visit, but he called every day, and he called on the day he found her dead. She didn't pick up the first time he tried; that was unusual but not un-heard of, so he gave it an hour and called again. Still no answer, and that *was* unprecedented. Feeling—no, knowing—something was out of order, he rushed to her apartment, calling a third time on the way, and her phone just rang and rang and rang. It was still ringing when he parked, dropped his own phone on the passenger seat of his car, rushed up the stairs, and used his key to enter her home.

She was in the bed, on top of the covers, eyes closed, hands folded on top of her chest. Stricken with fear, guilt, and a suddenly ponderous sadness, Nicholas Avery couldn't help but notice the peace he observed on his mother's face. He was struck by the contrast of what he felt and how she looked. Her Bible was on the table next to her bed, open, he found as he picked it up, to her favorite verse, Matthew 25:35. The page was dog eared and the passage highlighted with a see-through yellow marker. Nick stood over his mother and instinctively read aloud.

"For I was hungry, and you gave me something to eat. I was thirsty, and you gave me something to drink. I was a stranger, and you invited me in. I needed clothes, and you clothed me. I was sick, and you looked after me. I was in prison, and you came to visit me. Then the righteous will answer him, 'Lord, when did we see you hungry and feed you, or thirsty and give you drink? When did we see you a stranger and invite you in, or needing clothes and clothe you? When did we see you sick or in prison and go visit you?'"

Nick Avery closed the book and then closed his eyes. He knew what came next, had heard his mother quote the scripture at least a hundred times since before he was old enough to read, understand, and appreciate what the words meant. He understood them now and appreciated that his mother lived them every day of her life.

"The King will reply"—Nick lifted his face, eyes crying but still closed, to the heavens, where he believed his mom to be—"truly I tell you, whatever you did for one of the least of these brothers and sisters of mine, you did for me." Nick dropped to his knees next to his mother's bed and, for the first time since he was a child, bawled like a baby.

Marc Allen was back at Big Eddie's. A third mug of steaming black coffee shared the tabletop with a plate that once held eggs, over medium; bacon; and half a dozen "Big Eddie's Little Pancakes," as well as that day's *Raleigh News & Observer*, open to the obituaries section.

"Too bad we couldn't rustle up something you liked." Big Eddie himself had slid into the other side of the booth without so much as a nod from the detective.

"It's criminal how good your food is, Eddie," Allen replied, still not looking up. "I might have to arrest Boogie so I can have my breakfast without having to waste the taxpayers' money on gas to drive over here."

Boogie was Big Eddie's cook, had been for the past dozen years ever since the boss had found him one morning, curled up under a flattened cardboard box near the back entrance of the restaurant. Sitting across from the detective that morning, he remembered the morning from years ago. After rousting the man and bringing him inside for a cup of coffee and a plate of biscuits and gravy, Eddie learned Bobby "Boogie" Hoffman had been a cook in the army. Not a big believer in serendipity, Eddie nonetheless thought the encounter was fortuitous for several reasons. First, Eddie just happened to be down a cook. Second, the guy was big, not Big Eddie big but big, and despite having run into a rough patch, he was clearly well put together. Some extra muscle in the restaurant was never a bad thing. Last, he was ex-army, and Eddie had a soft spot in his heart for veterans, having been a navy man himself.

"So you served Uncle Sam by serving his fighting men," Eddie remembered saying, trying to make conversation. Boogie just nodded, clearly wary of the sudden unexpected kindness. "What happened?" Getting right to the point, Eddie wasn't exhibiting some kind of morbid curiosity; he honestly wanted to know. Boogie Hoffman must have sensed that, because he told him.

"Got out. Honorable discharge," he said proudly. "Got a job. At a Denny's in Florida." The cook took a loud gulp of coffee, then added more sugar and milk.

"Denny's, huh?" Eddie watched a strong right hand envelop a silver spoon and stir the coffee. He couldn't help but notice that, despite the man's current situation, his hands were clean, his nails trimmed.

"Denny's." Boogie looked up, and Eddie sank into the sadness in the man's eyes. He waited. After another long sip, Boogie told his story.

He had, in short order, worked his way up the Denny's ladder from prep cook to line cook, first working the restaurant's worst shifts to its busiest. Sitting across the table from Big Eddie in the hour before dawn, Boogie was no longer on the street, down on his luck. He was back in Florida, a proud veteran.

"They told me I was in line for another promotion, maybe even shift manager." Boogie looked past Eddie. Half a minute later, he continued. He had agreed to do a coworker a favor and switch shifts one day—one night, actually. The graveyard shift wasn't for everybody. You worked midnight to eight and, from behind the pass through between the kitchen and the restaurant proper, watched all kinds of God's creatures come and go. Bridesmaids and bachelors; bums and executives; a few cops and more than a few drunks. Most nights workers ended up with more time on their hands than during other shifts, and sometimes that meant a more intimate relationship with fellow workers. Boogie never liked graveyard, but from the first minute they met, he was fond of Candy Crosley. Candy, unlike Boogie, loved working the graveyard shift. She was everybody's work mom, had proudly worn the Denny's apron for more than forty years. Boogie thought she was the best waitress he'd ever seen and, quite possibly, the nicest person. She had a grandson in the army, part of the Tenth Mountain Division stationed at Fort Drum in upstate New York. He had served multiple deployments to both Iraq and Afghanistan and had returned home whole after each one. Candy had a special place in her heart for her army boys, which meant she had a special place in there for Boogie.

Boogie's recitation was interrupted by a knock at Big Eddie's front door. The owner had the only key, and in the process of meeting and getting to know Boogie, he had forgotten to open the restaurant.

"You hungry?" he asked Boogie.

"Yes, sir," he answered quickly, then quietly added, "but I'm sorry I've got no money to pay."

"Let me worry about that," Eddie said, getting up. "Consider it a down payment on the rest of your story." As he left the booth, he turned his head and looked back at his guest. "Don't you go anywhere."

"No, sir."

Eddie unlocked the front door and flipped the hanging sign from closed to open. Rico, the chef du jour, walked past, head down, and headed straight for the kitchen. The sky outside was just starting to welcome the morning sun. Blacks, purples, and deep dark blues would soon give way to another day. A minute later Eddie was back in the booth, across from Boogie.

"Hope you're okay with bacon and eggs, biscuits, gravy, and grits." He noticed a tear beginning to form in Boogie Hoffman's left eye. Before the man could express his gratitude, Eddie implored him to pick up where he had left off. So Boogie went back in time again. He recalled he had just made a Denver omelet for a guy at the counter who was still wearing a three-piece suit, complete with a bow tie. He next heard the entrance door chime and knew another customer was on his or her way in. As it turned out, it was customers, three men, equal parts boisterous, loud, and obnoxious. Boogie watched them, senses shifting to a familiar heightened state, as the trio made a beeline for a booth in the corner.

Boogie knew a hundred guys like this, had grown up around dozens, served with more than a few in the army. Punks. From the minute they sat down, they started barking orders and bitching about the restaurant. They might have been drunk; maybe they were high; or maybe, thought Boogie, they were just assholes feeding off each other's false bravado. Candy must have sensed Boogie's alarm, because she stopped at the pass through on her way to deliver menus.

"Don't worry, Army," she assured him affectionately. "I got this." Boogie hoped it was true as he watched her back.

Bow Tie must have also sensed discomfort, because he wolfed down what was left of his breakfast and left a twenty on the counter before heading for the exit. That left five people in the restaurant, and three of them were looking for trouble. It didn't take long for them to find it, because they caused it. Candy might have been a grandmother, but Boogie, and just about everybody else, still thought she was a looker, and the three in the booth had noticed that right away.

In Big Eddie's diner, the bacon, eggs, biscuits, and gravy came, interrupting the story. Boogie couldn't resist and dug right in. Eddie thought he knew where this particular tale was headed, but he was enthralled. He could see the man appreciated the meal that was now in front of him, but Eddie didn't want Boogie to make himself sick, so he suggested he slow down.

"Easy, Private Hoffman." Eddie put his hand on Boogie's left forearm. The man stopped midchew.

"Specialist Hoffman," he corrected. Eddie nodded. "I was a cook and a damn good one." A small piece of scrambled egg hung on his lip, and he gathered it up with a quick tongue. "These are good." He pointed at his plate with his fork. "But mine are better." Eddie smiled.

"Maybe you'll get a chance to prove it. Now tell me more about how you ended up sleeping under a cardboard box behind my establishment, *Specialist* Hoffman."

The boys—young men, Boogie corrected himself—were predictably rude to Candy, but true to form, she acted like she couldn't care less. Boogie knew it wasn't an act. He heard her tell them she'd be back as soon as they were actually ready to order something. That didn't go over particularly well with one of them, a Hispanic kid with a do-rag and what appeared to be a Rolex watch. He preferred Candy join them and suggested she do that by sitting on his lap. She smiled and turned on her heel to walk away, and according to Boogie, that's when somebody hit fast forward on the scene. The kid reached out to grab Candy, a no-no in both the employee manual and Boogie's mind. He missed her wrist but managed to get hold of the apron tie on her back. He gave it a yank. Startled, Candy lost her balance and went down to one knee. Boogie's concern boiled over into fury, and he grabbed a skillet and barreled into the restaurant. He was at her side, the hoodlums were pointing and laughing, and Boogie was in full protect-and-defend mode.

"What the fuck is wrong with you people?" Boogie said it to them in that restaurant then and in this restaurant now, out loud, to Eddie.

"Easy, boy!" he remembered hearing one of them say. He also heard Candy's softer voice.

"Don't be stupid, Army. You're not supposed to be out here."

"Yeah, *Army*, get back in your cage," the Hispanic kid had mocked.

Eddie remembered that as Boogie Hoffman told his tale his face relayed the pain and confusion of a person caught up in all the world's wrongs while simply trying to do the right thing. Eddie gave him a minute.

"I told those assholes to get the hell out of my restaurant," he told Eddie proudly, defiant. Then in a much softer, sadder tone, he added, "And I raised the skillet over my head to drive home the point." Without realizing it, Boogie had repeated the gesture without the frying pan. Eddie could sense the menace in it regardless.

Nobody knew what might have transpired, how Boogie's and now Eddie's lives might have been different, if he had heeded Candy's advice or been able to control his own temper and, at the very least, leave the skillet in the kitchen. But he hadn't, and when he raised it over his head, some leftover grease went from the pan into the Hispanic kid's left eye. At least that's what he said on the witness stand, wearing an eye patch, claiming he'd never see out of that orb again. It didn't help that the kid's father was on the city council, and despite character testimony from the restaurant manager and Candy Crosley, Boogie was convicted on three counts of aggravated assault. The other two men claimed emotional distress, and Boogie Hoffman was sentenced to five years in the Sumter Correctional Institution.

"Honestly, sir..." Boogie's voice cracked, and Eddie's heart broke. "I really couldn't tell you how I got from there to here."

"Well, you're here now." Eddie remembered putting a napkin to his face, wiping both eyes, and blowing his nose. Then he started to extract himself from the booth for the second time that morning, but he stopped and leaned toward his guest. "Just one more question."

Boogie sat motionless, trying to figure out what was coming next, wondering if it would send him back out on the streets.

Sensing no objection, Eddie pressed on. "What's your Christian name? And, assuming Boogie ain't it, how'd you get the name Boogie?" The man across the table involuntarily discharged a loud, relieved laugh.

"Robert, sir. My mama named me Robert."

"And Boogie?" Eddie waited.

"You don't want to know, sir. Trust me, you don't want to know." He let that simple answer hang in the air. Eddie nodded.

"Fair enough, but from now on it's Eddie, not sir, not Mr. Eddie, definitely not Mr. Ed, just plain Eddie."

"Yes, sir. Eddie, sir," the army vet replied.

Through the intervening years, Eddie Carbone had come to trust Boogie Hoffman about most everything, and during the same time frame, Boogie Hoffman never called his boss, his friend, "just plain Eddie."

"Now let's find out just how good a cook you really are." With that, Eddie had left the booth for good.

"Well, Detective." Eddie was back in the present, sharing the very same booth with a very different customer. "As much as Boogie might appreciate the compliment," the big man paused, "considering what he's been through, I'm fairly certain he wouldn't take kindly to being arrested for no reason."

"No," Marc Allen said, shaking his head. "I don't imagine he would."

"Anything interesting in the Snooze and Unnerver?" Eddie used his nickname for the local paper.

"Let's see. Duke Hoops signed another McDonald's All American, construction on I-Four Forty is delayed again, SAS is still one of the country's best places to work, and the Canes lost again. So nothing all that interesting."

"Guy on WRAL keeps saying he thinks Carolina still has a chance to make the playoffs." Eddie concentrated on the last news item.

"He's usually pretty smart, but on this one I gotta disagree."

"Me too."

"Now I'm just catching up on the obituaries." The detective smiled.

"Looking to see who's dead besides the Hurricanes?" Eddie slapped the tabletop with a meaty right hand.

"Just making sure I'm not included."

"Didn't George Burns say, 'The first thing I do each morning is read the obituaries, and if I don't see my name, I go make breakfast'?"

"I don't know if he said it first, but he sure got a lot of mileage out of it." Allen smiled at the thought of the bespectacled, octogenarian comedian.

"So, who's dead today?" Eddie brought the conversation back to earth. Allen peered at the pages.

"Looks like one of the ladies in Sister Sledge."

"We are family," Eddie started singing.

"You never cease to amaze me, Eddie." Allen chuckled as he went back to the paper. Eddie continued to hum.

"A Nobel Prize winner and some guy who played pro soccer in Europe."

"What about around here?" Eddie stopped humming long enough to ask.

"A shitload of people," Allen answered. "Almost all of them old, and from a variety of causes." The detective's eyes scanned the page. "Here's one. Blanche Lenore Avery. Says she passed peacefully in her sleep." Allen looked up at Eddie. "That's how I want to go," he said, "at my house, in my own bed."

"Me too." Eddie smiled a sad smile.

"You want to die at my house, in my bed?" Allen teased the restaurant owner. Eddie, in turn, gave the detective a stern look. "Okay, I'm outta here." Allen folded his paper and reached into his pocket for some cash.

"Don't bother." Eddie put his hand on Allen's arm. "Breakfast is on me."

"I appreciate that," Allen told the owner, "but absolutely not. Can't have any question of impropriety if someone ever sics the health inspector on you." He smiled and dropped a twenty on the table.

"Fat chance," Eddie said confidently. "See you tomorrow?"

"Nope," Allen said, sliding out of the booth. "Going on vacation. Headed to the Caribbean for a little sun, sand, and golf."

"Good for you." Eddie nodded. "See you when you get back."

"Count on it." Allen turned to go, and then he turned back. "You and Boogie hold down the fort."

"Consider it held down."

CHAPTER FORTY-ONE

Nick Avery sat in the silence of Blanche's apartment. The surroundings weren't exactly ever raucous, but its current state carried the weight of intense sadness. Nick was a realist; he knew nobody, let alone his mom, lived forever, but he still found himself enormously ill prepared for her passing. So he sat on her couch, in the middle of his memories, trying to figure out what to do next. She didn't have a lot, never wanted much, but for reasons Nick couldn't entirely grasp, he felt like he was tasked with cleaning out the basement of the Smithsonian Institute. He took one last sip of his store-bought latte and headed for the kitchen because that's where his mother kept the garbage container. While there, he decided to go after the low-hanging fruit and started to clean out the fridge.

At the store, he had picked up some Clorox wipes, paper towels, a bottle of Windex with a fancy spray nozzle, and a couple of boxes of heavy-duty trash bags. Standing in front of the open refrigerator, he began to fill one of the black bags. A mostly empty quart of milk well on the way down sour street, orange juice, a few stalks of celery, an unopened bag of string-cheese sticks, a Granny Smith apple, a tin of tuna (Nick wondered why she put an unopened can of StarKist in the fridge), a box of Arm & Hammer baking soda. Old, new, opened, sealed; it all went into the bag. Nick, the loving son, transformed into an impartial cleaning-service agent getting the apartment ready for its next occupant. In the back, on the bottom shelf, Nick discovered a four pack of Seagram's Escapes Strawberry Daiquiris. Three of the bottles waited to be opened and enjoyed. *You little devil,* Nick chided his mother with a thought. Then he threw all three bottles in the garbage bag.

It took a little less than thirty minutes before the refrigerator and freezer were empty. Nick made a mental note to have the woman who tidied up his own place come by for a thorough cleaning of his mom's. Then he took out his phone and made a physical note. He leaned against the kitchen counter and looked around at what he could see of the rest of the apartment. Taking inventory, he opened a new Notes page on his phone and entered everything he observed. Some of the furnishings and entrapments would be headed to the junk heap or a landfill, but much of it, while old, was still in very good condition and would serve some needy person or less fortunate family well. He'd be delighted to donate as much of his mother's belongings to Habitat for Humanity as they would take. He was confident his mom would approve. The last place he wanted to assess was the bedroom, so he put that off for the bitter end. The main living area of the apartment included a coat closet, and that's where Nick went next.

He found a winter coat, a raincoat, and a windbreaker hung side by side, patiently waiting but never again needed to keep Blanche Avery warm, dry, and comfortable. A shelf above the hangers served as a home base to a small variety of hats, gloves, and scarves. None would ever again pass for stylish, but all were serviceable, and he earmarked them all for the donation box at Blanche's church. There was also a plastic air freshener; he grabbed it and dropped it in a new bag. On the floor of the closet Nick found two umbrellas leaning against the wall. He recognized one as a souvenir he'd purchased at a recent US Open golf championship he had attended when the event was held at nearby Pinehurst. He set it aside, remembered wondering where he might have used and left it last. Near the "bumbershoots" (he recalled his mom using the term for umbrella after watching Dick Van Dyke sing and dance in *Chitty Chitty Bang Bang*), he noticed a pair of winter boots. Guilt flooded over him as he thought of the brutal, unseasonably cold season they had endured nearly a dozen years ago. *Had it been more than a decade since I bought you new boots?* He looked up, in his mind, past the ceiling, hoping for absolution. Looking down again, he found, behind the boots, a can of white wall paint, a small Hoover vacuum cleaner, and a pair of brown shearling-lined men's slippers. Not his. He smiled, thinking of Blanche Avery and some paramour sitting on the sofa enjoying an ice-cold bottled strawberry daiquiri and an old movie. Aside from a little dust and a long-dead spider, the only other thing in the closet was a plastic container, Tupperware on steroids—big enough, Nick was about to discover, to hold a lifetime of memories.

Across town Brodie Murdoch pulled her rental car in front of the home she owned and had lived in with Lancaster Heart. They'd left months ago, but looking at the steps leading to the small porch and front door, Brodie thought it felt like years. There were similar but distinct houses on either side. One was for sale, still or again; the other sat quiet too, but Brodie knew her dear friend Herschel Rosenberg was inside. He was almost always home. She cut the engine and sat an additional moment with her thoughts. She was here to meet with Teri Hickox's father. The man had indicated, through Brodie's realtor, he wanted to buy the house for his daughter, but he wanted to discuss the terms of the transaction with Brodie, and only Brodie, face to face. She thought that was weird and, quite frankly, more than a little disturbing. She had mentioned it to her friends Becky, Kim, and Dana over a second Kir Royale at the bar the night before, and they agreed it was strange. Becky, a couple of cocktails in herself, offered to perform the task of bodyguard and accompany Brodie to the meeting. She added that, of the group, she was clearly the muscle.

"That'll put the fear of God in him!" Kim teased her friend.

"Yeah, you can take off one of your Manolos and use it to pound him into submission," offered Dana.

"Screw you guys," Becky said, raising her hand to get the attention of the bartender. Brodie thanked her inner circle but assured them all she'd be okay.

"If not, I have you all on speed dial."

"Let it ring once and then hang up," Becky said conspiratorially. "That'll let me know he's got you tied up in the basement."

"Jesus, Beck!" Brodie looked at her pal.

"Why would you go there?" added Kim. "Besides, if she's tied up, she won't be able to call any of us." Becky ignored the rebuke.

"If I remember the listing correctly, that house doesn't have a basement." Dana got her two cents in.

"Just promise you'll have your phone on and then hide it somewhere on your body. That way we'll be able to ping it and track you." Becky bobbed her head in a knowing nod.

"You guys are not helping," Brodie said without an ounce of anger. "I'll be just fine. Let's eat." And they did.

Hours later, in front of the house, Brodie wondered, thanks to her friends, if Hank Hickox was lying in wait somewhere in the house. The front door of the adjacent home opened, interrupting Brodie's daytime nightmare. Out bounded Rosenberg, his ever-present smile beaming from beneath a bushy moustache from ear to ear.

"Brodie!" he shouted. "Bubbala, come give Mr. R. a hug!" Brodie smiled; her former neighbor always made her smile. She exited her car and obliged.

A few minutes later, she was enjoying a cup of tea, catching up with the neighborhood comings and goings, in Rosenberg's living room. His house was laid out much the same as hers, but it was decorated much differently. His style was busier, warmer, filled with tchotchkes. The house was welcoming, and the tea was delicious.

"What brings you back, dear?" Rosenberg leaned forward and patted her knee.

"To see you, silly!" Brodie flirted.

"You flatter me!" Rosenberg laughed out loud. "You're a liar." His face grew stern. "But don't stop!" And the smile returned. "Tell me more."

"Honestly, we might be selling the house." She took another sip. Rosenberg's smile once again disappeared.

"To the girl?"

"Yes. Well, more precisely, her father. He's indicated he'd like to buy it for her." She set her cup back in its matching saucer and looked at her neighbor. "Why? Is there a problem?"

"Heavens no!" Herschel said immediately. "She's a good kid, except for the fact that she calls me 'Rosie.'" He made a face like he had just smelled a fart. Then, in an effort to be charitable, he added, "She's been a good neighbor. Not you by any means." He smiled at Brodie. "But good."

"How well do you know them?" Brodie asked. "The girl and her father."

"Her much better than him. She's friendly enough, always ready with a smile, sometimes a glass of wine." He winked. "She mostly keeps to herself. Sometimes I'll hear her coming or going at strange hours—strange for an older Jewish gentleman, that is— but I've been witness to zero shenanigans. No loud, late parties. No cops. No complaints."

"What about him?" Brodie wondered.

"He's around occasionally." Rosenberg blew unnecessarily on his own cup and took a sip. "Mostly, it seems, to clear a clogged drain or fix a faulty water heater." Brodie marveled at the man. Did he actually know with what Hank Hickox was actually tinkering, or was he just making a supposition based on his own ten-year-old house? "But I've never had the pleasure," he finished, referring to meeting Teri's dad.

They both turned toward the sound of a vehicle pulling up out front.

"That's his truck," he said, unconcerned about revealing his distaste for the vehicle. Brodie had no doubt Hank Hickox had arrived.

"Looks like I'm about to meet him," Brodie said, rising and starting to take her dishes to the kitchen.

"Leave those, darling." Rosenberg rose as well. "It'll give me something to do while the two of you kibitz."

Brodie thought back to the conversation with her friends the night before and suddenly felt secure in the knowledge that Herschel Rosenberg would be doing more than washing a couple of teacups. She hugged her friend and headed out the door.

Nick had never seen this particular plastic container before. He'd never thought of his mother as particularly sentimental or much of a hoarder, so he struggled to imagine what might be inside. He reached for the bin and pulled it out into the living room. The plastic top was snapped in place, and it took a second or two for Nick to pop it open. He heard and felt his stomach rumble. A quick glance at his watch told him it was just past two o'clock. He had missed lunch and was still several hours away from dinner. He thought briefly about the discarded contents of the refrigerator, and his stomach quieted. Then he reached inside the box. Right on top, ensuring it would be the first thing Blanche or anyone else saw, was an eight-by-ten-inch framed photograph. In living color, wearing black and white, stood a much younger—and he thought happier—Nick Avery and his beautiful bride, Mel.

Blissfully married for half a dozen years, Nick and Melody Avery became concerned about their inability to conceive, despite sometimes exhaustive efforts. Being a guy, he figured it had to be him, so with Mel's blessing, he put himself through the requisite medical paces. It wasn't Nick. So Melody went to a specialist. The news wasn't just disheartening; it was devastating. Mel Avery's inability to become pregnant and bear children was the direct result of a tumor. The cervical cancer wouldn't just keep her childless; it would kill her. And after eleven more painful, remorseful, unbearable months, it did.

Blanche Avery had loved her daughter-in-law. In fact, everyone loved Melody Hanks Avery, but nobody loved her more than Nick. He never even considered remarrying, had no interest in meeting anyone else. He had fallen in love with Mel the day they met, and he loved her the same, with every beat of his heart, still. He kept the exact same picture on the mantel above his fireplace at home. He knew he had given his mother this copy, had it framed himself, but he'd had no idea what had become of it and had long forgotten to inquire about its whereabouts. He pulled it out of the box, kissed his wife through the dusty glass, and set it aside. There were other pictures inside. Dozens of them, all including his mother holding babies, standing with young mothers holding babies, or smiling with men and women, clearly not mothers and fathers, who were holding the same babies that were in different arms in different pictures.

Nick remembered clearly the joy in his mom's voice when she would greet him at the door after school with a hug and a "hallelujah!" because they had found a "forever home" for another one of "God's babies." As a kid, Nick didn't understand completely what she was talking about, but he loved those days because they usually meant an extra hour of watching shows he liked on TV that night. Growing up, Nick learned to appreciate and cherish those days, because he could see the burden of the unclaimed, seemingly unwanted children weighing more and more heavily on his mother's shoulders. When Nick met Mel, Blanche was ecstatic, but she never pressed either about grandchildren. She had always said she was already a grandma to dozens of children.

Beneath those photographs, Nick was surprised to discover several old-school bank savings-account passbooks. Three by five inches in size, blue in color, and filled with columns for dates and numbers that indicated an amount deposited and the resulting worth of the account. Groups of books were bound by thicker-than-normal rubber bands, the kind Nick saw when he bought asparagus at the store. Finding the first book in the set, Nick did the math and came to the conclusion his mother had started the practice of saving when she was around fifteen years old. A time, he recalled his mother reminiscing, when she had helped Nick's grandmother clean houses. The first deposit, noted with a stamp applied by a teller, was for five dollars. Subsequent stamps, in that book and many others, showed that a young Blanche Avery faithfully deposited five dollars every Friday into this particular account. At some point that escalated to ten dollars and eventually, until the last transaction, twenty dollars. Nick noticed the final deposit had been made the Friday before his mother passed away. As far as he could tell, Blanche Avery never withdrew a nickel. According to the books, Blanche had accumulated about $40,000, a sum that Nick (correctly) assumed belonged to him, because so far he hadn't discovered a last will and testament. Nick took a second to appreciate his mother's resolve, but at the same time, he lamented the fact that she didn't seek better, or any, advice as to what to do with her money. He made a commitment to add the cash in the bank to the rest of her belongings earmarked for the church. Nick then thought about the slippers and the booze and the money and conceded he was happy that there was a lot about his mom that he didn't know.

Brodie wasn't sure what to expect, but she didn't expect what she saw. She thought the man who exited the pickup truck was straight out of central casting for one of the old TV shows she remembered watching with her mom and dad. Hank Hickox was a big, rugged man dressed in denim overalls and a weathered John Deere trucker's style ball cap. She even noticed a red kerchief hanging half out of the back right pocket of his getup. He pulled it out and used it to wipe the sweat from his head before greeting Brodie. The day wasn't particularly warm, and Brodie couldn't help but wonder if it was nerves, rather than the heat, that made the man perspire. He stuffed the kerchief back in his pocket, kept the cap in his left hand, and then reached out with his right to greet Brodie.

"Hank Hickox, ma'am," he offered as his hello.

"Hello, Mr. Hickox," she replied, taking his hand. It felt like an unpolished block of granite, rough, unbreakable, making her wonder again if she had something to worry about. "I'm Brodie."

"It's my pleasure to meet you," he said earnestly, letting go of her hand.

"Shall we go inside?" Brodie led the way. Climbing the steps to the front door, she saw Mr. Rosenberg peering out his kitchen window. Through the reflection in the glass, she realized Hickox noticed the neighbor too. She watched Hank wave.

"That fella may not be my cup of tea," Hank said to Brodie's back, knowing she had seen him acknowledge Mr. R., "but I'm grateful for how he's treated Teri." Brodie didn't respond, so Hank continued. "He's made her feel real welcome here."

Brodie unlocked the door to her home—Teri's home now—and was struck by how little it had changed. From what she could see, there was no new paint on the walls, and while there may have been different furniture, it was in the same places as hers and Lancaster's. The place was spotless, and Brodie felt a little bit of the tension leave her body. The girl was clearly responsible, and it appeared to Brodie that she not only respected herself but respected others too. Neither she nor Heart had met Teri before or after she had become their tenant; the entire transaction had been handled by Dana. *What was the old saying?* thought Brodie as she dropped her keys on the counter. *The apple and the tree don't fall that far apart?*

"Teri loves this house," Hank interjected. Brodie jumped. "I didn't mean to startle you, ma'am," Hank apologized. "Just wanted to let you know."

"I'm glad." Brodie turned and faced the farmer. "We loved it too."

"I'm not much for small talk," Hank continued, "so if you don't mind, I'd like to get straight to business."

"That's fine." Brodie wasn't looking for an extended visit either.

"Like I told your realtor person," Hank said, looking down at his boots and then back at Brodie, "I'd like to buy this house for my daughter."

"Sounds great."

"What's the asking price?" Hank, true to his word, got right down to business. Brodie and Heart had discussed this. Even though the Raleigh market was on the rebound, it wasn't anywhere near the place where they could get what they really wanted as a result of the sale. Because of that, the two decided to ask any prospective buyer to pay a few thousand dollars less than what they had initially paid for the house.

"Four hundred eighty thousand," Brodie said, preparing to hear a counteroffer.

"Sounds fair," Hank said. Brodie was momentarily stunned, having expected a little more pushback.

"Great." Brodie regained her composure. "Great!" she repeated with a smile. "I'll get in touch with Dana and have her start drawing up the paperwork."

"I'd like to pay cash," Hank said, offering up another stunner.

"Wow." It was all Brodie thought to say.

"It might take me a few weeks to gather up all the money. Have to sell some assets," Hank said, almost as much to himself as Brodie, "but I'd like for you to consider this a done deal." He extended his right hand again for another shake. Brodie accepted. Without letting go, Hank sent his left hand behind his back and reached into one of the pockets in his overalls. Brodie reflexively tensed and tried to free her hand from Hank's grip. The farmer held tight and smiled as he revealed what he had retrieved from his pocket. "I'd like you to consider this a show of good faith," he said, handing Brodie an envelope.

"No problem," Brodie answered, only slightly relieved. Hank finally let go of her hand, and then he turned and headed for the front door.

"I'll be in touch," he said on the way out.

Brodie exhaled, realizing she had done very little breathing during the exchange. Still a little on edge, she set the envelope on the counter and decided that a look around the house might calm her nerves. She wanted to see what, if anything, Teri Hickox had done to her former home. Upstairs, she found an empty bedroom and smiled to herself because it had been empty the whole time she and Lancaster were there. A second bedroom wasn't empty. A queen-size bed sat against one bare wall. It had been made, but Brodie noticed it had also recently been slept in. She peeked in the empty closet and made her way into one of the two bathrooms upstairs. It was also anything but empty. A fresh set of towels hung on the rack, and a toothbrush occupied counter space next to a half-used tube of paste. In the medicine cabinet, Brodie found Advil, mouthwash, and a small box of tampons. Across the hall was the master bedroom, and that's where Brodie went next.

There was a second, this time neatly made, queen bed. Brodie and Heart had slept on a king-size bed, so the smaller one made the room look bigger than she remembered. Teri had filled some of the space with a small table and a chair. On top of the table sat a Tiffany lamp, a decorating style that wasn't present, as far as Brodie could discern, anywhere else in the house. She wondered if it was a gift or a piece Teri had brought with her to remind her of home. She walked into the walk-in closet and took stock of the girl's wardrobe. Business suits, with both pants and skirts, were arranged by color, sharing the closet with blouses, sweaters, and more casual wear. Dozens of pairs of shoes, heels and flats, were lined up neatly on the floor. Near the corner of the closet, Brodie saw a small stand-up safe and couldn't help but wonder what was inside. It wasn't jewelry, because that was contained in a beautiful wooden box that sat on top of the black metal safe. Before she could examine the master bathroom, she heard the doorbell downstairs.

"Well?" Rosenberg didn't wait to get inside to ask. "Spill," he demanded.

"There's not much to tell." Brodie tried to curb his enthusiasm.

"Poppycock!" he countered.

"He wants to buy the house for his kid." Brodie shrugged. "And he wants to pay cash."

"Alivay!" Rosenberg exclaimed. "Do you think he was serious?"

"Actually…" Brodie thought for half a second. "I do."

"Well then, mazel tov." Rosenberg touched her cheek. "Why are you still in here?"

"Just having a look around." Brodie shrugged again.

"And?"

"The place looks great. I'm impressed. I haven't been in the back room, though."

"What are we waiting for?" Rosenberg smiled and grabbed her arm. A walkway led to what was considered a bonus room. Halfway along, there were French doors that opened out to a small patio. Walking by, Brodie noticed two folding lounge chairs in the middle of the concrete, set out to face what would be the morning sun. The back room could serve as a separate master bedroom, a game room, or a mother-in-law suite; Brodie and Lancaster had used it as an exercise room. It appeared that Teri Hickox used it as storage. Cardboard boxes, opened and still sealed, covered a good portion of the carpeted floor. There were also dozens of books on the ground. Brodie noticed both textbooks and works of fiction. So did Herschel Rosenberg.

"*The Law of Torts*, fifth edition." He picked a book up off the floor and turned toward Brodie. "It's got a great beat, but I'm not sure you can dance to it," he said with a smirk.

"Put it back," Brodie chastised, "knucklehead."

"Yes, Mother." Rosenberg did as he was told.

"What do you make of this?" Brodie had walked over to a group of boxes. She held up a thick, off-white sheet of paper with the classic black silhouette of a person in the middle, clearly a gun-range target.

"Oy vey!" was all Herschel could say as they both stared at the perfectly formed set of six bullet holes in the middle of the target's head.

Next Nick discovered newspaper articles—some mentioning him, others her—and certificates identifying Blanche as the Employee of the Month at the shelter on several occasions. He'd had no idea; she was never one to boast. The next, and last, thing Nick uncovered was a manila envelope, big enough to hold a legal-sized piece of paper. Compared to everything else in the container, it looked new. The adhesive seal was secure, the little metal clasp engaged. On the outside, in his mother's elderly hand, one word was scrawled: "Nicky." At first he wondered if this was the will he had not yet found, and then his mind wandered to the last time his mother had called him that. He thought hard, remembering two different circumstances. The first was when he was around eight, lying in a hospital bed, trying to swallow a spoonful of vanilla ice cream. He had just gotten his tonsils removed. The second—and, as far as he could recollect, very last—time was when Mel died. He couldn't help but be filled with a sense of dread as he tore open the envelope.

It held two full single-spaced handwritten pages—part confession, part story, part cry for help. The first time Nick read it through, he embellished his mother's words with pictures from his own reminiscence. The second time, his examination was more clinical. Blanche told him she had been troubled, in what turned out to be her final days, by the apparent murder of a woman she was sure she recognized. He knew her life was the shelter, helping unwed mothers, young girls really, find homes for their babies. He had his memories and her photographs as evidence. He also recalled the horrible story about the dead woman, had seen the pleas for help in solving the case on his own television. "That handsome young man on the TV asked me to call if I had any information," his mother had written. "I had information. I called. No one called me back."

Nick smiled to himself as he read. His mom just couldn't resist acknowledging the newsman's good looks. Then his smile faded. As far as Nick knew, the dead woman's murder had never been solved, and that fact had clearly had a profound effect on Blanche. Nick realized that was what had saddened her, shrunk her, tortured her in her final days. He could only hope writing it all down, leaving it behind in the note, had given her some peace before she passed away. Now it was up to the son to do what his mother couldn't. He also noticed that Blanche had separated one of the eight-by-ten photographs from the rest and included it with her mea culpa. Now it was up to Nick to reach out, but not to the television station—to the police.

CHAPTER FORTY-TWO

Teri had worked until almost midnight the night before and spent a good part of this day at the law firm as well. At the moment, she was back in Tanner Goochly's office, sitting on his lap, trying to literally and figuratively get a rise out of him. She was tired, a little cranky, and a lot horny. The weird fantasy she had experienced at the pancake house seemed like forever ago. Tanner constantly acted like a tool, doing things that made Teri want to murder him, but she still considered him a useful tool. Cody Switzer watched the two of them from the other room, through the slightly cracked open door. Tanner, eyes focused on the numbers on the screen, was oblivious to both the girl and the boy, but Teri knew Cody was watching, and her current mood made her bound and determined to put on a show. With her left hand, she stroked Goochly's hair. He still seemed unfazed, but through her jeans, Teri could feel she was starting to accomplish what she had set out to do. Then she leaned forward and stuck her tongue in Tanner's right ear.

"Jesus Christ!" He recoiled and shoved her to the floor.

She couldn't see Cody's face redden, or know he leaned in to get a better look.

"What is your problem?" Teri, ass still on the floor, convinced Cody's eyes were on them both, questioned Tanner a little more loudly than she needed to.

"I'm just trying to get some work done, Teri," he said matter of factly. "I'm tired, getting hungry, and it's a little tough to concentrate with you getting all slutty on me."

"What are you gonna do, hit me *again?*" She emphasized the last word, not for the older man's benefit but the younger's. "You feel like smacking your little slut around?" She kept it up.

"What are you talking about? Just shut the hell up." Goochly stared at his cousin. "I've never hit you in my life, but if you keep this crap up, I just might have to start."

Cody didn't hear Tanner's response because he'd turned away in anger seconds before. A few minutes later, he sat in a chair in the outer office. Head down, face in a car magazine, as Teri strutted out of Tanner's office. For his benefit, she pretended to wipe away a tear when she passed. She successfully stifled a smile when she noticed that the cover, featuring a picture of a sweet Chevy Camaro, was upside down in the kid's hands.

Cody smelled her perfume on the breeze that floated past her when she opened the door to the office and left. He had never liked his boss, but after what he thought he had just witnessed, it was easy for that dislike to turn to hate. He was still sitting in the same spot when Tanner walked by minutes later.

"Hey, dipshit," he called to Cody as he headed toward the door, "your magazine is upside down."

"Hey, *dipshit,*" Cody mocked as he pounded the steering wheel of his truck. He was several cars behind Tanner, following even though the kid knew exactly where his employer was headed. "How about I put my fist in your face!" he shouted through the windshield. Cody couldn't understand what Teri saw in the prick. He was self-absorbed, treated her like crap, and as far as Cody could tell, only cared about money. Teri deserved so much better, and, again as far as Cody could figure, that "so much better" was him. Just ahead, Tanner's Raptor pulled into the parking lot of Fat Patty's. Cody drove by, intent on making a U turn at the first opportunity.

By the time Cody parked his own truck and entered the restaurant, Tanner was sitting at a table, talking up a waitress dressed in the establishment's uniform: a short plaid skirt and a cropped white button-down shirt with several of the buttons down. Cody had been sitting in the cab for almost twenty minutes before finally summoning up the courage to go inside and confront his boss. Fat Patty's served one of the best burgers in the region, and the place was usually packed. This day was no exception. Cody had come to the decision that it didn't matter what Goochly did to him; somebody had to defend Miss Teri's honor, and that's what he did.

"Excuse me, miss." Cody interrupted Tanner's conversation with the waitress. "I need a minute of this man's time." The waitress stared at Cody. Tanner, recognizing his voice, ignored him. Cody tried again, this time raising his voice. "Please, miss, it'll only take a minute." This time Tanner turned and glared at Cody. He slapped the girl on her behind and sent her on her way.

"What the fuck you want?" he asked in a dismissive way, turning back to his beer. "Shouldn't you be home? Mowing the lawn, doing your studies, washing your skivvies, or waiting on your mama to put dinner on the table like a good boy?" Cody ignored the insult.

"You can't hit Miss Teri no more." The kid pressed on. "I won't let you." A few heads turned in their direction.

"*Any*more," Goochly said dismissively, without turning around.

"What?" Cody was momentarily thrown off guard.

"I can't hit Miss Teri *any*more." Tanner suddenly swiveled his chair so he was face to face with Cody. Then he grabbed the kid's shirt between his chin and his chest and pulled him closer. "And if I do, what business is it of yours?" Cody steeled himself and grabbed Tanner's wrist with a surprisingly strong right hand.

"She's a lady, and you should treat her like one," Cody said as he puffed out his chest. Tanner let go of Cody's shirt, and Cody let loose of Goochly's wrist.

"Well, aren't you too cute," Tanner mocked. "Are you her knight in shining armor?"

"If I have to be." Cody tried to stand a little taller.

"Fuck off and mind your own business. And get the hell away from me!" Tanner said as he turned back to his beer. The waitress was headed his way with his meal.

"Don't hit her no more," Cody repeated. "*Any*more." He corrected himself this time. "If you do, you'll be sorry."

"Is that a threat, Cody?"

"Take it however you want," the kid said, and he turned and walked out before he could get a reaction. Many of the customers in the restaurant heard every word, and several of them stared at Tanner Goochly Jr. One of those staring was the cook from Big Eddie's diner, Boogie Hoffman.

"Y'all can mind your own damn business too," he said to them and attacked his meal.

Heart sat on the porch, staring at the golf course across the street. The day was growing long, but the sun still had a couple of good hours left to burn. An older couple, he assumed man and wife, got out of their golf car. The man grabbed the woman's hand and held it as they ambled up to the green. Heart smiled. He had grown up on this golf course; his parents played it nearly every Sunday. As kids, Heart and his two brothers almost always joined them. Saturdays were reserved for his dad and his dad's friends. No kids. When Lancaster was considered to be old enough, and polite enough, he was invited to be part of that Saturday group. On a few occasions, after a late Friday night, Heart had to hop the fence behind the first green and join them on the second tee.

"Here comes what's left of Lancaster," he could still hear his old man's voice saying.

Heart, from his rocking chair, lifted his martini glass to the sky at the memory. *Wish we were teeing it up tomorrow, Pops,* he thought and took a sip. His phone rang.

"Hey, honey." It was Brodie.

"Hey back," he answered.

"Still at the salt mill?" she wondered.

"Mine," he answered instinctively.

"Your what?" Her question made Heart smile.

"Never mind," he said, still smiling. "I miss you." He did.

"Miss you too, but I'll be home tomorrow."

"How did it go?"

"Weird." She didn't elaborate.

"What was weird? The father? The house? Being back there?"

"Yes," was all she said. Heart took a sip of his drink and waited. He knew more would come, and it did.

"The girls are great," she started. "They all send their love. Except Becky." She giggled.

"I never liked her." Heart played along.

"The house looks great. No real changes." She paused briefly. "It was definitely strange being back. Even though it's still our house, it didn't really feel like it." She sounded pensive. Heart changed the subject.

"How was the girl's father?"

"Straight out of *The Beverly Hillbillies,* or *Green Acres.* Take your pick." His mind conjured up an image of Buddy Ebsen and then Eddie Albert.

"Jed Clampett or Oliver Wendell Douglas?" Heart asked, guessing she wouldn't know.

"What's the difference?" She didn't.

"One was a hick; the other was a New York businessman who wanted a simpler life," he told her.

"The hick," she answered.

"Jed Clampett," he concluded. "Got it."

"He says he wants to buy the house for his daughter." She moved on.

"I like the sound of that, but something in your tone suggests a 'but' coming."

"No, not really." She offered up another slight pause. "It's just— well, he said he wants to pay cash. Gave me ten thousand dollars." She stopped there. Heart was momentarily speechless.

"You're kidding!" he finally blurted out.

"Yeah," she said softly. "I'm a kidder."

"Don't sell yourself short," he said lovingly.

"A leopard doesn't change its stripes," she said.

"You're right, darling, you're not a kidder." Now it was his turn for a pregnant pause. "Ten grand. Holy shit."

"That's what I thought," she added.

"So what's the problem?" he asked. "Other than Jed Clampett walking around with a check for ten grand in his trousers."

"Overalls," she corrected him. "And it was cash." This time Heart was speechless for more than a moment. "One hundred hundred-dollar bills," Brodie added.

"Now *that's* weird."

"I'm not sure this guy has ever *seen* the inside of a bank, let alone knows how to get a mortgage for a home."

"What did Dana say?" Heart asked, trying to find some firmer ground.

"Said it was unusual but not unheard of," she answered. "She said she'll draw up a contract, stipulate the ten grand as earnest money, and set up a closing for the thirtieth of the month."

"And if we don't close then?" Heart wondered.

"We keep the money."

"Well, then here's to Jed Clampett!" Lancaster Heart toasted for a second time that evening.

CHAPTER FORTY-THREE

Tourist Marc Allen stared out past his toes to the azure water. He had never considered himself a beach guy, didn't much care for the way sand seemed to find every nook and cranny, but he loved Turks and Caicos. He thought it the perfect place to get away. It was five hours, with a stopover in Atlanta, but it was a world away from Raleigh and the ever-growing solemnity of his day-to-day work. When he started walking the beat, the world in general and Raleigh in particular had been far less dangerous places. Now, with more than a decade on the job, his desire to make both safer hadn't changed. Unfortunately, his ability to do that—to keep up with the escalation, the inventiveness, and more than anything else, the pure brazen nature of the criminals—had. So every so often he needed something like this trip. His unsolved cases, as well as the crimes that were happening while he planted his behind on the beach, weren't out of mind, but they were out of sight.

"One world-famous rum punch." Denise Clawsew set the drink on the table that divided the two lounge chairs. Allen's butt was in one; hers was about to be in the other.

"Why, thank you," Allen replied, without looking at the drink or the girl who delivered it.

"Really?" she asked incredulously after noticing the book butterflied open on Allen's chest. "Michael Connelly?" The author was a former LAPD officer who now wrote books about, among other things, an LAPD detective trying to solve cold cases.

"He's a great writer." Allen defended his book choice. "I always find his work entertaining, interesting, and sometimes even enlightening."

"Thanks for that review, Gene Shalit," Clawsew scoffed.

"You're showing your age, sweetie," Allen chided, "and if I'm not mistaken, you like Connelly's books too. Especially the Lincoln Lawyer ones."

"I like Matthew McConaughey in the movies." She took a long sip of her drink. "And yeah, I like his books too, but we're supposed to be on vacation, *not* reading books that make us think about the cases we haven't solved yet waiting for us back home."

"Fair enough," he conceded. "Just let me finish this chapter." He took a sip of his own drink and watched Denise's back as she walked toward the Caribbean. "Or not," he said to himself, closing the book and following her into the sea.

Nick Avery parked his car in the police-station visitor's lot and grabbed the envelope that was sitting on the passenger seat. He'd read his mother's written note one last time while he was having his morning coffee. He was unclear about what the police would do with it; he hoped it might help. But before putting it back in the manila envelope, he made a copy. He wasn't exactly sure why. Then he added a note of his own, explaining how he had come across the confession and adding a few words about who his mother was. He included a request for an acknowledgment that Blanche's letter had made it into the appropriate person's hands. Then he dropped a couple of his business cards in the mix before sealing everything up.

Engine turned off, he slid his keys out of the ignition and headed for the door.

"Have you heard from Heart lately?" Allen asked, putting his arms around Denise from behind. The warm Caribbean water hit them both just below the waist.

"Not since he offered me a job a couple of months ago." She turned her head and kissed the detective on the shoulder.

"He asked you to come work for him?"

"Yep." She turned back around and stared at the horizon. "He wanted me to join his team, head up the camera operators in the newsroom, and impart the wealth of knowledge I've gained." Allen could hear the smile in her voice. "He even said he'd like me to do some reporting. To tell you the truth, it was a really good offer."

"And you said no?"

"I said no."

"Why?"

"Don't get me wrong, I thought about it long and hard, but then I Googled the cop shop in Reno. Not enough good-looking single guys, so the answer had to be thanks but no thanks." Still looking forward, she reached behind her, just below the surface of the water, and wrapped her hand around Allen's "weapon." Now it was his turn to smile.

"Can I help you?" Despite the question, the cop behind the desk gave the distinct impression that helping Nick was the farthest thing from his mind.

"I've got some information about a murder," Nick started, then stopped when the officer took a greater interest. "I mean I might have some information about a murder," he continued.

"You do? Or you might?" The cop leaned back in his chair and sized up Nick Avery for the first time. "And exactly how did you come by this *information?*" He said the word like it was an army of ants at a family picnic.

"My mother." Nick stared at the cop, wondering less with every second why some of the boys in blue had the reputation they had.

"Was she the victim?" the officer asked, looking back down at an open folder on his desk.

"What? No, of course not." Nick showed his frustration.

"Then why isn't she the one delivering this information?" Using the eraser end of the pencil in his hand, he pointed at the envelope.

"Because she's dead."

"But she wasn't the victim." The cop mocked Nick with an overly enthusiastic incredulity.

"Look." Nick steeled himself. "I'm here voluntarily with information that might help shed some light on an unsolved murder. I'm not exactly sure why you're being such a dick."

"Excuse me?" the cop said, looking angry. "I'd be careful what you say next, pal."

"I'm clearly not your pal, sir," Nick said, "but I apologize."

"That's better." The officer sounded like every bully Nick had ever encountered. It pissed him off even more.

"What I meant to say, Officer—"

"Sergeant," the cop interrupted.

"What I meant to say, Sergeant," Nick said, not missing a beat, "is that I have information I came across while going through my dear departed mother's possessions that may be of help in the investigation of what I believe is a still-unsolved murder." Nick took a breath but not long enough to give the officer a chance to interrupt. "I'm here because I would like to get that information into the appropriate person's hands. What I'm unclear about is why you're being such an asshole about helping me do that. Sergeant." Nick's look said "Don't fuck with me." The cop didn't.

"Since you put it that way, let me see what I can do." The sergeant smiled, and so did Nick.

Hank picked up the phone Teri had given him on his latest birthday and punched the speed-dial number she had also preprogrammed. It rang once.

"Hey, Pop," Teri answered happily.

"Hello there." Hank smiled at the sound of her voice. The weirdness he was certain had existed between them more than a year ago had never manifested itself in her tone of voice. He wondered if it was ever actually there at all.

"To what do I owe this unexpected correspondence?" Hank thought she sounded so lawyerly.

"Just thinkin' about you," Hank answered fatherly. "We haven't talked in a spell." Teri smiled at the colloquialism and then remembered she had spoken with him, even though the conversation was brief, just a couple of days ago.

"I'm sorry, Daddy, I guess I lost track of time," she said sweetly.

"It's okay," he said just as sweetly, even though it wasn't. "How's work?" he said, changing the subject.

"Same as it was the last time we talked," she answered, not changing the subject.

"Fair enough," he said. "How's the house?" He tried one more time.

"Great!" she said enthusiastically. "I love it."

"Well, that's good." Her father sighed. "Because I was thinking maybe I'd buy it for you."

"I wish we didn't have to leave tomorrow." Marc Allen stroked Denise Clawsew's hair. Her head was on his chest, they were on the bed, and the top sheet and pillows were on the floor.

"Really?" She looked up. "Not me. I mean, this is great and all, relaxing, but I'm ready to get back to work. Stuff's going on every day back home. Bad stuff, creepy stuff, exciting stuff, and I'm missing it by being here in paradise."

"You're such a romantic."

Denise rolled off of Allen and reached for the phone that was sitting on the table by her side of the bed. Allen shook his head and reached for his own phone. There was one message. He hadn't checked the device in a couple of hours, since they were out on the beach and the entire time they had been back in the bungalow. He retrieved the message.

"Detective, this is Sergeant Picozzi. I know you're enjoying a little R and R, but I thought you might want to know that a concerned citizen…" The sergeant paused, and Allen could picture him fumbling for a name. In a second the voice mail continued. "A gentleman named Nick Avery came by with an envelope, claiming it contained material that might be helpful in solving a case. A murder. I'm going to put it on your desk. Just thought you would want to know. Enjoy your vacation."

Allen kept the phone to his ear even though the message had ended.

"Bad news?" Denise was watching him.

"Don't know," he answered, half there, half in Raleigh. "Don't think so." Allen racked his brain, trying to think about to which case this might pertain. He also thought he recognized the name Avery, but at the moment, he couldn't recall why. "Nick Avery," he whispered.

"Who?" Denise was still staring.

"Nobody." Allen finally turned to face her. "Or maybe somebody," he said. "Come to think of it, I'm ready to get back too."

CHAPTER FORTY-FOUR

Teri had been awake for about a half an hour; it seemed like longer. Different sounds, noises, drifted into the bedroom through the window she had cracked open before settling into the queen-size bed. An occasional car, tires skimming over the pavement still wet from a late-evening, soaking thunderstorm. A dog's bark, or was it two, somewhere fairly close. A siren way off in the distance. Teri wondered if it might be a cop chasing down a criminal or an ambulance rushing someone fighting for a last breath to a hospital that would end up being too far away. She thought about dying, and living, and the difference.

Those noises that found their way into the room through the two-inch space were soothing compared to the rhythmic snoring coming from Tanner Goochly Jr.'s slightly open mouth. Teri didn't know if that was what had awakened her, but she was certain it was what prevented her from going back to sleep. She had reached out to Goochly and found herself back in his bed. For the last twenty minutes, she had racked her wide-awake brain, trying to figure out why. The sex was still good, but Teri was becoming bored with

Tanner's technique and the exercise's complete lack of meaning. A crooked smile formed on her lips as she remembered finding both of those things attractive; not so much anymore.

The relationship had always been easy, still was, and maybe that was why she kept coming back. There wasn't anyone else in Tanner's life, no other girls anyway, so Teri could come and go as she pleased, and she pretty much did just that. Tanner was the opposite of needy, and Teri had loved that about him at first. He hadn't changed, but she was suddenly wanting more and more to be needed. She shifted from her side to her back, hoping that would trigger a position change in her sleeping companion and bring an end to the sucking and wheezing. It didn't. The snoring never used to bother Teri; occasionally it still didn't, but tonight it was maddening. The little things—the chewing with his mouth open, the snoring, the fact that he still thought he was, and took perverse pleasure in, fucking his cousin, and for that matter, the complete disregard for her feelings—suddenly weren't so little anymore. Staring at the ceiling, she wondered if anybody, other than his old man, would miss Tanner Goochly Jr. if suddenly he ceased to suck oxygen. She couldn't think of anybody and imagined that even Tanner Goochly Sr. wouldn't miss him all that much or for all that long.

The Sig Sauer P238 was in her purse. She couldn't remember why she had decided to keep it with her this particular night instead of locking it safely away. One of the dogs, or was it the same dog, barked again. A soft breeze carried the sweet smell of rain on its back and into the room. Teri had to pee. She slipped from Tanner's bed, silently dressed, and tiptoed down the hall and into the bathroom to do her business. She had already made the decision not to return to the bedroom, but she wasn't sure she was quite ready to leave the apartment. On the way into the living room, she couldn't help but notice two Harris Teeter paper grocery bags. She peeked inside and wasn't surprised to find both filled with cash.

An hour or so later, Goochly woke himself up with a snort and realized he had to go to the bathroom. He rolled out of the bed, forgetting, or not caring, that Teri had been in it with him when he fell asleep. For reasons known only to Tanner Goochly Jr., he sleepily picked his boxers and a well-worn pair of socks up off the floor and put them on. Then he padded to the bathroom. After relieving himself, he opened the medicine cabinet, took two Advil from a bottle, and swallowed them without the benefit of a drop of water. He realized he hadn't flushed the toilet, and he turned back to accomplish that task but, again without a thought or concern for his houseguest, left the toilet seat up. Then he headed back to the bed and walked right into a pillow from his couch shielding the muzzle of a 9mm handgun.

"What the fuck!" he blurted.

"The fuck is your grandpa was a pervert, your old man is a pervert, and you are a pervert. And you're an asshole to boot."

The initial shock disappeared as quickly as it had arrived, and Goochly sized up the threat.

"That all may be true," he said with a scoff, "but what, exactly, are *you* going to do about it?"

The answer came in the form of two bullets fired from the pistol. The first hit Goochly in the chest, shattering ribs and sending splinters along with the slug into his heart. The second shot hit him just above the left eye, putting a hole in his head as it entered his brain. Goochly hit the floor with what was left of his face, breaking his nose and knocking out his two front teeth. But Tanner Goochly Jr. was well past the point of feeling any of that pain.

"That's exactly what I'm going to do about it."

CHAPTER FORTY-FIVE

"Come here, Duke," Hank called to the dog. "The bad man is long gone." The "bad man" was Tanner Goochly Sr. He didn't come around the Hickox homestead very often, but whenever he did, the Rottweiler hightailed it into a different part of the house. It made Hank marvel at just how good a judge of character the animal was. Trusting his master completely, the dog reappeared, took a whiff of the stale air left in Goochly's wake, and sneezed twice. Hank laughed out loud.

"Let's grab some fresh air out on the porch, boy," he said as they both headed outside. Plopping down in a high-backed rocker, Hank relived the last thirty minutes in his head. Goochly had shown up unannounced and knocked on the front door. It took Hank a few minutes to get there, but the visitor knocked just the one time. After pulling back the curtains, peeking outside, and seeing the strange yet familiar truck parked in front of the house, Hank finally opened the door. When he did, he was taken aback. *So this is what's become of Tanner Goochly* was all Hank could think.

The man, as a boy, had been quite the stud growing up. Starting quarterback on the high-school football team; power forward and leading scorer on the basketball court; homecoming king, not because he was the most popular kid in school but because the majority of his classmates were afraid of him. He wasn't exactly a bully, physically, but an anger hung on him wherever he went. It made everyone, save for the two or three like-minded souls who made up his personal posse, hang back an extra step or pick up the pace a tad if they found themselves in front. Other kids stayed a little longer at the drinking fountain, or in front of their lockers, or on their butts in the seats behind their classroom desks just to give Tanner Goochly as much room as they could without appearing to insult the kid outright. On the football field or the basketball court, Goochly was a local legend, and he had the letterman's jacket, the trophies, the newspaper headlines, and the scholarship offers to prove it. Hank had seen many of them on display when he visited the Goochly home during the courtship of Betty Lou. She told him all of the accompanying stories, but Hank wasn't impressed; he couldn't have cared less. All he cared about was Betty Lou and the feeling, the knowledge someplace deep inside him that there were darker, less glorious stories to tell. Eventually she told him those too.

Like Betty Lou, Tanner was the victim of the family patriarch's beatings, belittling, and drunken rages, but unlike his sister, Tanner didn't long to escape. He accepted the treatment as if he deserved it; then he channeled it into a force to be reckoned with on the field or the court. He used it like a fuel and fed off it like a fire does oxygen. Eventually, because of that, Gus Goochly stopped deriving his own sick, twisted pleasure from it and turned his full attention to Tanner's sister and Hank Hickox's future wife.

So on a football scholarship, Tanner Goochly went to NC State, where he lasted exactly three weeks. He ran into young men who were mentally and physically tougher, more motivated, and better prepared. It didn't hurt that most of them, unlike Tanner, could read past a third-grade level. So back home he came, scarred, somewhat disgraced, and settled under the thumb of his old man one more time. He learned the family business.

Hank had been a part of that same family business for years, and while visits from Tanner Goochly, the son, were uncommon, seeing Tanner Goochly, the father, was noteworthy.

Before leading the dog to fresh air, Hank had poured himself a tall glass of sweet tea, sweetened even further by a couple of fingers of another, stronger, amber liquid. As he recalled the events that had just transpired, he took a sip. The elder Goochly had seemed distant, distracted, but Hank thought he detected something else. Was it worry? Tanner Goochly was a lot of things, but in Hank's experience, a worrier had never been one of them. As he swallowed another gulp of his spiked tea, he reran the exchange in his mind.

"Tanner," Hank had said after cracking the door.

"Hank," Goochly replied, looking down at his boots.

"Surprised to see you." Hank didn't smile. "Would you like to come in?" He opened the door wider, and Goochly wordlessly walked through, past Hank. Back in the present, in the rocker on the porch, Hank reached down and scratched the top of the Rottweiler's head. In the memory, he saw the dog turn from Goochly and head to another part of the house. Hank was back in that memory. In the living room.

"Can I get you anything?" he said reluctantly, trying hard to sound hospitable. "Water? Sweet tea? Something stronger?"

"Not gonna be here that long," Tanner offered as a reply, finally looking up. "How long have we known each other, Hank?"

"Long time," Hank answered without giving it one second's thought.

"Long time," Goochly repeated. He pulled a crumpled pack of Marlboros from his shirt pocket and expertly popped one of the cigarettes in his mouth.

"I'd prefer you didn't smoke in the house," Hank said matter of factly. Goochly used the nail on his right thumb to strike a wooden match he had retrieved from the same pocket as the cigarettes. Hank walked over to one of the living room windows and threw it open wide. "Why are you here?" he asked, turning back to his unwelcome guest. Goochly took a long drag off the freshly lit cigarette and held the poison in his lungs before slowly releasing it into Hank's living room.

"When was the last time you saw my boy?" Goochly's words followed the smoke.

"Junior?" Hank answered absentmindedly.

"Only boy I got," Goochly cracked. Hank took a moment to think.

"It's been a while," he replied.

"What about Teri?"

"My daughter?" Hank said defensively

"Only one you got." Goochly sucked on the cigarette again.

"I saw her day before yesterday," Hank answered honestly. Goochly blew out the smoke and stared at Hank for a moment longer than was comfortable.

"I don't care when *you saw her* last." Goochly sounded accusatory. "I'm curious when you think was the last time Teri saw my boy." Hank had no idea where this was going.

"No idea."

"Well, could you ask her?" Both Goochly's tone and his eyes seemed to soften.

"No." Hank's didn't. Goochly nodded and then took another drag. Silence and smoke, both too thick for Hank's liking, hung in the living room air.

"I haven't heard from him in a couple of days." Goochly stared at the floor. "Won't answer his phone. That Cody kid said he hadn't heard from him either." Hank waited, sensing there was more. He was right. "That's not normal," Goochly finished.

"Maybe he's sick." Hank went for the obvious.

"Maybe," Goochly answered, as if he had considered that possibility.

"Why don't you check on him?"

Tanner Goochly took one long last drag off the cigarette. Then he removed it from between his lips, pinched the burning end between the finger and thumb of his right hand, and flicked it past Hank's head and out the open window. Hank didn't flinch.

"Would if I could." Goochly's words were accompanied by a melancholy smile. "But the little bastard won't tell me where he lives." Without another word, Tanner Goochly Sr. left Hank's home, got in his truck, and drove away.

Back in the present, out on the porch, comfortable in the rocking chair, Hank took another drink and swirled the bourbon iced tea around in his mouth. He had nothing but contempt for Tanner Goochly, but for a second, he found himself feeling sorry for the man. That second passed. Still, Hank couldn't imagine being estranged from Teri; the thought both scared and sickened him. He figured Goochly had brought all of the hardship and heartache on himself.

"Poor bastard," Hank said out loud to the dog as the contempt returned

CHAPTER FORTY-SIX

"Hey, Espo." Marc Allen walked toward the desk officer for the first time in a couple of weeks.

"Detective." Sergeant Jimmy Esposito didn't look up.

"How's it hangin'?" Allen asked with a smile.

"One more item for the ever-expanding human resources file." He shook his head and answered loudly enough for just Allen to hear; then he finally looked up. "Nice tan," he added so that everyone else could hear. The phone in front of him rang, and he answered it.

"Raleigh PD Sergeant James Esposito speaking." His tone and brevity made it clear the listener had better have a good reason to call on Raleigh's finest. The person on the other end of the line thought he or she clearly did. Jimmy looked at Allen and held up the index finger of his right hand, a gesture the newly tanned detective took seriously. Allen stopped midstride.

"Could you repeat that address?" Espo asked into the phone. Still looking at Allen, he raised his eyebrows. The index finger stayed in the air for another half a second before the sergeant

186

lowered it to desk level. Groping for a pencil, eyes still on the detective, he scribbled the numbers and a street name.

"Have you notified the landlord?" he asked, then listened. Allen held both hands out, palms up, in a "what's going on?" gesture. Espo's finger shot up again.

"Thanks for the information," he said, starting to end the call. "We'll send someone over to have a look." After hanging up, Jimmy Esposito leaned back in his chair, inhaled a healthy amount of police-department air, and slowly blew it out through pursed lips.

"Residence at"—he looked down at the notepad, squinting in an effort to read his own writing—"Honeytree, one word, Apartments," he read aloud, satisfied. "Four Three Four Four Saint James Church Road, Raleigh, unit seventeen A." He stopped reading and looked at Allen again. The detective repeated his "what's up?" gesture.

"Neighbor says something stinks inside the apartment. Knocked on the door, no response."

"Male or female neighbor?" Allen asked.

"What the hell difference does that make?" Espo wanted to know.

"None. Maybe," Allen told him. "Can't the landlord open the door?"

"Nobody on site. She called the management company before she called us."

"Female neighbor." Allen made a mental note. "Send a unit and call the management company and tell them not to open the door until our guys get there."

"Done," said Sergeant Esposito, "but it might be a guy and a girl."

"Jesus, Espo." Allen turned and headed back out the door.

For the third straight day, Cody Switzer sat in an uncomfortable chair outside Tanner Goochly's locked office door. Day one, he had sat there for nine full hours. The next day, he shaved that by 120 minutes and left at three o'clock. Today, he again arrived promptly at eight. The clock on the wall ticked its way toward ten minutes to noon. Cody looked at the small table to his left. He had read every magazine from cover to cover, twice. Even the golf one. For the third straight day, he wondered where everybody was, played solitaire on his phone, and dozed. On several occasions, he pulled the burner phone from his pocket and considered punching the only number that was preprogrammed, Tanner Goochly Jr.'s number. But each time, before hitting the button, the words he had been told when he was given the device rang in his ears.

"This is for an emergency, dipshit, and *only* for an emergency. Got that?" Cody remembered nodding. "And the only things I consider emergencies are if you're getting robbed or going to jail." Then Goochly tossed the phone at him. He caught it with his right hand and stuffed it in the pocket of his jeans. He had never once used it, and he figured since the two circumstances his boss considered emergencies weren't occurring, he wouldn't use it now either. Cody's stomach growled, so he got up and left the office, locking the door behind him, and went to do something about it.

It didn't take long for Detective Allen to get to the midsized apartment complex, which may or may not have been the scene of a crime, on Saint James Church Road. Pulling into the recently paved parking lot, the detective mused that the money for new asphalt and newly painted parking spaces could have done more good by replacing a clearly corroding roof or repairing shutters that no longer framed many of the building's windows. Allen had seen worse dwellings that housed his fellow Raleigh citizens, but he had seen better too. He figured the rents inside probably ranged somewhere between $500 and $750 a month. He was happy he didn't have to live in a place like this.

He figured, correctly, people died in apartment complexes like this one all the time, and he guessed it had happened again after counting three Raleigh PD cruisers in the lot. That fact confirmed in Allen's mind that there was something seriously amiss inside. *That's why you have the badge that says "Detective,"* he thought with a simple smile. A dead pet or a backed-up sewer system wouldn't require the services of three patrol cars. Allen also made a mental note that while at least six cops in three cars had beaten him to the scene, there was no sign of an ambulance or paramedic. The detective had seen dead people up close dozens of times before, and he knew he was about to add to that tally. Death left different looks, its visage dependent on the circumstances that accompanied its usually untimely visits. But even though it often looked distinct, what the Grim Reaper left behind always smelled the same. As soon as he opened the apartment building's door, that stench reached Allen's nostrils.

Did he really smell it? Could he so soon after sticking his nose inside? Or was his brain conditioned to smell it? Had he talked himself into finding a dead body inside and caused his brain to automatically send the message to his olfactory system? He wasn't exactly sure how close he was to where death had come and gone, but after a handful of steps, he hoped it was nearby, because the rotten-egg fetor was not a result of his brain working overtime. Not seeing or sensing any activity on the first floor, he headed up a flight of stairs, turned right at the top, and found what he was looking for. A uniformed officer crouched near the entrance to one of the apartments, his head hanging over what appeared to be an orange bucket. The kind you put light bulbs and duct tape in when shopping at Home Depot. Allen was momentarily confused until the cop barfed into the middle of the bucket. Allen winced, then wondered whether the vomit receptacle came from what he was more and more certain was a crime scene. He decided he didn't want to know.

"Officer?" The salutation hung between the two cops, one who had seen a lot, the other who hadn't. It was a question in search of an answer, not because Allen doubted the young man's service or purpose but because he just wanted to know which member of the brotherhood he was about to meet for the very first time. As a response, the young man wiped his mouth with the short left sleeve of his uniform, stood, and then instinctively pinched the identifying tag on his chest with the index finger and thumb of his right hand, tilting it toward the detective.

"Carroll, sir. Brian Carroll."

"Well, Brian Carroll, you got a little backsplash on a couple of those letters."

"Shit!" Carroll said, embarrassed, as he plucked the name tag from his chest and wiped it on his trouser leg.

"Wrong end," Allen chided.

"What?" Carroll looked puzzled. "Oh, right. Funny," he said without a smile.

"That uniform is going to need a visit to the dry cleaner."

"Yes, sir. Thank you, sir."

"First time?" Allen asked sincerely after getting a good look at the kid—and he was just a kid. The detective surmised Officer Brian Carroll was probably in his mid to late twenties; most likely became a cop because his old man, or his uncle, was. Or maybe he wanted to impress a girl, or the girls in general.

"First time this bad." The kid shook his head. "Does it get easier?" Allen thought about the question for a second.

"You never get used to it." He figured it was as honest an answer as he could give. "But it does get easier."

"I hope so, Detective." Carroll offered a sheepish smile.

"Me too, Officer," Allen replied. This time he uttered the word with respect. Then he turned and walked into the apartment.

"Nice putt." Heart was tending the flagstick on the fifth green at the Washoe County Golf Course. Joe Beckett, his longtime friend and colleague, had just rolled a twenty-five-footer to within inches of the hole. Brodie stood off to the side of the green, having already made a par.

"Didn't go in, did it?" Beckett said in mock anger.

"Good grief, you sound just like Tom Lilley," Heart said, remembering the crusty weatherman who worked for his father. He had played plenty of golf with the man, who rarely hit a putt that was satisfactory.

"On purpose," Beckett said with a laugh.

The green bordered a busy Plumas Avenue, and drivers in cars passed, some honking, with regularity. Heart wondered if they were honking because they recognized the tall, blond sportscaster who had delivered scores into their living rooms for years or because they were assholes who thought it was funny to honk in a golfer's backswing to try and distract him or her.

"Glad you're back on TV, Joe!" a red-haired woman yelled out the passenger-side window of what looked like a Chevy Camaro, answering Heart's question. Beckett waved, but the car and the girl were too far down the road for her to have seen the gesture.

"You guys are still one up, with one to play," Heart said to the other two. They were in the first stages of a round-robin match. The first six holes pitted Heart against Beckett and Brodie. Lancaster would team up with Joe against Brodie for the middle six, and then Brodie and Heart would partner for the final stretch. Brodie was staring at her phone as the group walked to the next tee.

"Whatcha got?" Heart asked his bride-to-be.

"Text from Andie in Dana's office. She wants me to call."

"Right now, or can it wait until we're finished?"

"Let me hit my tee shot, and I'll give her a jingle as we head up the fairway. I can give her a buzz and kick your ass at the same time."

"That's my partner!" Beckett chimed in.

"That's my wife," Caster added.

"That's affirmative to the first and not yet to the second." Brodie walked past both of them and pegged her golf ball. If she was distracted by the text message, she didn't show it as she blistered a tee shot right down the middle of the sixth fairway. The ball bounded past both Heart's and Beckett's drives. The sixth was a straight par four that paralleled its predecessor, heading away from the busy street. As she pushed her cart up the fairway, she dialed the number to the Raleigh realtor. The conversation was over by the time they all reached their tee shots. Beckett hit first and missed the green to the right. Heart sensed the opening to tie the match and launched an iron high into the sky. It landed and stopped about fifteen feet from the flag.

"Things are looking good for the good guys," Heart exclaimed, stuffing his eight iron back into his golf bag. Brodie smiled to herself and then proceeded to put her approach inches from Heart's ball.

"They sure are," she said as she went for her cart.

"What did Andie say?" Heart asked as they headed for the green.

"She said she thinks we should fish or set sail."

"She said *that?*" Caster wanted to know.

"I'm paraphrasing," Brodie said midstride. "She said Hickox called and said he wouldn't be able to meet the deadline. Said he'd like to give us another ten grand for thirty more days."

"Geez." Heart thought for a second. "What did Andie tell him?"

"She said she had to talk to us." They had reached the green. Brodie stopped and looked at Heart. "She thinks we should take the money but just this one last time."

"Well, okay," Heart said as he grabbed his putter. Beckett had chipped and missed while Lancaster and Brodie were discussing their Raleigh home. Brodie now had a birdie putt to close out the first stage of the match. She didn't miss. On the way to the seventh tee, she called Andie back and told her to take the cash and draw up another contract.

Allen took a minute to survey the crime scene. There were several other people in the room; all but one was still breathing. He noticed the two uniforms, one male, one female, and decided they must have been the ones who caught the call. He knew them both, liked one, the other not so much. Ken Jenkins had been on the force longer than Allen. The detective didn't know exactly how much longer; he just knew Jenkins, despite considerable effort, had yet to make detective. Eliza Starz was relatively new to the Raleigh PD. She was young, bright, and, Allen thought, no doubt among the next in line to pass Jenkins on the way up the ladder. But so far, the detective hadn't seen her show the slightest interest in ladder climbing. He had never heard of her kissing anybody's butt; she certainly hadn't kissed his. He turned his attention to the decaying, partially destroyed body on the floor. Shot at least once, the Caucasian male was dressed only in boxer shorts and a pair of white athletic socks. It seemed to Allen that his last act as a living, breathing human being had been to take about four steps out of the apartment's only bathroom.

"What do we have?" He asked the leading question, hoping to hear some information he couldn't see for himself. Jenkins started to answer, so he knew he wouldn't.

"White male, age somewhere between twenty-five and thirty; shot twice, once in the chest and once in the face. No identification."

"It's Tanner Goochly Jr." the detective interjected.

"How the hell could you possibly know that, having been here for all of about a hundred and twenty seconds?" Jenkins shook his head and then added just loud enough for Starz to hear, "Hotshot thinks he knows who it is when half his face is gone and the other half is unrecognizable."

"Well, Ken." Allen had heard too. "Hotshot *knows* it's Tanner Goochly because hotshot noticed a very familiar red Ford Raptor in the parking lot when hotshot pulled in." He paused to make sure that Starz was paying attention and that he wasn't going too fast for her partner. The slight smile that crossed her lips and the dumbfounded look on his face told Allen she was and he was. "Then hotshot," he continued, "just happened to notice that the second-place Punt, Pass, and Kick trophy sitting on the kitchen counter says it belongs to an eleven-year-old Tanner Goochly." Jenkins looked pissed, while Starz's smile was now full of teeth.

"Did you look in the bedroom for ID?" Allen asked Jenkins.

"We were waiting for you," he answered curtly. Allen nodded, knowing that was the proper response.

"Well, I'm here now," the detective said, conveying no disrespect. Jenkins turned, but Eliza Starz put her hand on his shoulder.

"I'll do it, Ken," she said. And she did.

Hank Hickox counted out $10,000 in hundreds, fifties, and twenties and wrapped them up with a big purple rubber band. He wasn't exactly sure how much money he had scattered around his property, but he was fairly certain it wasn't the $450,000 he needed to buy the house for Teri.

"What are we gonna do, Duke?" he asked the dog. Duke, as was his wont, replied to his master with a wag of his stubby tail. According to Tanner Goochly Sr., his son wasn't answering his calls, and there hadn't been a delivery for days. Hank suddenly worried that there may never be another one again.

CHAPTER FORTY-SEVEN

Marc Allen sat behind the wheel of his souped-up Dodge and watched the people come and go in the Fred Fletcher Park parking lot. It was early. Allen did this on occasion, before breakfast, just sitting and observing the denizens of the city he had taken an oath to protect and serve. He enjoyed watching people and took a modicum of comfort in imagining what other people's lives might be like. He used to—or liked to think he used to—think the best of folks. *There's a mom, taking a day off from work to spend time with her child instead of leaving that job to a day-care center or nanny again*, or *That man is running to try to stay in shape and live a longer, healthier life for the girl or guy he loves.* Now, with more than a decade on the force and a fresh, unsolved homicide on his mind, his imagination took a slightly darker turn. *The guy out for a run might just be a serial abuser who's staying in shape for the woman with whom he's having an affair*, and *The woman who just finished walking her dog is on her way home to jump on the computer and steal somebody's identity*, or *That man, sitting in his van, might have murdered Daisy Burns or Tanner Goochly Jr. Or both.*

Allen slowly shook his head back and forth, turned the key in the ignition, and fired up the engine. Then he headed for Big Eddie's.

Teri Hickox was relieved, happy, liberated—any one of the three or all of them. Fact was she couldn't put a finger on exactly how she felt having not seen or heard from Tanner Goochly in more than a week. There had been a message from his old man on her office answering machine, but she had ignored it, continued to ignore it. She had been celebrating with Harper, spending a couple of hours under the covers this morning, and then they had decided to go out into the fields around her dad's property and shoot stuff. That kept them busy for another hour or so. Both had work to do, so after another salty session in the back seat of Harper's Mercedes, Teri headed home to clean her gun and herself and then spend part of a weekend day in the office clearing her calendar. Driving home, she smiled at the thought that she felt even better than she had after walking away from her birth mother, Daisy Burns, for the final time. *I need to call my dad*, she thought as she reached for the radio knob and turned up Brad Paisley.

"What'll it be, Marc?" Big Eddie towered over the detective, who had climbed into a booth. The fact that the proprietor had called him by his first name told Allen that Eddie could sense something was troubling him.

"First, I need some fresh, strong coffee," Allen started without meeting Eddie's gaze. "Then I'll have one of Boogie's famous Denver omelets." Eddie put pencil to paper. "And finally, I need to figure out who's killing people in our fair city." Allen finally looked up at the diner owner. "Don't suppose you have that anywhere on the menu?" Eddie turned on a heel and headed toward the kitchen.

Less than ten minutes later, Allen's coffee mug was refilled, and a steaming omelet, with toast and hash browns, was placed in front of him. Boogie Hoffman slid onto the seat across from Allen.

"Who's dead now, Detective?" Boogie stared. Allen took a big bite, chewed, and swallowed.

"God, that's good," he half whispered reverently with his eyes closed. "What's your secret, Boogie?" Hoffman blinked in appreciation.

"I suppose a secret is only really a secret if nobody knows," Boogie said wisely. Allen decided he couldn't argue with that logic.

"Kid named Tanner Goochly Jr." Allen answered Boogie's initial question. "Killed in his apartment, shot once in the chest, once in the face." Boogie said nothing. Allen kept talking. "Nine millimeter. Some evidence suggests he had company, either that very night or sometime very recently. We found a hair. DNA's not back yet." The detective took another bite, chewed slowly, and swallowed again. "His old man said he hadn't heard from him in a while, didn't even know where he was living." Allen looked at Boogie. "Can you believe that?"

"I knew him," Boogie answered. Allen put the fork down. "I mean I know who he was," Boogie clarified.

"Pray tell," Allen prodded. Boogie did.

"Clarice, this girl I'm seeing off and on, works over at Fat Patty's. She says this kid comes in all the time. Thinks he owns the place, treats all the waitresses like crap. Name is Tanner Goochly Jr." Allen took a sip of his coffee, hoping there was more. There was. "A few weeks ago, Goochly was in there again, eating, drinking, bitching at Clarice, slapping another waitress on the ass. Then another kid, short hair, younger than Goochly, looks like he works out, comes through the door and walks right up to the table. He starts yelling at Goochly, something about needing to treat somebody like a lady." Boogie looked down, then grabbed Allen's still-full water glass and took a long, slow drink. He set the glass back on the table and continued.

"Goochly told the kid to mind his own business and to get the fuck out of his face. Then the kid got all puffed up and said for

Goochly not to hit 'her' anymore and if he did, he'd be sorry." Boogie stopped.

"Clarice tell you all this?" Allen asked and took another small sip of coffee.

"No, sir." Boogie shook his head and looked at Allen. "I saw it, heard it. I was there." Allen let out a whistle.

"You think you could identify that kid with the short hair if I showed you some pictures?"

"No doubt about it."

Allen speared another bite of omelet and brought it to his mouth, but Boogie's big hand stopped it before it could reach the intended destination.

"That's gone cold, Detective." Boogie smiled. "Nothing worse than a cold Denver. Let me make you another one."

"Much appreciated," Allen said. *For everything*, he thought. Boogie slid out of the booth.

CHAPTER FORTY-EIGHT

Marc Allen was riding a high. There were few things, in his opinion, like the adrenaline rush of catching a break on a case, especially a murder. He was well aware of the fact that, courtesy of Boogie Hoffman, he had just received a huge gift. He mused about the aligning of the planets, the delights of a perfectly cooked Denver omelet, and the reality that if Boogie Hoffman hadn't been sweet on a girl who waited tables at an unpretentious burger joint, he wouldn't be any closer to solving Tanner Goochly Jr.'s murder. In the space of a couple of hours, he had spanned the bridge from suspecting a random dog walker to finding a photograph of a kid named Cody Switzer who had publicly threatened a guy who ended up dead.

Stopped at a red light, Allen replayed Boogie's description of the confrontation in his mind. *Young kid, looks like he works out, clearly familiar with Goochly. Do I know this kid?* Allen thought. *Have I seen him while I was keeping tabs on the Goochlys?* he wondered. He knew there was a sure-fire way to find out. Before the light turned green, Allen blasted the siren, fired up the flashing lights, and after a quick glance in both directions, pulled out into the intersection.

Cody Switzer sat in his truck, parked out in front of Tanner Goochly's office. Another wasted morning was slipping into another forgettable day. A day, it appeared, that would tick tock by without a Tanner sighting or any work for Cody to do. *What the hell is going on?* Cody thought. He put his head back to take full advantage of the headrest. Earbuds in place, he turned up the volume, flooding his aural faculties with the sounds of his new favorite band, Post Animal. Eyes closed, he wouldn't have been able to see the unmarked police car pull up behind him. Ears full of music, he couldn't hear it either.

"My lucky streak continues," Allen said to the windshield as he drifted in behind what he figured to be a late 1990s Toyota Tundra. He could see somebody, he hoped it was Cody Switzer, in the driver's seat. *Is he sleeping?* A couple of minutes and a handful of steps later, Allen was astride the driver's side door, looking through the window at a kid behind the wheel. Head nodding slightly up and down, earbuds stuffed in. *Not sleeping.* The detective unholstered his weapon and held it in his right hand. He grabbed his shield with his left and held it up to the window. Then with the butt of the gun, he rapped on the glass. Cody heard that. The kid turned his head and almost crapped his pants. Without turning the music down, he ripped the earbuds from his ears and stared wide eyed at the detective. With the gun, Allen made a gesture of rolling down the window. Cody did.

"Hands where I can see them, son."

"Yes, sir, Officer." Allen smiled and let that slide.

Cody's trembling hands went to the steering wheel.

Seeing no weapon, Allen couldn't help but notice that Cody, or the young man he assumed was Cody, was clearly scared to death. He was about to find out if he had a reason to be.

"What's your name, pal?"

"Switzer, sir. Cody Switzer," he answered, looking straight ahead. Allen smiled and made a mental note. Cody Ross was a former girlfriend's favorite baseball player, and Barry Switzer was a famous coach of his least favorite college football team.

"What are you doing here, Cody Switzer?" Sensing little danger, Allen put his weapon back in its holster.

"I work here." Cody continued to answer as if this were a normal conversation. "Or at least I used to work here," he added.

"What do you mean by that?" Allen let the question hang.

"I mean I haven't seen or heard from the boss in days." He looked at the cop. "In fact, I haven't heard from anybody in days. Just come here, sit around, then leave."

"Who's your boss?" Allen asked, even though he already knew.

"Tanner Goochly, sir." He looked at the front door and then made a move for the glove compartment. Allen took one step back, drew his weapon, and screamed at Switzer.

"Hands on the wheel! Hands on the wheel! What the fuck do you think you're doing?" Cody froze, then put his hands back on the steering wheel.

"Don't kill me!" he pleaded. "I was just going to get the phone Mr. Goochly gave me." Then the kid started to cry. Allen let out a long slow breath and holstered his gun.

"That phone won't do you any good." Allen found himself feeling sorry for the kid.

"Why not?" he asked, trying to wipe away a tear with his right shoulder. The last thing he was going to do was take his hands off the wheel again, maybe ever.

"I should have asked who *was* your boss." Allen paused. "Tanner Goochly Jr. is dead, son." With that news, Cody Switzer closed his eyes, and his forehead joined his hands on the steering wheel.

"Oh, fuck."

"I think you better come with me," Allen said as he opened Cody's door.

It took about twenty minutes to get back to the station. Cody Switzer sat in the back of the cruiser, silent the entire time, staring out the window. After Allen parked and led him inside, the boy finally spoke.

"Can I call my brother?"

"Is he your attorney?" Allen held the door.

"No, sir. He's my brother." The detective couldn't help but smile.

"Give me the number. I'll call him."

"Thank you, sir."

"You don't have to call me sir."

"Yes, sir."

Nick Avery was at his desk, reading the e-mail illuminated on his computer screen for the third time. He still had no idea what it said. Avery was distracted; more accurately, he was annoyed bordering on angry. Weeks ago he had gone to the police and dropped off the envelope containing his mother's dying words, her confession. And so far, he hadn't heard a thing, not a peep. He reached for his wallet and pulled out Detective Marc Allen's business card and tapped the edge on his computer. Despite his simmering anger, he was reluctant to call. He couldn't put a finger on exactly what he expected the detective to do with the information, but he did presume the policeman would, at the very least, have the courtesy to acknowledge, no matter how briefly, that he had received the envelope containing the words that his mother had felt the need to write. He punched in the numbers on his phone.

Allen was four steps away from his desk, headed to the holding room to speak to Cody Switzer, when he heard the phone ring. He turned his head toward the sound, started to take one step back, then decided to let the call go to his voice mail. As he resumed his intended task, he noticed Officer Eliza Starz.

"Hey, Starz," he said with a smile.

"Detective." She didn't smile back.

"You got a minute?"

"Depends." Still not smiling, she added, "What's going on?"

"Got a possible suspect in the Goochly murder. I'm headed in to talk to him, and I'd love your take."

"Not really my purview," she said honestly.

Who the heck says "purview" anymore? Allen wondered. "Understood," he told her. "But if you're not too busy, I'd really appreciate your eyes and ears on this one." It sounded that simple, and it was. Starz held a manila folder up for Allen to see.

"Let me drop this off on my desk."

"No problem." He nodded. "Thanks."

She nodded back and added an appreciative smile.

Cody sat in the metal chair. It reminded him of the ones every teacher in his grade school had behind his or her desk. He stared straight ahead and rocked back and forth from the waist. His hands were in front of him, fingers interlocked, but every once in a while, he lifted his right hand to his mouth and absentmindedly gnawed on the nail of his index finger. Allen and Starz watched through the small window in the door.

"Why am I here?" the officer asked the detective.

"I'm sorry?" Allen wasn't sure what she meant by the question.

"What am I doing here?" She reiterated the same sentiment in a slightly different form. "I mean, you said you had a suspect in the Goochly murder." She looked away from Allen and into the room again. "This boy didn't kill anybody."

Allen was struck by the use of the term "boy." He guessed Eliza Starz wasn't that much older than Cody Switzer. But as he looked past her to the kid in the room, he could see exactly why she had said it. Allen tended to agree with her that Cody Switzer neither looked nor acted like a killer, but he wasn't about to go anywhere near "couldn't" just yet.

"That may be true," he acquiesced, "but let's see what you think after we talk to him."

"We?" she wondered. "This isn't my collar or my case."

"It's nobody's collar—kid isn't under arrest—and it's my case." He looked straight at Starz. "And I want you in on this." He opened the door without waiting for an argument or response. She followed him inside. Cody looked up and blushed.

"Hey, Cody." Allen did his best to sound friendly. "How're you holding up?" Switzer looked down and spoke to the table.

"Did you call my brother?"

"My name is Detective Marc Allen." He ignored the question. "And this is Officer Starz."

Cody looked at the woman and blushed again.

"Ma'am," he said. Eliza Starz let out a laugh.

"That might be the first time I've been called ma'am," she said with a soft smile. Cody smiled too. "Officer Starz will do."

"Yes, ma'am," Cody said, unable to help himself.

"He's very polite," Marc Allen added.

"Did you call my brother, sir?" Cody turned his attention to the detective and returned to the question.

"See what I mean?" Allen looked at Starz. She looked at the kid.

"We left him a message. Said something has come up that concerns you but for him not to worry. We said you're okay." Cody stared at her. Allen did too, liking the way she took the lead on answering the question. He realized she knew the answer would sound better to Cody coming from her.

"He's a busy guy." After a pause, Cody added, "Am I?"

"Are you what?" she asked.

"Am I okay, ma'am?"

"That depends on the next ten or fifteen minutes." This time it was Allen who answered.

"You don't have to answer any of our questions," Starz said, reclaiming her time. "But if you haven't done anything, have nothing to hide, it would be a good idea to cooperate. Just give an honest answer to whatever the detective asks. It's your right to ask for a lawyer, have him or her here. Up to you." She gave her best "we're on your side" smile to the kid. He didn't hesitate.

"I don't have a lawyer." He lowered his eyes and shook his head. "And even if I did, I wouldn't need to call him." He looked up at Starz, then over at Allen. "Fire away."

Allen flipped his own metal chair around so the back butted up against the table; then he straddled it. Still looking at Cody, still smiling, Starz retreated to a corner of the room.

"Good call, kid," the detective said reassuringly. "You want a Coke, or a glass of water, or anything?"

"You got a diet Dr. Pepper?" he asked hopefully.

"I think we can find you one of those," Starz answered and started to leave the room.

"I don't want to start until she gets back," Cody said, looking at the detective but pointing at Starz's back.

"Fair enough," Allen said, nodding.

It took Eliza Starz a little less than ten minutes to get the requested beverage and return. During that time, Allen devised a strategy. His instinct, matched by Starz's, was that the young man seated in front of him had nothing to do with the murder of Tanner Goochly Jr. But Allen also surmised that there were few people more closely connected to the victim, so the answers he got might give some insight into who might want Goochly dead. That's what he hoped to get out of Cody Switzer. The door opened, and Starz entered. She set a cold can of diet Dr. Pepper in front of Cody and popped the top. Then she went back to the corner of the room.

"Ready?" Allen asked. Cody took a long pull of the soda.

"Ready, sir." Out of the corner of his eye, Allen saw Eliza Starz pull a notebook out of one pocket and a pen out of the other.

"Do you live at One Fifteen Winifred Drive in Morrisville?" Allen started.

"Yes, sir," Cody answered without stopping to think.

"With your mom?"

"Mom and Dad." Allen's plan was to ask simple yes-or-no questions, get Cody in a rhythm of answering quickly, reactively, without giving any one question too much thought.

"Do you work at Goochly Music and More?"

"Yes, sir." Cody took another drink from the Dr. Pepper can. Starz held on to the pen and paper but so far hadn't written down a thing.

"For Tanner Goochly Jr.?" Allen kept going.

"Yes, sir." Cody looked the detective in the eye and shrugged. "Well, I guess I *did*, sir."

"Do you own a gun, Cody?"

"No, sir." Again, no hesitation from the kid, and Allen knew he was telling the truth. At least Cody hadn't purchased a gun in Wake County. He had consulted with Sheriff Denny Hartson, who confirmed that nobody named Cody Switzer had applied for a gun permit. So far Allen had no reason to think Cody Switzer was trying to hide anything.

"Did you kill Tanner Goochly Jr., son?"

"No. Sir!" Cody's eyes never left Allen's. He never blinked.

"Did you ever want to?"

"Yes, sir, I did." Cody still didn't look away. "All the time, sir."

"Tell me what happened at Fat Patty's," Allen prompted, and Cody did. Officer Starz started writing.

CHAPTER FORTY-NINE

Lancaster Heart's cell phone rang. Brodie, beside him in the bed, grunted softly and rolled away from her fiancé. Heart looked at the time displayed on his phone, cleared his throat, and answered.

"Denise!" He feigned excitement. "What a pleasant surprise at six seventeen in the morning."

"Get your lazy butt out of bed," Denise Clawsew chastised. "Are you going soft on me out there in Ne-vah-duh?" She mispronounced it on purpose.

"As a baby's butt." Heart didn't take the bait. He kicked off the covers, swung his legs over the side of the bed, and sat up. "To what do I owe the pleasure of this wake-up call?"

"I've been giving your offer a lot more thought." She paused, and Heart pulled the phone away from his face and looked again at the caller ID. "You still there?" He heard her through the tiny speaker and put the phone back to his ear.

"I'm here." He said nothing more.

"Anyway," she plowed on, "if the offer is still good, I'm inclined to take you up on it."

"What changed?" Heart asked

"Look, Caster, this isn't an interview." He smiled to himself. "Either you still want me to come out to the wild, wild West and school your camera ops or you don't. The why and the what don't matter."

"Well then, when?" He figured it was the only thing left to say.

"Give me three weeks," she quickly replied. "I figure it'll take that long to give my notice, pack my stuff, and get out there."

"Take a month," Heart said.

"You're a peach," Clawsew said happily. "And thanks."

"I should be thanking you," he shot back.

"Oh, don't worry, you will be." And Denise Clawsew hung up. Heart laughed out loud and set the phone back on the bedside table.

Allen's desk was always a mess, but for some reason, he thought it was more untidy than normal. Two unopened and thus unreturned interoffice communication requests covered up a third envelope—one that had been sitting there since Nick Avery had handed it off weeks ago. Allen was going over Starz's notes for the third time and waiting by the phone for information about Teri Hickox. The name rang a bell, but at the moment, he wasn't coming up with the reason. His mobile rang, and he reached for the instrument on his desk. His personal phone rang again, and realizing his mistake, he picked it up.

"Allen," he announced.

"Hey there." It was Denise. The detective felt some of the tension in his shoulders leave his body.

"Hey." He smiled into the phone. "How are you?"

"Good," she said. "You?"

"Not bad. Busy."

"I noticed."

"I know I've been out of touch." He felt a little guilty. "But I got a huge break in the Goochly murder case, and I've been chasing it." Denise said nothing, which gave Marc pause. "Did I tell you about the Goochly murder?"

"No. No, you didn't, but I heard about it over the scanner." Allen closed his eyes at the rebuke.

"Crap, Denise, I'm sorry," he said honestly. "I've just been going a hundred miles an hour since it happened."

"No worries, really." She didn't sound mad. "I get it."

"Did you guys run with it?"

"Nope. The Hammer fought for and got an extra minute for his scintillating Scotty McCreery interview. The perceived-domestic-violence story wound up on the cutting-room floor. I think they might have run a reader during one of the morning cut-ins."

"Well, Scotty is pretty big around these parts." Allen tried to lighten the mood.

"Clearly," she replied, sounding unamused.

"Come on, Guy! Where's your sense of humor?"

"Must have left it in my other pants," she said, and Allen wondered if she actually was angry, sad, or both. Then there was silence between them. He thought it might be the first time in a long time, or ever, that they had run out of things to say to each other. He hoped that wasn't the case and took the conversation in a different direction.

"You wanna get dinner or a drink tonight?" he asked. "Allow me to make it up to you?"

"You don't owe me anything." He decided she didn't sound upset, but Allen still felt the distance. "Besides, I can't."

"Other plans?"

"Something like that," she said. "I have to start packing."

"Packing?" he asked. "We just got back."

"That was weeks ago, Marc. Besides, I changed my mind about Lancaster Heart's job offer." She let that sink in for a second or two. "I'm moving to Reno."

"What?" The revelation caught him completely off guard. "Because I didn't tell you about the Goochly case?"

"Christ, Marc. Don't be an asshole and think this has anything to do with you." Suddenly she was angry. "I'm doing what's best for me."

"You're right. I'm sorry." He was. "It's just..." He took a deep breath and let it out. "What about us?"

"People get murdered in Reno too, ya know." And with that, Denise Clawsew was gone. The thinly veiled invitation made Allen feel a little better. Or did it?

Among other information, Cody had given the detective a few ideas about where he might find Teri Hickox. At the third establishment of the not-so-young-anymore evening, Allen found what he was looking for. It was in a popular sushi place on Glenwood Avenue. Two-thirds restaurant, one-third bar. As the detective walked through the door, a troubadour was finishing up a decent version of Edwin McCain's "I'll Be."

"I'll be better when I'm older," Allen sang along to himself. "I'll be the greatest fan of your life." He walked up to the bar, shouldered his way into what wasn't a space, and got the bartender's attention. "Double Crown on the rocks."

The amber liquid burned a little going down. It felt good. He looked around the bar at the groups of single or pretending-to-be-single people and the couples, or the ones pretending to be couples, and thought about Denise and Reno. The minstrel started on his rendition of Chris Stapleton's "Traveller." *Perfect*, thought Allen. He took another sip of the Canadian whisky and walked down the bar. He stooped next to a blonde.

"Can I buy you a drink?" he asked into her right ear.

Without a hint of surprise or annoyance, Teri Hickox turned slowly. Allen thought he saw a flash of something—could it be recognition?—in her eyes. She looked the detective down, then up.

"No offense, but I'm not into bald guys."

"None taken," Allen replied honestly. Teri looked away.

"No offense," Allen added, "but I'm not into women who trample all over fragile hearts." When Teri turned back, she was looking directly at Marc Allen's shield.

"Can I buy you a drink?" he asked again, less collegially this time.

"Do I need to consult my attorney?" She started to smile, then stopped.

"Up to you." He took another drink of whisky. Teri turned to her companion, Harper Madison.

"Can this gentleman, this *detective*"—she tilted her head ever so slightly Allen's way—"buy me a drink?"

"Only if he agrees to buy me one too." Harper nodded a hello of her own at Allen.

"Fair enough," he replied before draining what was left of his double Crown. He set the glass on the bar and started to try to get the attention of one of the bartenders.

"Rocco!" Harper did it for him, and a second later, Rocco stood in front of her. "One more." She pointed at her drink and Teri's. "And whatever our new best friend wants." She nodded at Allen again. "After all, he's buying."

The three stared straight ahead as Rocco worked behind the bar. Allen wondered about the two women; the two women wondered about Allen. Rocco poured out two cosmopolitans, light on the cranberry, and squirted some Diet Coke into a tall glass of ice.

"Done drinking?" Teri asked

"It would appear I'm about to go back on duty."

"Does it now?" she said with a laugh. Then she picked up the martini glass and took a drink, downing most of the vodka. "Call an Uber," she said to Harper, who was starting to work on her own cosmo. "We wouldn't want to get busted for DWI." Harper put the glass on the bar with her right hand and grabbed her phone with the left. "Thanks for the drink, Detective," Teri said as she got up and walked toward the door. A few seconds later, Harper followed her without a word. Allen smiled, shook his head, and pulled an evidence bag from the inside pocket of his jacket. He grabbed a fresh bar napkin from a stack near the beer taps and used that to handle Teri's martini glass. He lifted it from the bar, spilled out what was left of the drink, and dropped the glass into the bag.

"What the hell are you doing?" It was Rocco.

"Borrowing this for a few days, Rock." Allen lifted the bag. "Tell your boss I'll bring it back."

"Whatever," replied the bartender, who turned his attention to another thirsty customer.

Teri stared up at her bedroom ceiling. Her arm was around Harper, whose right cheek rested comfortably on Teri's left breast.

"What was that all about?" she asked Teri's nipple.

"What was *what* all about?" Teri continued to stare.

"The cop at the bar."

"Not sure." Teri had been wondering the same thing.

"Whose heart did you trample all over?"

"You heard that?"

"I heard that." Harper gently bit the nipple. Teri took a deep breath.

"Kid named Cody Switzer, I'm guessing," she said after a few seconds. "He's got a terrible crush on me."

"Can't say that I blame him," Harper responded.

"Why, thank you, darling." Teri kissed the top of her head.

"But how did the cop know?" Harper asked the question Teri had been wondering about most.

"Great question," she said. "I have no idea." Teri knew her girlfriend was wondering if she was telling the truth. "Do you think I need to talk to a lawyer?"

"You're talking to one."

"No, I know, and thank you for listening, but I mean—do you think I need to speak with a criminal attorney?" Harper thought Teri actually sounded a little worried.

"Probably wouldn't hurt."

"Probably wouldn't hurt," Teri repeated.

"Do you want me to talk to the old man?" Harper asked. The "old man" was her father, Dollar Ridge Madison, known in courtrooms and by television executives all across the country as "Dolly." He was a bombastic self-promoter, and he was also an outstanding criminal defense attorney. Judges and prosecuting attorneys tended not to like Dolly Madison very much, but juries and defendants loved him. So did the television camera.

"You don't have to do that," Teri said, hoping Harper would.

"I don't *have* to do anything," Harper said as she slid past Teri's stomach and did something they both wanted.

Marc Allen stared up at a different ceiling. After walking through the door, he had called Denise three times in his head and once for real. She hadn't answered any of them. He grabbed his notebook, brushed his teeth, and climbed into bed. Lying on top of the covers, he replayed his interview with the Switzer kid over and over again. Then he did the same with the conversation he'd had with Officer Starz about the interview with the Switzer kid. They both had come to the same conclusion: Cody Switzer wasn't a liar or a killer. Teri Hickox, thought Allen, was a different kettle of fish. He closed his eyes and placed himself back at the bar on Glenwood. He heard the Chris Stapleton song, saw himself walking up to Teri Hickox for the first time. She *had* recognized him; he could see it again in her eyes. But how? From where? He reasoned it could be from any number of places, including on her television screen, but he couldn't stop wondering if her appearing to know his face was important. He moved on in the memory. She was tough; no reason to wonder about that. He threw her breaking a poor, unsuspecting, naive kid's heart straight in her face, and she didn't flinch—showed no signs of remorse. His badge didn't seem to tilt her off her axis either. She acted like he was showing her his library card—that's how impressed she appeared. He had made what he thought was a decent effort to engage, but she just dusted three ounces of vodka like it was Fiji water and headed for the door, all hips and ass.

Unlike Switzer, Teri Hickox owned a gun, actually two, both 9mm. He'd found that out by going back to the Sheriff Denny Hartson well. Now that in itself wasn't all that damning these days. A lot of women owned 9mm handguns; in fact, female gun owners were among the Raleigh area's fastest-growing populations. But two guns? Two 9mm guns? That deserved a fresh set of questions. And she knew Tanner Goochly Jr., actually knew him intimately if the Switzer kid was to be believed, and Allen felt the Switzer kid was. Another reason to have another chat with Miss Teri Hickox.

The other thing eating at the back of Allen's brain, the part of the subconscious that dared him to remember something and threatened to beat him up if he couldn't, was the feeling that Teri Hickox was no stranger to him. At least her name wasn't. Where he had heard it and why it nagged at him as he drifted off to sleep. He never heard Denise Clawsew call him back, because she didn't.

CHAPTER FIFTY

B right and early the next morning, Allen pulled into the parking lot of Denise Clawsew's apartment building and saw the midsized U-Haul truck. Her black Jeep Wrangler was hitched to the back. The image of a giant walrus occupied a third of the storage area of the truck, all snout and tusks, with one big black eye staring him down. Above the creature's head, "#119 Venture Across America" was written; "Maine" was listed as the destination where this wonderful adventure could be found. He had stopped at Starbucks and picked up a coconut-milk latte, her favorite, for Denise and a black coffee for himself. He carried both up the stairs and knocked on her door. After about a minute, she opened it, still toweling off her mop of hair.

"Hey," was her greeting.

"Morning," he said back with a smile. She stepped to the side, and he walked past her into the apartment. It was empty. "You're really leaving," he said as he handed her the beverage.

"Now *that's* brilliant detective work, Detective," she said, taking the cup.

"It's why I make the big bucks." He half smiled. "Did you get all your stuff in that truck?" he asked, tilting his head toward the parking lot.

"All the stuff I figured was worth taking." She took a sip, "Umm, that's so good." She raised the cup in his direction. "Thanks."

"Pleasure," he replied. "But where's the moving van? Isn't Heart paying for your move?"

"He offered," she said, "but I decided driving across the country in a rented U-Haul would be a cathartic adventure." She took another sip, this one longer.

"I'm sure it will be."

"I *did* make him pay for the truck," she added.

"This isn't the end of us," he said, looking into her eyes. "I won't let it be." He smiled.

"I'm going to hold you to that." She smiled back. Then she set her cup on the kitchen counter and walked into his arms.

Hank sat on the window side of the bed. The sun streaming in gave the room a more sanguine feel than it deserved. He remembered sitting just this way, every day after he and Betty Lou were first married. But then he'd had a cigarette in his hand. He had started each day the same way, with a smoke. Now Betty Lou and the cigarettes were long gone. He ran his hand across his mouth and over his chin and realized he hadn't brushed his teeth or shaved in days. *Probably ought to do one or the other, if not both,* he thought. The house was heavy with loneliness, occupied now by just him and the dog, and Hank figured that Duke didn't care if he did either one. Before heading to the bathroom, he grabbed his phone and called his daughter. She picked up on the second ring.

"Hi, Daddy!" She sounded happy to hear from him.

"Hi, honey." He did his best to sound happy too.

"I'm so glad you called. I've been thinking a lot about you lately."

"That's nice to hear." It was.

"How are you? How's Duke?"

"Duke's good," he answered.

"And what about you?"

"I'm doin' just fine," he lied. "I miss you," he added, telling the truth.

"I miss you too! Why don't you come over this weekend? We can grill, and there just might be a thing or two around here that needs some TLC." She knew how much he liked to be a handyman hero.

"Sounds great," he said. "How's work?" he asked, not really caring; he just didn't want her to go.

"Good." He could tell she was smiling. "*Really* good. I'm busy. They're giving me a lot to do."

"That's terrific," he said, happy for her. "How's Tanner?" he couldn't help but ask.

"Who?" she asked, sounding caught off guard.

"Goochly, Tanner Goochly?" He repeated the name. "Aren't you two seeing each other?" He realized he might be giving away the fact that he had been keeping tabs on her, but he was beyond caring.

"I was," she said, not seeming to care either, "but not for a while. I decided I was way too good for him," she said proudly.

"You'll get no argument on that front from me," Hank said happily.

"I gotta go, Daddy." And with that, what was left of his heart broke a little more. "I have another really busy day ahead, but I'll see you this weekend, right?"

"You'll see me this weekend."

"Great. I love you."

"I love you too." He heard the smack of her kiss into the phone, and then she was gone.

Buoyed by the morning meeting with Denise, Allen leaned on the hood of his car, feeling the heat of the engine through his jeans and the warmth of the sun through his Ray Bans on his shut eyelids. Heard the click-a-clack of high heels on the sidewalk and hoped they belonged to Teri Hickox's feet. He opened his eyes and wasn't disappointed.

"Hi again," he said as she approached. Her head was angled slightly downward, her face in her phone, so she heard him before she saw him. But even though he knew she had heard his voice, she didn't acknowledge his presence. She just kept walking.

"Teri? Aren't you Teri Hickox?" That made her stop and look up. She couldn't help herself.

"Yes?" She continued to pretend not to recognize him. "And who, pray tell, are you?"

"Hi." He smiled. "Marc Allen." He waved a little. "Detective Marc Allen," he added. "We met the other night."

"Oh, sure." She continued to look like she was seeing him for the very first time. "What do you want? And maybe more important, how did you find me?" She pulled her own sunglasses down the bridge of her nose, revealing hard eyes.

"Like I said, I'm a detective," Allen replied, remembering Denise's admonishment from earlier. "And I'd like a few minutes of your time." He kept his sunglasses over his own hard eyes.

"I'm pretty busy," she said, pushing her glasses back up. "Is it important?"

"Depends," he said casually. "I got a dead guy, shot twice with a nine millimeter, and if I'm not mistaken, that's the same caliber of the two guns that you own. I also have hair and other DNA found in my dead guy's apartment." Allen stopped; Teri didn't say a word. "Oh," he said, making a display of tapping his index finger to the side of his bald head as if to say he had *just* remembered something else. "And I also have a martini glass, and my educated guess is what we find on that glass and what we found in proximity to my dead guy is going to match. So, is it important? Like I said, depends."

"I am Dollar Ridge Madison, Esquire, and this young responsibility while we are your guests."

"Good to know," Allen said. "I heard—in fact, the entire precinct heard—that you're not thrilled with our usual accommodations."

"That's putting it mildly, young man. I must insist my dear friend here is treated with respect."

"I've got no problem with that." He turned to Starz. "You have a problem with that, Officer?" She shook her head. "Why don't you come with us? I know a comfortable place where we can talk."

That place turned out to be an office previously occupied by the chief of detectives. She had recently taken a job in Washington, DC, as the head of personal security for North Carolina's junior senator, who just happened to be her husband. The position she relinquished had yet to be filled. Allen had, on more than one occasion, hoped it would be offered to him, but so far it hadn't been offered to anyone. So the space served as a go-to spot for sensitive sit-downs and meetings. Because Teri Hickox was not yet under arrest, Allen didn't see any harm in acquiescing to Dolly Madison's demands.

"Please sit down." The detective offered one of the four chairs situated around a small conference table. Madison walked past him, grabbed the high-backed leather chair behind the desk, and wheeled it over to the table. Then he motioned for Teri to sit in it. "Please make yourselves comfortable," Allen deadpanned. Madison and Allen stood as Teri took the chair and Eliza Starz sat. After that, the big man plopped down heavily into one of the three remaining armchairs. Allen was the last to sit.

"Why, exactly, are we here, young man?" It was the second time Madison had used the dismissive. Allen had let it go the first time, but he wasn't about to do it again.

"It's Detective, sir."

"Of course it is," the lawyer huffed in response. "Why, exactly, are we here, *Detective?*" He said it as if it were three separate words. Allen looked at him, then at Teri, then back at Madison.

"We're here because a young man named Tanner Goochly Jr. is dead." Before he could continue, Dolly let out a snort.

"And what, exactly, does that have to do with us?"

"My professional guess is that it has little or nothing to do with you, sir." He turned his attention to Teri. "But it potentially has a great deal to do with her."

"I'm dying to learn how," the attorney interjected. Just then the door to the office opened, and a uniformed officer handed Allen a folder before retreating the way he had come.

"How very dramatic," Madison said just loud enough for everyone to hear.

"You would know," Allen replied in equal volume as he looked over the information. Teri sat stoically, appearing to be a little bored by it all. "Did you know Tanner Goochly Jr.?" Allen looked up over the folder at Teri.

"I believe that information has been established," the attorney answered for her. Allen ignored him and asked again.

"Did you, Teri Hickox, know Tanner Goochly Jr.?"

"I believe that information has been established," Dolly Madison repeated, this time tapping the folder in Allen's hand with a sizeable index finger.

"Were you with Mr. Goochly the night he was murdered?" Allen, despite the interruptions, pressed on. His eyes didn't leave Teri's.

"What night was that?" The lawyer again. Allen sat back in his chair, rubbed his hand over his bald head, and prepared to try again. Madison beat him to it.

"Miss Hickox slept with Mr. Goochly on many nights. In fact, she did more than sleep with that young man. She had sex. Oral sex, vaginal sex, and anal sex with Mr. Goochly. At *his* residence, at *her* residence, at *his* place of business, in *her* car, in *his* truck, and even on the eleventh green of the Finley Golf Course. My guess is that folder of yours alludes to all of that. But sex, even frequent and what some of a puritanical mind might regard as abhorrent, deviant sexual behavior, is not against the law."

"Actually, it is." It was Officer Starz. Madison cast a withering glance in her direction.

"And who are *you* again?" he sneered.

"Eliza Starz, sir. Master Officer Eliza Starz, and depending on where Ms. Hickox and Mr. Goochly had the sex you describe, it might very well be illegal. You see, in some North Carolina counties, sodomy is, indeed, against the law." Allen smiled a little smile, and he noticed Teri was smiling too. Dolly Madison was not.

"Heavens to Betsy," the exasperated attorney exclaimed. "Be that as it may, it still doesn't amount to murder. In any county." He turned back to Allen. "That dog won't hunt, no, sirree, that damn dog will not hunt. So, if you have nothing further, we'll just be on our way." With that, the big man started to rise, and so did Teri.

"Do you own a nine-millimeter handgun, Ms. Hickox?" Allen asked

"Oh, come on." Madison threw up his arms. "You need to stop treating me, us, like idiots. I know you already know the answer to that question, Detective Allen. No, my friend and client does not own a nine-millimeter handgun." Allen shot a surprised look at Eliza Starz. "She owns two nine-millimeter handguns," the attorney continued. "Both purchased legally, both permitted in Wake County and the great state of North Carolina."

"I'd like to see those guns," Allen persisted.

"And I'd like a Lykan Hypersport," Madison shot back. Allen assumed that a Lykan Hypersport was either some sort of fancy car or a private jet. "It's a car," Dolly said dismissively.

"I have enough to get a warrant." Allen tried for the last word, but he sounded a little like a petulant child, and he knew it.

"Then get your warrant, young man." Madison gently grabbed Teri's elbow and led her out of the room. Eliza Starz stared at the tops of her shoes.

"What do you think?" she asked the detective.

"I think Teri Hickox killed Tanner Goochly. I also think she thinks she's going to get away with it."

CHAPTER FIFTY-ONE

"Is it really?" Allen and Starz were at her desk; Teri and Dolly Madison were about an hour gone.

"Is what really?" she asked without looking up.

"Is anal, uh, sodomy really illegal in North Carolina?"

"Not only North Carolina but about ten other states, even though the Supreme Court ruled those laws unconstitutional in 2003. Some states, including our own beloved Tar Heel State, still have them on the books." She still hadn't looked up.

"How do you know stuff like that off the top of your head, Starz?"

"I read, Detective; I read. You should try it sometime." He silently accepted the rebuke. "Okay, I think it's ready." Starz finally looked up. They—mostly she—had been working on a warrant to search the home of Teri Hickox in an effort to seize the 9mm guns Wake County said she owned. At Allen's request, she kept the warrant simple and specific in hopes of expediting its approval. The piece of paper called for the legal search of the premises at which Ms. Teri Hickox currently resided. Allen had gotten that information from Cody Switzer. They had the DNA evidence, which was, as Dolly Madison suspected, detailed in the folder that was handed off to Allen during their conversation. That alone might not persuade a judge, but Allen hoped it, along with the knowledge that Goochly was killed with a 9mm, the same type of gun owned by Hickox, as well as the transcript from Cody's interview detailing the perceived physical abuse of Teri by Goochly, would convince a jurist. Plus, his plan was to put the warrant in front of Judge James Wachter, who had been amenable to Allen's requests in the past.

"Looks great," he said to Starz, because it did.

"No worries," she replied with a smile. "Thanks." Allen looked at his watch.

"Damn," he whispered.

"What's wrong?"

"Twelve twenty. The judge is at lunch." Allen knew Wachter walked to Beasley's Chicken + Honey every day for his midday meal. And every day he ordered Hook's Cheddar Pimento Mac 'n' Cheese from the menu. He also knew, from personal experience, that the judge hated to be interrupted while enjoying the delicacy. But the detective worried that every minute they waited was a minute that Teri Hickox could use to ditch the guns and claim that they were stolen or lost, and Allen's evidence against her would remain circumstantial.

"So let's go intrude," she said with the confidence of someone who had never been privy to the wrath of Judge "My Cheddar Pimento Mac 'N' Cheese Lunch Is Getting Cold" Wachter. "I mean, it's just lunch." She shrugged. Allen pondered the reasoning but ultimately knew a happily satiated Wachter was his best chance.

"Better not." He touched her on the shoulder. "You'll learn." Starz just shook her head. "We'll give him another half an hour, and then we'll hit him up at the courthouse."

"I hope that's not too late." Starz said what Allen was thinking. The phone buzzed at her desk, and she picked it up. "Starz."

"Hey, Eliza, it's Espo," came the desk sergeant's voice on the other end. "Is Allen nearby?"

"He's right here," the officer said, looking at the detective. "You need to talk to him?"

"Not really," Espo replied. "Just tell him he's got a package up at the front. Courier just dropped it off."

"Roger that, Jimmy. Thanks." She hung up the phone. "Package up front for you," she said, her eyes never having left Marc Allen's.

Thirty seconds later, the detective and the officer were looking at two 9mm guns. One was a Sig Sauer P238, the other a Smith & Wesson Bodyguard, both belonging to Teri Hickox, according to a signed affidavit.

"I guess I can tear up that search-warrant request," Starz said as one of her gloved hands picked up the Bodyguard. "Nice gun."

"It is, and I wouldn't just yet." Allen referred to both the weapon and the warrant. "Why would she just up and deliver these to us?" he wondered aloud. *Maybe these aren't the only two guns she owns,* he thought.

Teri sat at her desk, staring at the screen saver on her computer screen. It was an image of her dad and Duke during happier times. Her mind was on the exchange that had happened just a few minutes before. She had protested, actually argued, when Harper's father suggested voluntarily handing over both of her legal weapons.

"They can't just have my guns," she had said to the lawyer, voice raised. "It's a violation of my Second Amendment rights." Dolly let her release that particular bit of steam, and then he placed his hand on her knee in a fatherly gesture.

"They're going to get them anyway, dear—your guns." He spoke in a calm voice. "Better optics if you give them to Detective Allen rather than he up and takes 'em."

"Optics?" She was still upset. "How about the *optics* of me telling him to go fuck himself. Is that illegal in North Carolina?" That made Madison laugh out loud, which in turn made Teri laugh. Suddenly a ton of tension had been released into the limousine. It seemed to float out the slightly opened driver's side window.

"Listen, girl," the lawyer said, sounding more fatherly than ever. "There really are only a couple of realistic options here." She looked up at him. "You can control this situation, cooperate, volunteer your guns—the ones he wants, at least." Teri gave Dolly a more scrutinizing look, wondering what he knew or *thought* he knew. "Or the Raleigh Police Department, in a dick-swinging show of force, can come rolling down that quiet street of yours, with all your neighbors peeking out from behind their curtains, and show up on your porch banging on your front door, bellowing as loudly as humanly possible that they have a warrant to search the premises and demanding you let them do it." Teri agreed that it wouldn't look good, and then Dolly made the decision a no brainer. "Worse yet, they also obtain a warrant to search your daddy's farm."

Heaven only knows what they might find there, she thought. "Lord love a duck," she said.

CHAPTER FIFTY-TWO

"Larry, how the hell have you been?" Allen and Starz had driven the guns over to a ballistics lab in Durham. The city, just twenty or so miles from Raleigh, was most famous for being the home of Duke University, but lately it was gaining an ever-growing reputation as the gun-crime capital of North Carolina. Because of the rising backlog of cases in the State Bureau of Investigation, the city of Durham decided to circumvent the usual process and open up its own facility, much to the chagrin of the NCSBI. Adding insult to injury, the new lab then offered the SBI's best ballistics expert, Larry Green, twice as much money and hired him away. Marc Allen and Eliza Starz were standing in front of him now.

"Well, hey there, Eliza," Green said, completely ignoring Allen.

"Greenie," Starz answered.

Is she blushing? Allen had heard through the "blue vine" that Eliza Starz and Larry Green had been seen together socially. If he was being honest, he'd admit it was one of the reasons he'd asked her to join him on this particular mission. But at the moment he needed the lab tech's full attention. He cleared his throat, which made Green turn his head.

"Coming down with something, Detective?"

"As a matter of fact, I am," Allen replied. "It's a bad case of I-*really*-want-to-catch-a-murderer pneumonia."

"And the boogie woogie flu?" Green sang the words.

"That too, Larry." Allen shook his head, and Starz smiled. "So how about you give us a hand."

"Us?" Green was back looking at Starz.

"I'm just along for the ride." She shrugged, still showing more teeth than not.

"She's much more valuable to me on this case than that," Allen interjected. "You could say we're working this one together."

"You could?" Starz asked.

"You could?" Green mimicked.

"Yes." Allen looked from one to the other. "You could. Now can you give us a hand?" Larry Green raised both hands, palms facing each other, and clapped four times. "Funny," said Allen. Starz giggled.

"I'm pretty busy right now," Green said, tweaking Allen a little more. "But if Officer Starz here can see her way clear to joining me at Il Palio one night soon, I'll see what I can do." Allen knew the restaurant in nearby Chapel Hill's Siena Hotel. It was an Italian place; the food was delicious and expensive.

"Deal," Starz said with another smile and without hesitation.

"What do you have, Detective?" Green held out his hand.

They were back in Allen's Charger headed southeast on Interstate 40 back to Raleigh.

"Are you and Green an item?" he asked the officer.

"Not yet." She looked straight out the window. "And it's none of your business."

"Not yet," he parroted. She wondered for a second what he meant by that, and then she just as quickly decided she didn't care.

"Look, Allen." She cared about something else. "I appreciate you bringing me in on this. I love the work and hope to make detective one day myself, but I *don't* appreciate being a show pony, a tool." She took a deep breath and let it out. Allen opened his mouth as if to say something, but she gave him the Heisman with her left hand. "I'm not done."

"Finished," he added quickly.

"What?" She stared at him.

"You're not finished," he admonished. "'Done' means cooked through and through."

"Oh, for fuck's sake." She shook her head. "I'm not done," she repeated. "I don't appreciate you using me to get something you want. I realize I have to earn your respect, but parading me out in front of Green just to butter his bread wasn't fair. And it wasn't professional." She folded her arms against her chest.

"You're right. I'm sorry." She could tell by his body language and the tone of his voice that he was. "It won't happen again, and I do."

"You do what?" Her arms were still folded.

"Respect you." A few minutes passed in silence as he weaved his way through traffic.

"What happens next?" She finally spoke again, asking a question even though she thought she knew the answer.

"What happens next is our friend Larry Green loads up those two guns with nine-millimeter ammunition and fires them into a tank full of water. That way they have spent and unmarred bullets that they can compare to the slugs we recovered from the Goochly crime scene." He looked over at her, and she nodded. Then she proved she indeed knew "what happens next."

"Then he puts both the unblemished bullets and the slugs you dug out of Tanner Goochly under a super-duper microscope to see how the markings on each compare." She could see Allen was impressed, and she continued. "If they're an exact match, we have a murder weapon."

"And a murderer," he finished for her.

"One more question, Detective."

"Call me Marc."

"One more question, Marc."

"Shoot, Officer."

"Call me Starz." They both smiled.

"Shoot, Starz."

"You seem pretty certain those slugs you retrieved at the scene are going to match the bullets fired from one of those guns." Allen nodded, waiting for the question. A question that he figured was the same one he had been asking himself. "If that's the case, then why in the world did Teri Hickox *voluntarily* give them to us?"

CHAPTER FIFTY-THREE

Eliza Starz had gone home to her golden retriever. Allen decided to put a few more hours in at the office. He had no dog waiting at home, and with Denise gone, he had no reason not to run the Goochly murder through the hoops in his mind a few more times. This most recent exercise, like the last and the last before that, added up to Teri Hickox. He went to the break room and popped a Keurig capsule in the machine. He had liked it better when the room was equipped with two glass coffee pots: one with an orange rim signifying decaf, the other rim all black for leaded. Before progress reared its ugly head, the room always had smelled of burnt coffee, and it had helped Allen think. As the Columbian roast poured out into his Durham Bulls mug, his thoughts returned to Denise Clawsew. He realized it had been a few days since they last talked, and then it was she who had called. *Is she in Reno yet?* He wasn't sure as he pulled his phone from his front pocket, unlocked it, and hit the speed-dial number for her mobile. After one ring it went to voice mail.

"Guy, it's me. Hope the drive across America is everything you hoped it would be. When you get a chance, give me a call." Before he could add the "I miss you" he intended to say, his phone buzzed, indicating an incoming call. Hoping it was her, he looked at the caller ID. It wasn't, but he wasn't entirely disappointed. The caller was Larry Green. He hit the icon that disconnected one call and answered the other.

"Allen," he said, hoping to mask the excitement he felt.

"Detective, it's Larry Green."

"Hi, Larry. Do you have the results already?" he asked, not considering the question might be perceived as an insult.

"Is Starz around?" Green asked, sounding insulted.

"Nope, she called it a night a while ago, but my detective instincts tell me that you probably already knew that. Come on, Larry, what did you find out?"

"Do you want the good news or the bad news?" Green asked, reveling in the fact that he was further antagonizing the detective. They had played this game before.

"You know the answer to that." Allen was exasperated. "I always want the bad news first."

"No match." And with those two words, Allen knew either he was being played for a fool or he was foolishly chasing down the wrong suspect. Either way, he was pissed.

"Both guns?" He clung to one last thread of hope.

"No match."

"What the fuck is the *good* news?" He practically screamed his frustration into the phone.

"There is no good news," the lab tech answered. "Have yourself a good night, Detective," he added before clicking off.

"Fuck, fuck, fuckity fuck!" Allen paced the break room. Suddenly the last thing he wanted was a cup of coffee. A shot of something stronger might be the appropriate chaser for Larry Green's bad news. Marc remembered the former head of detectives kept a bottle of Tattoo Tequila in her desk for occasions just like this one. He wondered if she had left it behind for whoever came next. "Only one way to find out," he said to the Keurig machine as he walked out the door toward the office. Further chagrin awaited him there; the door was locked.

"Son of a bitch." He gave the handle another twist. "Can't anything go right tonight?" he grumbled. Allen decided Teri Hickox had to have attempted to pull a fast one on him by purchasing identical weapons at some point and sending him those instead of her original firearms. One of which she had used to murder Tanner Goochly in cold blood. He worked his way back to his desk and on the way made two phone calls. First, he dialed the Wake County sheriff's office. He knew he wouldn't get hold of anybody at this hour, but he wanted to leave a message for his friend Denny Hartson. He hoped he would be the first thing the sheriff thought about the following morning.

"Denny, it's Marc Allen over in Raleigh. I hate to be a pain, but I've hit a bit of a snag in the Goochly thing. I was wondering if you could check your records on Teri Hickox again. I'm trying to determine if she purchased more than just the two nine millimeters. I know it doesn't preclude her from buying guns at a show or in another county, but anything you can do to help would be greatly appreciated." He knew how desperate it all sounded, but he figured he had to try. "Thanks, man, I owe you big time." Allen disconnected that call and quickly made the next.

"Hello, this is Eliza," Starz answered immediately.

"Officer Starz, this is Detective Allen. I'm sorry to bother you at home."

"No, you're not," she said simply.

"Okay, you're right—I'm not."

"What's up, Detective? And this better be important, because there is an episode of *Say Yes to the Dress* that I haven't seen on TV right now."

"Geez, that *is* important! I'll make this quick."

"See that you do."

"Got the call from Larry Green on the ballistics." He got right to the point. "No match."

"On either gun?" She asked the same question he had. Despite all the bad news that night, he smiled.

"No match."

"That's disappointing."

"That's putting it mildly," Allen replied. "But I've been thinking that maybe she bought two sets of identical guns at some point, somewhere else, maybe even off the grid. And those are the guns she voluntarily gave us." Allen paused, waiting for affirmation. Hearing none from Starz, he continued. "She killed Goochly with one of them, knew we'd find her DNA all over the kid's apartment, probably even run down the lovestruck Cody Switzer too, and all that would lead us to her." He was rolling now. "So somewhere along the way, knowing she'd be the prime suspect in Goochly's murder, she bought duplicate handguns that could never be matched to the bullets." He stopped for a breath.

"Detective?" Starz took advantage of the pause.

"Yes?"

"I'm totally impressed by you. You're a good guy, and even better, you're a great cop. Both exceeding your reputation, and that's rare." Allen felt uplifted by the praise and the apparent confirmation of his theory. "But," Starz added.

"But?" Allen realized he had been doing laps around the desks. He stopped.

"But don't you think you're giving this girl a little too much credit? You're turning her into this criminal mastermind who strategically plots a cold-blooded murder, then stays one step ahead of one of the smartest detectives around, all while graduating from law school, holding down a great job, and caring for a sick aunt with two pit bulls."

"She has a sick aunt and two dogs?" Allen asked, oblivious to the sarcasm.

"Jesus Marc, take a step back. I know you're frustrated by Goochly *and* the flower-girl case, but listen to yourself. You want your theory to be true so badly that you've convinced yourself that it is, despite the actual evidence. Maybe this girl is just a girl and the guns are just guns and Tanner Goochly pissed off a lot of people, most of whom wouldn't mind seeing him dead." Allen felt like he had taken a Tommy Hearns right hand to the gut. *Could Starz be right? Of course she could be,* he realized.

"But that would mean I'm back to square one," he admitted, his voice saturated with dejection.

"It means *we're* back to square one," she said reassuringly. "*We've* got to work even harder."

"Hey, Starz?"

"Yeah, Marc?"

"I hope she ends up saying yes to the dress."

"I'm afraid I'll never know."

During the conversation, Allen had meandered through the station and managed to work his way back to his own desk. All the adrenaline had drained from his body, and he felt exhausted. He plopped down into his chair and rubbed his head from his forehead to the back of his neck. Then, completely frustrated, he used both hands to pound, fists balled, on the desktop.

The violence shook loose several items in front of him, revealing a plain eight-by-eleven-inch envelope, on which was written his name. He couldn't remember ever seeing it. The flap was sealed shut. Intrigued, Allen pulled on the top drawer of his desk and grabbed the antelope-handle letter opener Denise had given him when he made detective. For half a second, he thought about calling her again; then that thought passed. He sliced through the top of the envelope, pressed the sides to create an opening, and peered inside. He saw several pages of what looked to be a handwritten letter, as well as an eight-by-ten photograph and a business card. Allen turned the envelope so that the open end was pointing at an angle toward his desk, and he shook it as if it were a salt dispenser. The business card tumbled out and landed, face up, right in front of him.

Nicholas "Nick" Avery
Financial Planning, Future Dreams

It took the detective a half a minute or so to connect the familial dots.

CHAPTER FIFTY-FOUR

Two hours later, he was still at his desk, coffee cup refilled twice, half as many times as he had read Blanche Avery's gut-wrenching letter. Now he was staring at the old photograph; in it were five people. Thanks in part to the letter, Allen was able to establish two of them as a young Blanche and an even younger woman, who he now knew would grow older and become Daisy Burns. Flipping the picture over, he had seen the writing that identified the others as Hank and Betty Lou Hickox and a bundle of joy wrapped in swaddling clothes listed only as "the little angel." Marc Allen knew that baby was now the prime suspect in his murder investigation, Teri Hickox. He took a sip of the growing-cold coffee and stared at the person to the left in the image, Hank Hickox. He saw a man seemingly filled with joy and hope, but on closer inspection, he thought he sensed something around the edges. *Is it the eyes? The mouth? Both?* Allen thought for sure he detected a deep sadness, some kind of impending sorrow, that had gripped this poor soul and wasn't about to yield an inch.

"Could it be *you?*" the detective asked the photograph of Hank. He felt his heart rate tick up to about a hundred beats a minute, and he racked his brain trying to figure out how or why he knew the name Hank Hickox. Then, with what felt like a burst of light and heat, he had it. Allen reached for his phone and dialed Master Officer Kelly Ann Bynum. He didn't look at what time it was, didn't care, and he knew she wouldn't care either.

"Hello." It was Bynum's groggy voice.

"KAB, it's Marc Allen."

"Do you know what time it is?"

"Does it matter?"

"No," she answered, now sounding completely awake. "What's shakin'?"

"Me," he answered, "if you want to know the truth. Do you remember a while back I was out keeping an eye on Tanner Goochly Jr.?"

"Vaguely," she interjected.

"Try hard, Kelly Ann," he pleaded. She knew he only used her given name when he was desperate. "You've got the best memory on the force." That had been a proven fact.

"Why, thanks," she replied, accepting the compliment. "And who is this again?" Allen laughed.

"Seriously, I was checking on Goochly, and his Raptor randomly pulled off the road and onto a dirt driveway somewhere out in the boonies."

"I remember," she said. "Hickox spread. Hank Hickox."

"I *love* you, Bynum!" he shouted and hung up. Then he dialed Eliza Starz.

"Starz," she answered in her sleep.

"Wanna go make an arrest?" was all he had to say.

CHAPTER FIFTY-FIVE

Hank Hickox rested his left hand on the top of Duke's head. A solitary tear trickled through the whiskers on his right cheek.

"How did it ever come to this?" he wondered aloud. The dog's head turned toward the sound of its master's doleful voice. Hank took a deep breath and scratched Duke's head. Then he wiped away what was left of the tear with the same hand. His right hand held tight to a twelve-gauge double-barreled Pedersoli Wyatt Earp shotgun. It weighed just seven pounds, easy to manage with one hand, and it was locked and loaded.

He tried to put the pieces of what had become his life over the past eighteen months together into a narrative that made some kind of sense. He couldn't remember exactly what had possessed him to start distrusting Teri. He did recall that following her made him a little sick to his stomach at first. That feeling quickly turned to an anger, near jealousy, when he witnessed her flirtatious behavior with the Goochly kid. His imagination transformed that into rage. He succumbed to an entirely different set of emotions when he shadowed his daughter as she rendezvoused with Daisy Burns. Surprise and sadness joined with his jealousy then, and they all took turns whispering in his ear. Ultimately abject fear came along and thrust the other emotions aside. The fear of losing his daughter caused every sensibly logical synapse in his brain to short circuit. Hank had tried to give Teri everything she needed, everything he thought she wanted, her entire life, but he knew he couldn't give her what Daisy Burns could. Not physically, emotionally, or monetarily. He had already lost Betty Lou; he couldn't bear the thought of losing Teri too.

Earlier that evening, he had cobbled together two pieces of correspondence. The first was a simple confession. In four sentences, Hank admitting to being the person responsible for the killing of both Daisy Burns and Tanner Goochly Jr. Then he scrawled his signature, and on the outside of the envelope, he scribbled, "To Who It May Concern." He placed it on the kitchen counter, half a bottle of Pappy Van Winkle bourbon and a 9mm Beretta PX4 holding it in place. Then, on another sheet of paper, he sketched out a detailed map illustrating the location of every single coffee can filled with cash on the property. An eight-by-eleven-inch treasure map with dozens of tiny *X*s marking the spots. He knew the money wouldn't buy Teri's forgiveness, but he hoped she'd take it anyway. He folded the map with three even creases and placed it in an envelope addressed to his daughter in care of the law firm at which she worked. He licked a forever stamp, stuck it on the upper right-hand corner, and dropped the envelope in the mailbox in front of the liquor store before going inside to splurge on the $200 bottle of Pappy. It all felt like days ago, although it had only been a few hours.

Hank Hickox had absolutely no regrets about taking a pillow off Tanner Goochly's objectionable couch, putting it between the barrel of the Beretta and the smug kid's chest, and firing away. In fact, he felt like he had done the world a service by putting bullets in his heart and his brain. Killing Daisy Burns was different. Taking her life, in a fit of mindless jealousy and envy, did no quarter of this, or any other world, any good. Conversely, he knew it actually made this world a decidedly worse place, and because of that, he realized he had no chance of joining Betty Lou in the afterlife. Somewhere, not far off in the distance, he heard a siren. Maybe more than one. As he put the Pedersoli barrels in his mouth, tasting fresh gun oil on his tongue, he hoped his beloved wasn't waiting for him on the other side, because he figured he was never coming. Then he pulled the trigger. Duke howled like he had been the one shot.

CHAPTER FIFTY-SIX

"You've got some decent gear here." Denise stood next to Lancaster Heart's desk and read from a spiral reporter's notebook. "And some that's going to need to be replaced in the next six to eighteen months." Heart smiled at her as she read. Clawsew looked up and caught him grinning. "Wipe that stupid grin off your face," she scolded. "You asked for this assessment."

"I'm just happy you're here," he answered honestly and continued to grin.

"Me too." She smiled back.

"What about the operators?" he asked, and her smile disappeared.

"That's a different story." She flipped over a couple of sheets of notebook paper. "This Jim Irwin guy is a keeper. He may be the most creative, pure shooter I've ever seen. Besides me, of course." Heart nodded. "He's also got good instincts about what is and isn't a story, so that's a bonus."

"Good to know," Lancaster added unnecessarily.

"The chick, Vargas," Denise kept going.

"You can't call her that," Heart interrupted. Denise looked up from her pad.

"Even if I am one?" she asked.

"Even if you are one," he answered.

"This world is becoming an effed-up place," she said, shaking her head. Heart couldn't disagree.

"Vargas is good too." Denise picked up where she had left off. "Not Irwin good, but good. That's the good news," she said, flipping another page. Lancaster Heart nodded, knowing what was coming next. He asked anyway.

"What's the bad news?" Denise blew out a long breath.

"This nitwit Graham Roberts is a disaster. Can't shoot, can't write, can't focus his camera or his brain. It seems to me he probably peaked as an intern somewhere. I mean, how did he even get this job?"

"GM's nephew," was all Heart said.

"Figures," she replied with a snort. "Okay then, he gets ribbon cuttings, grocery-store openings, and Friday-night high-school football games. Maybe he'll quit." She closed the book.

"Fine with me, but you tell Beckett." Pat Green's "Three Days" sang from Heart's mobile phone.

"Say hey to Brodie for me," Denise said, walking away.

"Clawsew says hey," Heart said, answering the phone.

"Hey, Denise," Brodie replied without missing a beat.

"Brodie says hey," he called to his newest employee as she walked away. "What's up?" he said into the phone.

"Well, I have news," Brodie began.

"I'm all ears."

"Looks like we sold the Raleigh house," she said excitedly.

"You're kidding! Already?"

"Yep, Dana just called."

"Wow, that's terrific." Heart was excited too. "Solid offer?"

"Buyer agreed to put forty percent down, in *cash*."

"Wow, forty percent! That's better than solid; that's pretty much set in stone."

"I know." She giggled. "Don't stay at work too long. I made reservations at Lulou's."

"Sounds fabulous," Heart said. "We've been meaning to give that place a try."

"And tonight we will. Now I have to put my head back to the grindstone and get some work done in the next hour or so. Don't be late."

Nose. Heart thought about correcting his fiancée. He didn't, but he did promise not to be late.

"Heart?" Connie Albanese stood in the same spot Denise Clawsew had occupied moments before. Heart looked over at her. "Got some mail for you."

"Thanks, Connie. Heck, I could have come and gotten it."

"No problem." She shrugged. "I was headed this way anyway. Is Pierce here?" She looked around the newsroom. Heart smiled to himself.

"I think he's out in the studio doing some mentoring."

"He's good at that." Connie smiled too.

"Yes, he is. Hey, thanks for the mail," he said as Connie walked away. He looked at the envelope and saw the return address was Park and Claire Murdoch's in Aspen. He tore it open and pulled out the contents. There was a sheet of white paper, on which he recognized Parker's unmistakable handwriting:

"Son, thought you might find this of interest" was all it said.

Son, thought Heart. He set that sheet aside and looked at the other thing included in the correspondence. It was a copy of an article reprinted from the *Raleigh News & Observer.*

"Local Farmer's Suicide Linked to Two Raleigh Area Murders," read the headline.

"Come on, boy," Teri called through the open front door from the porch. A couple of seconds later, the Rottweiler trotted out, leash in his mouth. "Good boy, Duke!" Teri scratched behind the dog's left ear. Duke's entire rear end wiggled back and forth in appreciation. She clipped the leash to the dog's collar, and they both headed down the steps.

"Hello there, dear," Herschel Rosenberg called. He was watering the plants in a flower box at the front of his house.

"Oh, hi, Herschel." Teri waved happily. He was thrilled she had stopped calling him "Rosie." On the street, he noticed the rear of a brand-new Loire-blue Jaguar F Pace S open up. He had never seen the car before.

"New car?" he asked his neighbor.

"It's mine, handsome." Rosenberg turned back to the house and saw Harper Madison come out the front and close the door behind her. He lifted the hand not holding the hose and wiggled the fingers in a wave. He was relieved neither woman could see the skin under his full graying beard redden.

"Do you want to meet Duke?" Teri broke the all-too-brief spell. She pointed to the dog. Rosenberg cleared his throat.

"Not right now," he said. *Not ever*, he thought. "I'm not much of a big-dog person," he added, forcing a smile.

"No problem," she replied. "But he's really a sweetheart."

"Wouldn't hurt a fly," Harper added with a flirtatious giggle.

"I'm sure he is and he wouldn't." Rosenberg's eyes bounced back and forth between the two women. "Unless of course he sees a meal," he deadpanned. The dog, tongue hanging out, tail still wagging, stared at his new neighbor.

"There's plenty of time for you to become friends," Teri said as the dog jumped into the back of the Jag. "Besides, Duke doesn't like Kosher food." She laughed. Rosenberg didn't.

"I'll be sure to keep that in mind, dear." *Oy vey, I miss Brodie*, he thought as he went back to watering his pansies.

Marc Allen had backed his Charger into the driveway of one of the two houses for sale on the block. He watched the three-way conversation between Teri Hickox, her friend, and her neighbor through his field glasses. "Nice house, kid," he said to nobody. Allen had, once upon a time, looked into buying something in this neighborhood. He was pretty sure Lancaster Heart and Brodie Murdoch owned, or maybe used to own, a place somewhere around here. He had quickly found out the address was a little too rich for a guy on a cop's salary, even a detective. He was curious about whether Teri had inherited her father's land and then sold it to buy this place, but a check of records by his pal Kelly Ann Bynum showed the house in which Hank Hickox blew his brains all over the ceiling had not yet been put on the market. Somewhere, somehow, Teri had gotten the money to buy this big house.

She could have still used her old man's estate as leverage, Allen thought as he took a closer look at Harper Madison. *Or Dolly Madison's daughter, who drives a brand-new fancy imported SUV, also owns the house, and Teri Hickox is just living in it.* As those scenarios whirled around his head, he made a mental note to call on Bynum again to check those theories out. He put the glasses on his lap and rubbed his eyes with his right hand.

He remembered every word of Hank Hickox's written confession. As far as his captain, the district attorney, and most everybody who had an opinion was concerned, that closed both the flower-girl and the Tanner Goochly Jr. murder cases up tight. Allen also remembered the relief in the voice of Daisy Burns's husband when the detective gave the widower the news, and the appreciation he received from Nick Avery when he called to thank him for his help. It certainly seemed everybody on his side of the fence was happy with the way things shook out. But something about it didn't sit right with Marc Allen. The conspiracy theorist in him thought it was all a little too convenient. Over a drink, he had mentioned his gut feeling to Eliza Starz, who dismissed it at first.

"You've got the Sunday blues," she said, pulling the maraschino cherry out of her Manhattan. When all Allen gave her in return was a quizzical look, she explained further.

"My pops was a big-time television sports producer." She set the cherry on the cocktail napkin next to her drink. "He did all kinds of events: basketball, golf, baseball, and football. Big games,